P9-BZQ-252

LOS GATOS PUBLIC LIBRARY
LOS GATOS, CALIFORNIA

DEATH
BY ELECTION

PATRICIA HALL

LOS GATOS PUBLIC LIBRARY
LOS GATOS, CALIFORNIA

St. Martin's Press
New York

Blank page torn 12/3/09 No

DEATH BY ELECTION. Copyright © 1993 by Patricia Hall. All rights reserved. Printed in the United States of America. No part of this book may be used or reproduced in any manner whatsoever without written permission except in the case of brief quotations embodied in critical articles or reviews. For information, address St. Martin's Press, 175 Fifth Avenue, New York, N.Y. 10010.

Library of Congress Cataloging-in-Publication Data

Hall, Patricia.
Death by election / Patricia Hall.
    p.   cm.
"A Thomas Dunne Book."
ISBN 0-312-11461-3
I. Title.
PR6058.A46D4   1994
823′.914—dc20   94-12922   CIP

First published in Great Britain by Little, Brown and Company.

First U.S. Edition: September 1994
10 9 8 7 6 5 4 3 2 1

Death by Election

ONE

HARVEY LINGARD CAME BACK TO Bradfield to die. His mind had been only half made up as he had battered his way through the crowds on the platform at King's Cross and slumped exhausted into a window seat on the busy 125 to Leeds. But as the train had sped arrow-straight across the flat East Midlands fieldscape of pale young wheat, fractured by the occasional garish rectangle of rape-seed and, here and there, brilliant late tulips, the resolution had grown within him that he would not make the journey south again.

He slept fitfully through Peterborough and Grantham, peering blearily at the latter and wondering which of its streets had nurtured the town's most famous daughter, now almost as faded as he felt himself. Most of the time he simply rested, eyes closed, pale eyelashes almost imperceptible against his skimmed-milk cheeks, as the train sped on into the hillier country, the Pennines now a series of undulating purple-grey humps on the westerly horizon as the 125 took the sharp curve into Wakefield and hissed to a halt amid the reek of hot brakes at the station perched precariously above the town.

From then on the train was constrained like a leashed whippet as it negotiated the curves and points of an apparently endless industrial townscape and slid reluctantly into Leeds. Harvey levered himself wearily out of his seat, hoisted his blue sports-bag with difficulty from the rack and followed his neighbours off the train, down

1

the platform, and took the familiar sharp turn to the local bays where a two-carriage diesel stood filling the air with acrid fumes, ready for the sharp climb up to Bradfield.

The railway to Bradfield, he had always thought, was a triumph of optimism over common sense. The Victorian engineers had been undeterred by geography or geology, and had taken their tracks up precipitous slopes by way of cuttings and tunnels which might have made an alpinist blink. Harvey had always enjoyed this last twenty minutes of the ride to what he had come to regard some ten years before as his second home, and even now the first view of the town, from the brow of a hill where no self-respecting railway had any right to be, brought a faint smile of recognition to his thin, bluish lips.

From that point on the driver had little to do but use his brakes to control the descent as the little train rattled and crashed downwards into the urban valley where the blue slate church spires of God and a few remaining black stone mill chimneys of Mammon still vied to see which could reach nearer to heaven. With his chin on his hand Harvey began to pick out the landmarks below: the town hall, an absurd gothic extravaganza in golden, recently washed Yorkshire stone; Crosslands mill, a rugged and smoke-black Italianate pile, empty and becoming derelict, its towering chimney lifeless for years now but still dominating the eastern slopes as it had once dominated lives in the huddled terraces which surrounded it; the four rectangular blocks of the Heights, the town's problem estate, known locally simply as Wuthering, and, so the sociologists had it, a text-book example of deprivation in three dimensions; and away to the west, on the first of the real Pennine slopes, a few glass and concrete facades, gleaming in the pale sunshine like splashes of molten gold amongst the darker, older buildings of the university which was his goal.

On the platform at Bradfield, Harvey Lingard hesitated. It was one thing to decide on the spur of the moment to come back to die, quite another if the home you returned to remained, and was likely to remain, oblivious to your arrival, with not so much as a welcoming cup of tea, still less a bed, to ease you towards the big sleep. For the first time, Harvey began to think that his trip might have been misconceived. Far better, he thought, to have stayed in the foetid bustle of London and expire amongst concerned acquaintances. Neither here nor there, he thought bitterly, would he be likely to find the comfort of friends. Nor the devotion of a lover he had decided he could no longer bear.

He put his bag into a left-luggage locker and pocketed the card which would guarantee its retrieval later. 'I can always get the train back again,' he told himself, although he had not bought a return ticket, so certain had he been of the rightness of his decision at the moment he had reached the head of the queue at King's Cross. He drank a solitary sweet cup of tea in the station buffet before finding the energy to walk out into the bustling town centre.

It was lunch-time and the usual throng of shoppers who came to Bradfield from many of the commuter villages in the Pennine valleys to the west had been augmented by clock-watching workers thrusting their way into pubs and pie-and-sandwich shops with one eye on their comestibles and the other on their watches. Harvey was not hungry. He seldom was these days.

He made his way more purposefully now through the main shopping centre towards the hill on the west side of the town and the university quarter which flanked the Manchester road. Here the crowds were different, younger, a sartorial and ethnic patchwork swirling to and fro, browsing over bags of chips and slices of pizza, and chattering their way from lecture block to students' union or cafeteria and back again. Harvey suddenly felt at the same time young again, slipping back ten years to when he had taken his natural place in this crowd, and infinitely old as he recognised that the groups were opening and closing to allow him passage not as one integral part of the whole, as they used to, but, in spite of his fashionable jeans and leather bomber jacket, as an alien, an intruder in the body youthful to which he still felt in his heart he belonged. He flicked back his pale blond hair, a cut too long for this company, above a face a decade too old and a lifetime too sick, and pushed on grimly.

At the bottom of a flight of broad stone steps leading to the revolving doors of a nondescript glass and concrete building he hesitated. The notice by the door announced, in slightly more faded lettering than it had done in his day, that this was the Faculty of Social Sciences. The notice boards and walls around were as plastered as they had ever been with posters from the large and garish to the handwritten and almost illegible. The population was still being urged, he noticed, to consider the future of socialism, to protest against student loans, to save the third world or the environment, and assist the Gay and Lesbian Front to out the hypocrites.

For three years he had gone in and out of those doors with an exuberance and over-confidence the equal of any of the young men and women who were making their way in and out now. He stood for a moment watching them and felt the pricking of tears of self-pity at the back of his eyes. Abruptly he turned and shouldered his way through the throng which was thickening as two o'clock approached and went back at a swift walk down the hill towards the town, his resolution evaporating like early morning mist on the surrounding hills.

It had all been a stupid mistake, he told himself angrily, a stupid, romantic, almost gothic conceit, which he should never have entertained for a moment. He would go back to London tonight, he decided. But first, there was just one more short journey he wanted to make.

Back in the town centre he made his way through the now thinning crowds, recognising no one he knew although he was not himself unrecognised, to the central bus station. The bus numbers at least had not changed in ten years, he was comforted to discover, and boarding a familiar blue double-decker he settled himself in the front upstairs seat where he could watch the route unfurl as the vehicle ground its way up and out of the town, past the unmistakable, flaking concrete cliffs of the Heights, into the open moorland country beyond.

This would be the last, the very last, sentimental journey, Harvey promised himself as he alighted in a small village with a couple of women shoppers. Leaving the cottages behind, he took a road which quickly became no more than a track and then a steep and treacherous pathway as it climbed to the brow of the hill. Here the stone cottages nestled for protection against the westerly winds which blew more often than not at a brisk pace across the even bleaker moors and fells beyond. Behind him he could hear the bus manoeuvre itself around to begin its downhill journey back into Bradfield. Once the grinding throb of the diesel engine had faded, there was nothing to disturb the silence except the sound of the wind and the occasional cry of a curlew.

It was, Harvey recalled, almost always cool up here, even on the most cloudless summer days. At a time in his life when both he and the world had seemed young, and sex a delightful new adventure, he had lain here in the heather and tussocky moorland grass with more than one lover listening to the skylarks soaring irrepressibly above them. They had even read Shelly once, he thought, bitterly amused as he looked back at the presumption of youth.

He was becoming very tired now as the path zigzagged steeply the last few yards to the summit. With his breath coming in shallow gasps and his legs heavy he breasted the rise and stood for a moment taking in the panorama beyond. This had been a favourite place, he thought, and it still took his breath away. For mile after mile the moors spread out to the north and west, rolling hills of purple and dusty green fading into a misty blue on the far horizon. The landscape was broken only by the occasional dark green valley, where boggy ground gave a home to marsh marigolds and the first spikes of rushes, and by the stands of yellow-green young bracken and dark gorse just breaking into an occasional splash of brilliant gold.

The path went on, skirting a rocky outcrop, turning sharply and dropping towards a shallow stream where a couple of raggedy sheep stood looking at him stupidly as he passed. He knew he could walk no further and where the path made to ford the stream by way of a couple of stepping stones he sank on to a convenient stone himself, tears born of tiredness and self-pity – and an element of joy – trickling slowly down his pale cheeks. He rested his chin on his hands wearily, and gazed at the all-encompassing countryside. He was shivering with exhaustion but in no doubt now that the whole gruelling day's travelling had in the end been worthwhile. He took a deep breath of the cool, peat-scented moorland air, felt the breeze ruffle his thin fair hair and was, for the first time for many months, content.

He was unaware of danger, as it came silently up behind him, and knew nothing of the crushing blow which sent him into a not unwelcome oblivion.

There was another, much more public death that day.

'That old bugger Mortenson's dead!'

The message, harsh and unequivocal as it was, did not at first penetrate the misty coils of sleep which befuddled Laura Ackroyd's brain. She had picked up the bed-side telephone reflexively before her eyes were fully open and although she recognised her boss's voice she failed to register its message.

'Ted?' she muttered, pushing a tangle of dark red-gold hair out of her eyes. 'What did you say? I was asleep.'

'Then wake up, girl,' Ted Grant went on unapologet-ically. 'I said he's dead. Old Mortenson MP. Gone to meet his maker. Can you get in at sparrowfart in the morning? We'll have to get the obit out and some sort of reaction piece done. About seven?'

Laura was awake now and had taken in not only Ted Grant's message but also the fact that it was one-thirty in the morning, which left her at best another five hours of pursuing her objective for the night which had been to catch up on some much needed sleep.

'Right,' she said thickly, knowing from long experience that argument would get her nowhere. 'About seven.'

It turned out to be even more of a struggle to meet Grant's requirements than she had anticipated when she re-set her alarm and fell back into a heavy sleep. The local radio station was already broadcasting a grudging appreciation of Charles Mortenson, Bradfield's now defunct MP, by the time she had showered, dressed and run a comb cursorily through her damp hair. She glanced at herself in the mirror in the hallway of her flat as she pulled on her coat and grimaced at her reflection. It was the classic face of the redhead which returned her gaze – creamy skin scattered with freckles that were less obtrusive at this time of the year than in high summer, a mass of dark red hair still wildly curly from her shower, and eyes of an unusual greenish grey, bright and critical. Fine if you like that sort of thing, she thought with a shrug, but I never have myself.

In the car she tuned back into the local radio station. The appreciations of Mortenson's career had been thrown together, she thought critically, switching into her professional mode. There was no excuse. They must have known for months, as the Gazette had, that the old boy was terminally ill. It had only been a matter of time before he died, facing the government with a by-election which, in a seat which in the eighties had been regarded as relatively safe, they would probably now lose.

She drove fast through the still almost empty early morning streets, down the hill from her top-floor flat in a

7

tree-lined road of Victorian houses, most of them now converted into offices or apartments, down Aysgarth Lane, main artery in an area of old stone terraces known locally, with a sort of affectionate contempt, as Little Asia, and across the largely deserted town centre to the Gazette's offices in a low, newish building on the edge of the river-side industrial estate. The car park was almost empty and she pulled up her more than middle-aged, and distinctly unwashed, white Beetle next to Ted Grant's gleaming new Granada with a grin. He would not appreciate the contrast, she thought.

In the newsroom she grabbed herself a coffee from the automatic machine and joined Ted Grant and the chief sub-editor, Frank Powers, at the far end of the room where they were bent over a jumble of proofs, page lay-out sheets and a dozen glossy black and white photographs of Charles Mortenson at various stages of his career.

There was Mortenson the candidate, with obligatory rosette and adoring group of middle-aged women voters, Mortenson the victor in his three-piece of local worsted and white rose buttonhole outside the Palace of Westminster, and Mortenson the enthusiastic saviour of the threatened local regiment, stiffly at attention with colonel and veteran supporters opposed to any and all defence reviews. Only one, Laura thought, as she flicked through the prints, showed Mortenson as he had latterly been, accompanied by a wife with frightened eyes, his fleshy face much ravaged by his illness, the shoulders slumped, as his body, abused for a lifetime, had refused to be abused any longer. That photograph, she knew, the Gazette would not use.

'You'd better start phoning round,' Ted Grant said abruptly to Laura, dispensing as he usually did with the common courtesies. 'The Party agent, the mayor, the Chamber of Commerce, you know the score.'

'Is the actual obit up to date?' Laura asked.

'Yes, yes,' Grant responded impatiently. 'I did it myself a

couple of weeks ago. After all, we've known this was coming for long enough.'

'What about the Labour Party?'

'Yes, you'd better get a comment from Richard Thurston. He'll likely be succeeding Mortenson, the way the opinion polls are. You know him quite well, don't you?'

'He was my tutor when I was a student,' Laura said, anticipating and ignoring Grant's habitual wince of anguish whenever her university career in social science was brought to his attention. He was a newspaperman of the old school, as he never tired of telling his staff, determined to resist the inexorable march of the graduate recruit across his profession until the not-too-distant day when he would have to pack up his battered typewriter for the last time and leave the field to the computer literate and politically correct younger generation. Laura Ackroyd he tolerated with better grace than most because not only had she attended the local university but she had been born and brought up within the borough boundary as well.

'Tutor? Aye, well, that'll come in handy at the by-election,' Grant conceded. 'I'll expect summat exclusive out of that.'

'Right,' Laura said unenthusiastically. Her own experience at the previous general election, when Thurston had also stood for Labour, was that her acquaintance with their candidate had been a handicap in the office rather than an asset. The Gazette in general, and its editor Ted Grant in particular, made no secret of where their political allegiance lay, and it was not with the challenger in the political battle to come.

She hesitated just a moment longer.

'How long before we have a date for the by-election?' she asked. Grant shrugged.

'They've known for a long enough it was coming,' he said. 'The old bugger's been at death's door for months. I'd not be surprised if they don't go for a quick one. Get it

9

over fast so people will have forgotten about it before they have to go for the big one.'

'And Richard Thurston will win?' she asked, turning away from the two older men to hide the gleam of excitement in her eyes.

'Oh, aye,' Grant said between clenched teeth. 'Your bloody sociology man'll win. Short of an earthquake up Manchester Road, there doesn't seem much doubt about that.'

An hour later, Richard Thurston himself listened to the eight o'clock news on the local radio with slight and sober surprise as he buttered his third piece of toast. His wife Angela had, as usual, set breakfast for him at the kitchen table under the window and then taken herself into the garden where she liked to open the windows of her greenhouse as early as possible so that the early morning sun did not overheat her choicer blooms. It was as if her own day could not properly begin until she had tended all her children, reduced to a single dog and a multitude of plants now their flesh-and-blood offspring had left them.

So Thurston heard alone that he would shortly be fighting for a parliamentary career for the second time in his life and much earlier than he had expected. Charles Mortenson's demise, at a time when his party's fortunes were at a low ebb, would not be welcomed by his party at Westminster, Thurston thought grimly, but all the more reason why he himself should relish the fight which was to come.

He was a tall man, his dark hair greying above a thin face, with fine lines of humour around the mouth, and clear hazel eyes. It was a face which could not conceal the excitement he felt now at the prospect of a long-cherished ambition about to be fulfilled, although there was anxiety in his eyes as well as he contemplated what would inevitably be a bruising fight in the full glare of national publicity.

The particular shadow which marred his immediate pleasure at the prospect of the coming election was cast by Angela's likely reaction to the morning's not unexpected news. He knew that what he had to tell her would be like throwing a large boulder into the tranquil pool of her life. And yet, he thought irritably, had it not become too tranquil too soon? They were not old, after all, although he sometimes felt that Angela took refuge in pretending that she was, spurning fashion and adornment in a perverse attempt to turn herself into a grandmother long before her children showed any sign of casting her in that role. She had been an attractive woman and could be attractive still if she chose, he thought a touch bitterly.

He sighed and poured himself another cup of coffee, glancing out of the window as he stirred it. He could see his wife making her way from the greenhouse towards the bottom of the garden with a handful of rubbish for her compost heap, a golden labrador gambolling helpfully around her heels and pushing an inquisitive nose into the bundle. Thurston smiled affectionately at the sight of her broad beam in her favourite corduroy trousers moving with the deliberation which was her most noticeable characteristic.

Poor Angela, he thought. She would never share his enthusiasm for the coming battle. For more than twenty years she had loyally backed his every academic move, typed his thesis, his letters and his articles, even a book or two, set her own not inconsiderable talent for literary criticism on one side to devote herself partly to their two children, now grown up, but most centrally to him.

She would, he knew, be there at his side again during the election campaign. She would have her hair done and pin a red and gold rosette to her best Laura Ashley dress and try to look enthusiastic as the votes were counted. But she would not, he was equally sure, enjoy it, any more than she would relish the life of an MP's wife if that, as now seemed very likely, was what she was shortly to become.

11

He drank his coffee quickly and went to meet her as she returned from her sharp-eyed stroll around her garden, where she had snipped a dead-head here, and noted a presumptuous weed to be dug out there, as she did most mornings at this time. He met her on the paved terrace outside the back door and put his arm around her companionably, but her look of surprise held a hint of wariness.

'Old Mortenson's dead,' Richard said. Angela shrugged herself quickly free of her husband's arm and preceded him back into the house, without facing him directly, calling the dog to heel as she went.

'There'll be a by-election then.' It was a statement rather than a question and her tone gave nothing away. 'How soon?'

'Within a month, I should think.'

She went to the sink and slowly washed the mud off her hands under the tap, her shoulders slumped under her thick Aran sweater. She was not a tall woman and the gradual broadening of middle age made her look stocky in her trousers and gardening boots. Her hair, pale gold when they had married, was becoming paler rather than grey, but she had not yet completely lost the prettiness of her youth and her blue eyes had a sharp intelligence that many men, deceived by appearances, had learned to rue.

'So soon,' Angela said, drying her hands meticulously and still avoiding her husband's troubled gaze.

'Do you hate the idea so much?' he asked.

'Of course not', she came back quickly, although not wholly convincingly. 'If it's what you want. But I'm bound to have mixed feelings if you win. You'll be away so much.'

'We can take a flat in London. Now the kids are away, you don't have to be here. You can come with me.'

Angela turned to look at him, leaning against the kitchen sink with her arms folded beneath her ample bosom. She smiled at him sadly.

'I'd be like a fish out of water in London,' she said. 'You

know that. Perhaps I'll take up the Wordsworth study again. It's about time I did something for myself for a change, got the brain back into working order. Old Leavis would be ashamed of how little use I've made of my brain, wouldn't he?'

'Yes,' he said enthusiastically. 'That's just what you should do. I've always felt guilty about distracting you from that.'

'You – and the kids, and the house, and the garden, and the dogs? Come on!'

Thurston glanced guiltily at his watch.

'I'd better go,' he said, 'I've got a seminar at nine.'

'Dinner?' she asked, turning away to hide the anxiety in her eyes.

'No, thanks. I'd better see the campaign committee tonight. There'll be a lot to do even before they move the writ for the by-election. There'll be a hell of a lot to do then. A hell of a lot.'

'Of course,' Angela said, moving smoothly into her morning routine of clearing the breakfast table. It was not until she heard the front door slam behind Richard and the house fell into its customary daily silence that she finally sat down at the kitchen table and put her head in her arms with a groan.

TWO

'WE KNEW THEY'D ONLY WAIT as long as was decent,' Ted Grant said brusquely, one hand proprietorially on the Press Association message which had told the Gazette that the by-election was now just over three weeks away. Across the table from him his features editor, Laura Ackroyd, stared down at her notepad with a slightly anxious frown.

'It's not as if he's been much cop as an MP for the last year or so, is it? He was lucky to get back in the general election, if you ask me. So,' Grant went on, looking round the whole editorial conference which he had hastily convened in his office on what had been a quiet Monday afternoon, 'we've got our plans laid. All we have to do now is swing into action.'

He glanced round the table speculatively. Steve Hardcastle, the news editor, was nodding his agreement enthusiastically, as he usually did. Laura Ackroyd had been waiting in vain for years to hear Steve contradict Ted. The picture editor, Larry Savage, lit another cigarette from the stub of the one he had just finished. All the staff's attempts to gain a no-smoking office had foundered on that rock. The chief sub-editor, Frank Powers, was idly blocking out page layouts on a large pad in front of him, feigning dispassion as he usually did, while Laura herself began an elaborate doodle.

'Come on, Laura, what's eating you?' Grant asked in irritation. She looked at him impassively for a moment before replying.

14

'I just wonder whether I should be the one to follow Richard Thurston,' she said. 'Perhaps I know him too well. You might do better with someone more objective.'

Grant snorted disbelievingly. He was a big, florid man, given to furious outbursts of rage and equally unexpected bouts of jocular good humour. This time his mood was sunny enough as he contemplated the excitements of the three weeks which lay ahead.

'You're the one who's always telling us we're too hard on his lot,' he said. 'So get stuck in there, girl, and maybe you'll come up with summat good on Doctor Thurston.' He used the title with heavy irony. 'Don't you worry – if you go over the top Frank here'll soon chop you back into shape, won't you Frank?'

The chief sub jerked back to attention and nodded.

'Close to him, were you, when you were a student?' he asked. The men round the table laughed at that and Laura ignored the question, though she felt a tell-tale flush of embarrassment at her throat.

'And the women's angle,' Laura asked, only the slightest inflection in her voice indicating what she felt about this aspect of her responsibilities. 'You still want interviews with the wives? The Tory fellow does have a wife, I suppose?'

Grant flicked through the pile of documents in front of him and pulled out a sheet issued by the Conservative Party.

'Timothy Charles Lennox, thirty-three, Harrow and Trinity College, Cambridge, barrister-at-law specialising in commercial cases, nowt unusual there, dum-de-dum-de-dum . . . here we are, married to Antonia, baby son Justin, main home in Surrey – will buy a home in the constituency if elected.'

'Nice of him,' Laura muttered. 'I wonder how Antonia will like that.'

'Well, if the polls are owt to go by, Antonia won't have to like it. Any road, you can ask her, can't you? And who's going to look after baby Justin while she's out helping hubby on the hustings.'

'Perhaps she won't help hubby on the hustings,' Laura objected. 'I doubt very much if Angela Thurston will. It's not her scene.'

'Aye, well save it all for your women's page feature,' Grant broke in impatiently. 'We'll run that next week – Thursday, say? – when things really get under way. OK, Frank?'

'And you want a piece every day on the campaign as seen from the Thurston camp?' Laura asked again.

'Aye, not necessarily very long,' Grant said. 'Just a colour piece. Fred can do the main coverage, the press conferences and such. We'll run it with a similar short piece from Fred on the Tory camp, and summat on the Libs or the Greens if they actually put up. They seem a bit at sixes and sevens at the moment, though they've had long enough to make their plans, God knows.'

Fred Jones was the paper's senior political writer, habitué of council chamber and planning committee – which was what had kept him away from this particular meeting – and frequenter of the town's Conservative Club on every available occasion. Laura had no illusions that her conscientious coverage of the opposition party's campaigning would get equality of space with whatever Fred culled from the Conservative camp and would be allowed to spread over the best part of the front page each day.

'Oh, and by the way,' Grant added as an afterthought. 'It's Mister Thurston as far as we're concerned. We don't want folk thinking he's a medical doctor when he's nowt but a loony sociologist.'

Laura gritted her teeth at that but lacked the energy to debate the point with Ted, a dispute she knew she would not win. The meeting broke up desultorily. It was the time of the afternoon when the presses downstairs had fallen silent, the Gazette's green and gold vans had all pulled away from the dispatch bays, and the reporters who had afternoon assignments around the town had not yet returned to switch on their computer terminals and begin writing early copy for the next day's paper.

Laura went back to her desk and sat gazing at her luminous computer screen. It was time she got away from the Gazette, she told herself for what must have been the hundredth time that week. And for the hundredth time she bit back her anger and told herself that she would not leave, not yet, not while there was still one overriding reason why she should stay in Bradfield, even if it meant putting up with Ted Grant's aggression and Frank Power's snide remarks for years to come.

She sighed and pulled a red notebook across the desk and looked up Richard Thurston's phone number, but before she could call up an outside line, the phone on her desk rang shrilly. The voice at the other end of the line was instantly recognisable and instantly objectionable.

'Doll?' it said. 'It's me, Vince. How's it going?'

'I'm fine,' Laura said, so many reservations in her tone that most callers would have found themselves frozen off the line. Laura knew that nothing she could say would freeze Vincent Newsom out.

'I'm coming up to do the by-election, doll,' Vince said enthusiastically. 'You know I'm freelancing now? I've got this commission from the Globe to do some colour pieces for them – could be a staff job in it if all goes well, you know? How do you feel about putting me up for a few nights?'

'You're joking,' Laura said, although she knew he was not.

'Come on, doll, be serious. Just a few nights won't hurt, for old times' sake. I'm not planning to stay up for the whole damn campaign or anything.'

Laura did not reply, and after thirty seconds of silence, Vince continued, his optimism unabated.

'Tell you what,' he said. 'Let me kip in your spare room, and we'll have dinner at the Clarendon on what I save on exes. How does that grab you? A little smoked salmon, Châteaubriand, a nice burgundy, that sort of thing? And don't tell me you get that very often on the pittance the Gazette pay you. And you can fill me in on the background to this little battle – the chickens that'll be coming home to roost now old Mortenson's popped his clogs.'

Laura smiled in spite of herself at the sheer brass neck of it.

'I thought they'd cracked down on expenses on the nationals,' she said.

'Yeah, well, I'll swing it somehow. To entertaining contacts, you know the score.'

'When are you coming up?' she asked, knowing before the words were out that the battle was lost. She heard Vince's chuckle down the line and felt the old familiar combination of irritation and incipient pleasure which he had always sparked in her.

'Wednesday, doll? Pick me up at the station off the three o'clock from King's Cross?'

'Not the Clarendon,' she said. 'There's a new country house place out Arnedale way. It's supposed to be very good. We could try that.'

'It's a deal. See you,' Vince said, and rang off.

Damn you, Newsom, Laura said under her breath as the line went dead. She glanced across the office where a new young trainee, Jane Archer, had taken the desk Vince Newsom had ebulliently occupied up to eighteen months ago. He had come to the Gazette straight from Oxford as a trainee himself, but with the confidence and sheer bravado to make the sort of impression which Jane would never achieve if she stayed ten years at his desk.

Tall, fair, good-looking and with an ego which took the office and Laura by storm, he had perfected the art of dodging the boring routine jobs that are the staple of every local newspaper and projected himself on to the front page and the feature pages with a string of contributions which even his worst enemies – and he made many – had to admit were accomplished.

He had also propelled himself with an ease which Laura still could not account for into her affections, her bed and, for two stormy years, her flat, the live-in lover she swore to herself she did not need but found she could not do without.

Then, with brutal suddenness, he had gone. The chance of a job on a new magazine in London had been seized. Come with me, he had said, and she had refused. He had not begged, that was not his style. He had shrugged his shoulders, packed his bags and gone. The magazine had been launched and had folded as the recession began to bite and she had lost touch with him for months until the call which had just set her heart racing. Damn you, she said to herself, pushing her mind back to the phone and the appointments she had still not begun to make. But before she could pick up her receiver, it rang again, and this time her smile of recognition was filled with a genuine warmth.

'You haven't forgotten you're coming to supper on Thursday, have you?' Vicky Mendelson asked without preamble.

'You haven't got another eligible man laid on for me, have you?' Laura returned sharply. 'It took me weeks to freeze out that unutterably boring accountant you invited last time.' Her friend laughed.

'No, I think this is one David and his father want to chat up. Single, though, so I need another woman. Some policeman just moved into town, name of Thackeray. Have you come across him?'

'Nope,' Laura said. 'I don't get much crime reporting, remember? I'm the women's interest supremo. I'm down for riveting interviews with the candidates' wives in the by-election campaign next week. What to wear for the State opening of Parliament, all that garbage.'

'Poor soul,' Vicky said insincerely. 'You'll be telling me your vocation is child-minding next. What about asking them how they propose to stop their men leaping into bed with their secretaries to while away those long lonely nights at Westminster?'

'I'm not sure that sort of frank and open discussion is quite what Ted has in mind,' Laura said, laughing. 'How are you, by the way?' she went on quickly, suddenly guilty. Vicky was expecting her third child.

'Oh, I'm blooming as usual, you know me. All the grotty bits are over now.'

'I suppose David's desperate for a girl, is he?' Laura asked. Of her former student friends, Vicky and David had married first and produced children – two sons so far – the earliest. David Mendelson had qualified in law, refusing his father's offer of a partnership in the family firm of solicitors, and was now working for the Crown Prosecution Service while Vicky, to Laura's mind, which she seldom hesitated to speak, wasted her academic talents in motherhood. On that topic the two friends agreed to differ, though not without some heat.

'The boys would like a girl,' Vicky said, laughing. 'They're old enough to relish the idea of someone they imagine they can boss about without getting thumped, I think.'

'I thought you were bringing up new men,' Laura offered.

'Fat chance,' Vicky said. 'They seem to inbibe the idea that females are some sort of pre-programmed washing-up machine with their mother's milk. Perhaps we could work on changing the formula some time.'

Laura glanced across the newsroom, which was slowly filling up as the afternoon wore on. Ted Grant was watching her from the door of his office. Jane, the trainee, was besieged by Frank Powers, who had a not very avuncular hand on her shoulder as he discussed something on her computer screen. Laura sighed.

'I have to get on,' she said. 'What time Thursday?'

20

Harvey Lingard's body lay on its back in the boggy ground close to the edge of the stream. It had lain there for three weeks now, in the hollow where it had been rolled after his death, hidden from the path by a screen of moor grass which grew thicker and taller with every warm, wet, spring day that passed. Although Harvey's life had departed his body instantly and without pain as a crushing blow descended on his head, life itself had not. Nature the scavenger had set to work on Harvey Lingard as soon as his bloodied scalp met the muddy surface of the bog and nature had now reduced his remains to what looked from a distance like little more than a bundle of soggy rags, denim and leather proving more resistant to decay than the flesh and blood within.

In good weather the track across the moor was well-trodden, but in bad weather, such as there had been for most of the time since his death, the path itself turned to black, sticky mud, blocked by pools of standing water and interspersed with treacherous screes, which deterred all but the most determined walker.

Martha Halliday would not have been deterred had it not been for the flu which sent her to bed with a generous measure of whisky in her hot milk the very day that Harvey had taken his last trek up the moor behind her low stone cottage. At seventy-five, and a frequent and public commentator on her own remarkable fitness for her age, she had succumbed with ill-grace to her doctor's instruction to stay in bed, and later indoors, for a full three weeks. She had watched with increasing frustration as her neighbour, himself in his eighties, came each morning and evening, put Bess, her golden retriever, on her leash and took her for what Martha condemned as a mere stroll around the village.

At last, the doctor placated and the weather fine again, Martha put on her fleece-lined boots, sheepskin jacket, red

21

knitted hat and gloves and set off herself with Bess,
determined to climb to the top of the moor and at least
reach the stream which divided the almost tame heath
from the really wild and open country beyond. It was, she
knew, no more than a mile, but a steep mile and after
three weeks of inactivity she felt the muscles at the back of
her sturdy legs complain and even allowed the dog, an
energetic five-year-old, to take some of the strain where
the climb over stony outcrops became most difficult.

Breasting the final rise and scanning the moor for
sheep, which she did not see, she unleashed the dog and
allowed her to bound away through the heather at the side
of the path. Even before Martha had reached the stream,
breathing more heavily than she usually did and irritated
with herself for it, Bess had returned, tail between her
legs, whimpering.

'What is it, lass?' Martha asked, fondling her ears.
'What's up?'

She stood within feet of the rock upon which Harvey
Lingard had sat to take his last view of the world and
scanned the moor for whatever had frightened the dog.
She could at first see nothing untoward. But Bess pointed
upsteam of where they stood, quivering with nerves, tail
still drooping forlornly, and eventually Martha made out a
faint touch of dirty blue amongst the browns and murky
greens of the boggy stream bank.

She picked her way slowly towards it, the dog trailing
anxiously behind, and was horrified when a cloud of flies
arose from what appeared to be no more than a bundle of
rags half submerged in the soggy ground and more than
half hidden by clumps of marsh marigolds and rushes. She
stood for a moment, her boots braced firmly against the
suck and tug of the bog, her heart beating against her ribs
so loudly she almost believed she could hear it, and
gradually her still sharp eyes were able to make out the
vaguely human shape of the lumpen bundle.

'There's some poor bugger theer, lass,' she said to the

dog, holding her collar to prevent her approaching again. 'Long gone, by t'look of it.'

She went no closer, needing no confirmation that whoever lay there was long past her ministrations. Putting Bess back on her leash she turned away, grim-faced, and tackled the slow, treacherous clamber back down to the village. Safely in her own living room, she picked up the phone and dialled 999.

Chief Inspector Michael Thackeray was still coming to terms with Bradfield, and Bradfield with him. In taking over from his predecessor, Harry Huddleston, he knew he was succeeding a man who had become a local institution. His first few months on his new ground had been regularly punctuated by a heartfelt interrogation from every new acquaintance and contact he made on both sides of the law about the now retired chief inspector's health and ambitions. It was not always affection which prompted the inquiries either – more often a wary respect, tinged in many cases with relief. It had not taken Thackeray long to conclude that the hole Harry Huddleston had left was a large one and would take some filling.

Michael Thackeray was not a local man and was not treated as such. Knowing his county as he did, he understood that his birth all of fifteen miles away near the old market town of Arnedale set him firmly apart as a rural man in the company of the urban men of Bradfield. The folk who knew in their bones how to spin, card and weave wool, though there was meagre enough call for their skills these days, understood little and cared less about the beasts which produced the stuff on the fells and moors to the north where Thackeray had grown up on one of the hill farms of the high Pennines.

Thackeray knew all this and accepted it. He was in any case a man who kept his own counsel and at more than six foot, with the physique and experience of a rugby player,

23

was seldom pressed to do otherwise. Bradfield, he knew, would slowly come to terms with the loss of the belligerent Huddleston, who had gone out in a blaze of glory, and when it had done that it would come to terms with his own arrival too. In the meantime he watched, his square, slightly rugged face an impenetrable mask, only his blue eyes occasionally giving a hint of cool amusement at what he saw. And while he watched, he also waited for the chance to make his mark.

That chance might have arrived, he thought, as he felt the first faint stirring of the excitement that a difficult case brought. He stood, the trousers of his grey suit tucked into gumboots, dark hair tousled in the moorland wind, but looking completely at home in the wild countryside that lay, for all that, within Bradfield's urban boundaries. He was watching the town's fat pathologist, Amos Atherton, crouching uncomfortably in the mud in wellingtons, overalls and plastic gloves to examine the body which had been found on the moor above Heyburn village.

Thackeray's face was dispassionate as the remains were examined. The young constable who had made the trek up from the village to investigate Martha Halliday's claim to have found a body had been sent back to base, ashen-faced and shaking, after reporting in, but Atherton and Thackeray, accompanied now by older and more experienced officers, were made of sterner stuff.

'Male, young – judging by his clothes, there's not much else to go by now – and his head's smashed in at the back,' the pathologist said as he scrambled back to the path where Thackeray stood, peeling off his disposable gloves as he approached.

'Could he have fallen?' Thackeray asked, glancing around, but he shook his head, answering his own question. 'There's nothing high enough to fall *from*, is there? And the ground's soft by the stream.'

'The blow's too much on the crown of the head, I'd say,' Atherton said. 'And there's nowt around there to cause that sort of injury even if he'd slipped. Looks much more like a blow from above with summat heavy.'

'Murder then?'

'You don't expect me to commit myself to that at this stage, Chief Inspector, do you?' Atherton came back with unexpected caution.

Thackeray smiled faintly. He was not yet, he thought, sufficiently accepted to indulge in off-the-record speculation.

'Of course not,' he said. 'No doubt you'll want to get full value back in the lab when we've scooped him up.'

'You'll need shovels, tell the mortuary men,' Atherton said grimly. 'He's been lying down there weeks, if not months. It'll be a mucky job.'

'So our lad who came up first-off said,' Thackeray commented dryly. He had taken his own close look at the body before Atherton's arrival, not touching, but seeing enough of the bloated, invaded flesh beneath the sodden clothing to know that identification was going to be difficult and the post-mortem probably inconclusive. He remembered the uncovering of a woman's body in similar country in his days in uniform. He had been the one to turn away retching then. He was tougher now, he thought, though the anger he had felt all those years ago at the sheer arbitrary wantonness of death was still there, deep down, sharpened indeed by brushes of his own with the unfeeling reaper.

'I'll warn them what to expect,' Thackeray said. 'I'll just let the scene-of-crime lad have a look around, though there'll be little enough for him to get a hold on after the rain we've been having. The whole place is like a swamp.'

'He's wearing a digital watch,' Atherton said. 'Seems to have stopped at 14.55. Could be the time of death, I suppose, if it's not waterproof and it stopped when it went into the mud. But I doubt we'll ever pin down exactly when he died, the state he's in. Could be anything from ten days to a month ago, given the warm weather.'

'But long enough for someone to know he's missing?' Thackeray asked.

'Oh, aye, if anyone cares,' Atherton said. 'The way young folk carry on these days, coming and going, kipping down here and squatting there, it's a wonder the mortuaries aren't overflowing with unidentified corpses.'

The two men scrambled back down the muddy track to Heyburn village together, leaving the uniformed men to cordon off the area and await reinforcements. Village was in fact something of an exaggeration, Thackeray thought as he slowed down at the point where the path broadened out into a rutted track just above the level of the dark stone roofs of the straggle of cottages below. There were no more than two dozen of them altogether, low old buildings with heavy lintels and doorways under the broad stone slabs of the roofs. They were well cared for, though, the windows framed in gleaming white paint and the tiny gardens full of late spring flowers. It was a welcome normality after the horror of what lay a mile behind them.

The only building of any size in Heyburn was the pub, the Fleece, a square structure in the same heavy local stone with an air of having squatted there in the teeth of the moorland gales for a couple of hundred years and having every intention of defying them for another couple of hundred. It was set back from the lane across a yard where its only concession to fashion – several wooden tables and benches streaked with green mould – stood damply amongst standing pools of rain water which reflected the ragged clouds above.

'Fancy a pint?' Thackeray asked the pathologist. 'They should be open. I'll just call in and get a house-to-house organised for later, though from what you say I'm not sure yet just what we're asking folk about.'

Atherton nodded eagerly enough and stood in the pub doorway watching while Thackeray made the call from his car radio. This was Atherton's first serious contact with the

26

detective chief inspector on a case, though he had met him briefly at the infirmary when he had called to introduce himself a couple of months earlier. The gossip had it that Thackeray had been well thought of in his previous division on the other side of the county, though not, it was said, a clubbable man, and a teetotaller to boot. But Atherton, and Bradfield itself, took pride in making up their own minds on such matters – and that slowly.

Thackeray brought Atherton a pint of the local brew and himself a fruit juice and they settled at a table in the almost empty saloon bar. The spring sunshine cast bright shafts of yellow light across the oak tables and high settles, and sparkled amongst the glasses and bottles behind the bar and on the gleaming brass and copper on the walls. The place had a welcoming warmth inside which its dour exterior belied. It had all the signs of a well run house and Thackeray nodded affably enough to the landlord when he asked what the police had found up on the moor.

'There's a body up there,' he confirmed. 'Been there some time, by the looks of it. Do you get many strangers in at this time of year?'

The landlord shook his head with slow deliberation.

'Not so's you'd notice,' he said eventually. 'We're right dependent on the weather up here. A fine spring day brings 'em all out – hikers, bikers, courting couples, model aeroplane men – noisy buggers they are an' all. But this last month's been a dead loss. Rain and sleet and then more rain. It must be three weeks since we saw the sunshine. You'd not buy a barrel of ale with my takings this month, and that's a fact.'

'Give it a moment's thought, if you would,' Thackeray suggested. 'Anyone who's been in that you didn't know. Or any strange cars in the village. I'll send one of my lads over later to take a statement.' He picked up his drinks and moved back to Atherton.

'The place'll be packed in a couple of weeks time if the weather brightens up. He'll be cheerful enough then,'

Atherton offered, taking a first mouthful appreciatively and glancing curiously at Thackeray's more innocuous tipple.

'Popular, is it?' Thackeray asked, conscious of the pathologist's unspoken question but feeling disinclined to answer it.

'A lot of walkers come up this way in the summer,' Atherton said. 'That track'll take you right over to Haworth if you've got the puff. They only really run the bus service up so far for the hikers. The village itself is hardly big enough.'

'There's no car parked anywhere near that can't be accounted for, the old girl who found him says. They'd have noticed and I reckon in a place as small as this she's right. So our lad must have come up on the bus – or walked.'

'Someone will have seen him,' Atherton said comfortably. 'You can bet on that in a place like this. Nowt happens without someone sees.'

Thackeray smiled faintly, his eyes taking on a reflective look.

'I was brought up in a village like this,' he said. 'My father used to say you couldn't go to the privy without someone knowing.'

'Arnedale way, was it?' Atherton asked.

He wants my life story, just like the rest of them, Thackery thought, and he is not going to get it. Not now. Not yet. And some of it not ever. Atherton was oblivious to the tightening of Thackeray's jaw and the remote look which passed like a cloud across his eyes as he took another satisfied draught from his glass.

'Nice little town, Arnedale,' he said. 'I bought a good jacket at that shop behind the church a couple of years ago. What's it called? Johnson's?'

'Beyond Arnedale,' Thackeray said, turning his mind back with difficulty to Atherton. 'My father farmed up on the tops towards Ribblesdale. Sheep.'

'And you weren't for following him, then?'

'I wasn't too keen on tramping those moors at all hours in four foot of snow and a howling gale, and minding the ewes all night in a bitterly draughty barn at lambing,' Thackeray said, smiling thinly at the memory. 'What I didn't know was that I'd be kept up just as long and just as late looking for villains in a different kind of wilderness.'

'Aye, I wouldn't have said you'd picked a more comfortable berth,' Atherton said heavily, swilling down the last of his pint. 'Another?' he asked, squinting obliquely at Thackeray's glass again, but Thackeray shook his head.

'Some other time,' he said. 'I want a word with our Mrs Halliday before I go back to town. She'll enjoy telling her tale a second time around, and she just might have seen our lad before. Young, you reckon, do you, on what you can see so far?'

'Young, fair haired, longish fair hair, that is, blue jeans, leather jacket, training shoes, nowt to distinguish him from a hundred others, I dare say. But it's early days yet, Chief Inspector. Wait on a few days and I'll give you as much as pathology can offer, perhaps even his name and address if there's owt in his pockets for forensic to have a go at.' Atherton belched comfortably and patted his expansive stomach.

'It's not as easy to stay anonymous as some folk like to think,' he added darkly. 'Not nearly as easy.'

THREE

'WHAT AM I GOING TO do, Laura?' Joyce Ackroyd asked bitterly. 'I'll not get as far as the committee rooms with this bloody thing!' She pushed her metal walking frame away derisively as she sat down again in her high-seated armchair. She sat close to the gas fire which gave a flickering blue flame although Laura did not find the day cold.

'What am I going to do? I've not missed an election since 1945.'

Laura picked up her grandmother's frame and parked it within reach by the chair, thrown off balance by this unusual querulousness and by the unexpected appearance of the frame. The last time she had seen Joyce she had been using two sticks, a means of getting about which had been distressing but which lacked the finality of the tubular steel apparatus she had now acquired. For the first time Laura considered the possibility that Joyce might soon become too frail to cope alone, a prospect which filled her with as much horror on her grandmother's behalf as she guessed it was causing Joyce herself, although she knew that she would never admit it.

For all her white hair and pale, translucent skin meshed with infinitely fine lines, this was no old lady going gently into any good night. Joyce Ackroyd, as redheaded in her youth as her granddaughter, had been a fighter all her life and her eyes were still bright with determination. What infuriated her now was that the arthritis which was slowly

30

crippling her looked set to keep her away from a battle in which she scented victory.

Laura had driven out of town after work to the old people's bungalows which stood in the lee of the four looming blocks of the Heights. Joyce Ackroyd not only lived at the Heights: she had, as a young and not so young woman on the town council, helped to plan and oversee the entire estate to completion, taking immense pride in replacing insanitary stone back-to-back slums with modern homes.

But like so many good intentions, the planners' scheme to keep the elderly close to their roots had gone tragically awry at Wuthering, as the locals had soon derisively christened the 1960s estate which dominated this side of Bradfield. Far from feeling at home, many of the old people who had been accommodated here, just where the bitter east winds of winter whipped most fiercely around the base of the blocks of flats, were frankly terrified, by day and night.

They complained constantly to social workers, the police, the Gazette, to their families, to friends who bothered to visit them, and to each other about the swirling litter, the rampaging gangs of children, the half-wild dogs and the simmering violence which every now and again exploded in a mugging, a fire or an inexplicable outbreak of mind-blowing vandalism. They even complained to Joyce Ackroyd who, although she was no longer able to serve on her beloved town council, was still ready enough to pick up her phone and do battle with bureaucrats and politicians of any political persuasion whenever she discovered a worthy cause.

Political battle of one sort and another was her life-blood and she fretted now to the point of tears at the thought that she could not take any active part in the by-election which had just been announced.

'Has no one got a car to run you to the committee rooms?' Laura asked. 'I'm going to be up to my eyes in it myself at work. I'll not be around to give you lifts.'

'I'd not ask you, lass,' Joyce said angrily. 'I know you'll be

31

busy, so don't you fret about me.' Laura glanced around the tiny living room, normally kept as neat as a hospital ward. Was she imagining it, she wondered, or was there really a film of dust on the mantel over the gas fire? There was no doubt that the pile of newspapers in the rack beside Joyce's favourite armchair was higher than usual, and less meticulously tidy, nor that the pot plants on the window-sill, where they caught the morning sun, looked slightly dry, the foliage more yellow than it should have been, the dead flowers untrimmed. Tiny signs, Laura thought, but significant, and they filled her with apprehension.

'What about Gordon? Didn't he run you about last time?' she asked, turning back to the immediate problem of Joyce's transport for the campaign.

'He can't drive any more, can't Gordon,' Joyce said bitterly. 'His eyesight's not what it was. We're all bloody old crocks when it comes down to it.'

'No, you're not,' Laura said, her smile showing more reassurance than she felt. 'You'll outlive my father, the way you're going.'

'Aye, well, there'd be some justice in that,' Joyce snapped, a gleam of satisfaction in her eyes. 'Have you heard from them at all? I've had nowt but a postcard since Christmas.'

That was unsurprising, Laura thought to herself. Her father, Joyce's only son, was an infrequent correspondent. When he did write, she knew that Joyce was quite likely to respond with five or six closely handwritten pages of political analysis which always included at least one page of good reasons why British citizens who had made their brass out of the working folk of Bradfield should not remove themselves and their funds to foreign parts. Joyce Ackroyd had never minced words and saw no reason why she should make an exception for her son.

Jack Ackroyd was a self-made man and a successful manufacturer of plastics until a heart attack at the age of

forty-five had persuaded him to sell up and retire to a villa in Portugal two years before. He had been a severe disappointment to his long-widowed mother. She must be the only parent in the country, Laura thought with amusement, who had been tempted to disown her son when he became a millionaire.

Unlike Laura, who had allowed her parents to buy her a flat when they went abroad, Joyce had refused all financial help from that source. She had lived in a council house all her life, she had declared when Jack offered to find her a cottage in a more salubrious suburb, and she could see no reason why she shouldn't die in one. Jack, who had inherited his mother's temperament but had learned to control his temper rather better, had glanced at his wife in despair, pocketed the sheaf of estate agents' details he had brought with him and effectively walked out of his mother's life without another word.

Laura though, who reckoned that in her veins the destructive Ackroyd pride had thankfully been diluted, had stayed. Joyce was the reason she had refused to go to London with Vince Newsom. Joyce was the reason why, however frequently she was infuriated with life at the Gazette, she skipped over the weekly pages of newspaper job advertisements, resolutely refusing even to look at them, avoiding temptation. She was Joyce's only relative within a thousand miles. While her grandmother was alive, she was determined she would not leave Bradfield.

'I had a letter from my mother a couple of weeks ago. They've filled up the swimming pool already. It's getting up to eighty degrees in the afternoons. They want me to go out for a holiday soon,' Laura said, knowing that Joyce had an unexpected and lasting affection for her mother, an ineffectual woman totally incapable of standing up to Jack's moods and tantrums and one for whom she would have expected her grandmother to show nothing but contempt. There were ties there, Laura suspected, that neither party had ever chosen to tell her about.

33

'Why don't you do that, love,' Joyce said unexpectedly, her irritability overtaken by her pleasure at Laura's presence. She scanned Laura's face sharply, not missing the faint violet shadows beneath her eyes, 'You look a bit peaky. You'll be tired when this little lot's over. Is he going to win, do you think?'

'That's what everyone seems to expect,' Laura said comfortingly. 'The opinion polls are all going the right way. He should walk it.'

'But will he be any good?' Joyce insisted. 'You know him. What do you reckon?'

'He'll be good. Not a firebrand. Not your style, you old rabble-rouser,' Laura said affectionately. 'Thoughtful and rational and conscientious, I should think. And he knows the town well. He's been here twenty years.'

'The Party's not what it was when I were a lass,' Joyce said, generations of regret in her face. 'I once heard Nye Bevan, you know. There's no one can speak like he used to. No one in the same league, nowhere near. It's all university lecturers and public relations men these days. The old working class giants are long gone. I don't suppose you'll be doing owt to help?'

The last was said sadly, almost as an afterthought, because they both knew what the answer would be. Joyce had been fighting a battle with her son for the soul of the granddaughter who looked so like her for almost the whole of Laura's life. And neither she nor Jack, from the distance of exile, would ever admit that they had both lost, that Laura was her own woman.

Laura laughed and shook her head, her hair catching the light like burnished copper.

'You know I can't in my job, even if I wanted to,' she said. 'I'm supposed to be objective, not writing propaganda for political parties, even your political party.'

'And you don't think t'other lot'll be getting any propaganda in that rag you work for, then?' Joyce came back angrily.

34

'I'm doing regular features on Richard Thurston's campaign,' Laura said, ducking the substantive issue deftly. 'Interviewing his wife tomorrow, in fact. At least you can be sure that'll be honest. Now what do you want me to do about the committee rooms? I can't stop. I've got to meet someone off a train from London.' She deliberately did not tell Joyce whom she was expecting. Joyce had met Vince Newsom and had not forborn to tell Laura in great detail the many reasons upon which she based her dislike of him.

'Oh, I'll ring around,' Joyce said, airily. 'I'll find someone with a car.'

'Just the committee room, mind,' Laura said, putting her coat on. 'Don't you go trying to canvass round those flats or down the hill on the estate. You're not fit enough for that.'

Joyce glanced at the walking frame regretfully and gave a nod.

'Half of them won't even come out to vote any road,' she said scornfully, glancing out of the window at the blocks which lowered above the bungalows. 'Bits of kids with kids of their own, half on 'em, the other half not even bothered to put their names on the register in case they get done for t'poll tax. You sometimes wonder what we've worked for all these years.'

Laura hesitated. It was not like her grandmother to sound so deeply depressed. She glanced at her watch. Vince Newsom's train would be arriving in ten minutes.

'Richard's going to win, Nan,' she said determinedly. 'If you're looking for lifts, I'd book one down to the Labour Club on the night. You'll not want to miss the celebrations.'

The old woman looked at her soberly for a moment, the picture-book image of white-haired, elderly respectability, and then her eyes gleamed maliciously and a triumphant smile lit up her face.

'Aye,' she said. 'That'll show them buggers, won't it?'

*

Vince Newsom's train was late. Laura sat impatiently in the station car park in the fading late afternoon light only half listening to the six o'clock news on the radio. National interest in the by-election was already beginning to pick up, but her mind was elsewhere.

She had been at her desk earlier in the afternoon when Rob Stevens, a young colleague who had joined the paper at the same time as Vince Newsom, had pulled up a chair determinedly and sat down close to her elbow. He thrust a crumpled handbill in front of her.

'What are you going to do about that on your squeaky clean features pages?' he asked aggressively. He was a thin-faced young man, brown-haired, blue-eyed, and not unattractive, she thought, although she worried about the faint lines of tension about the eyes and mouth and thought she knew what caused them. The determination with which he was tackling this issue did not really suit him, she thought. Rob was essentially a gentle soul, given to constructing thoughtful but pithy essays on the arts in Bradfield, which he connived with Laura to smuggle on to the features pages in the teeth of Ted Grant's well-known contempt for anything which smelt of culture.

Laura looked down at the handbill. It was familiar enough. In fact she had had one thrust into her hand a few days earlier when she had been walking up the hill near the university. It was headed 'Out, Out, Out, Get the Hypocrites Out!' and published by the students' Gay and Lesbian Front. The gist of its message appeared to be that members of the community who were gay and did not publicly admit to it were doing those who had 'come out' a disservice. They were pretending to be something they were not, leaving those who had identified themselves to bear the brunt of anti-gay prejudice and worse. If they did not voluntarily identify themselves, it suggested, then the Front would do it for them. It was a good story. It was a story she knew – and she knew that Rob knew – that Ted Grant would never use in a million years.

'Have you tried to sell the idea to Ted?' she asked.

'I'm trying to sell it to you,' Rob said. 'A feature on the Front, some sort of discussion on "outing". You know it's going on in the States. They could really be thinking of trying it here. It could turn this town upside down, especially with the by-election coming up.'

'It'll only turn this town upside down if they get round the libel laws,' Laura said irritably. 'You know no one will publish what they want published without cast-iron evidence, and probably not even then. Remember Elton John and all the other huge libel damages? And even if they started naming people on handbills they could get clobbered legally.'

'Then just do a feature on the principle of the thing. Talk about the American experience, the ethics of it . . .' He trailed off rather miserably and Laura watched him for a moment. She knew he cared about the issue and why he cared, why the hands which were smoothing out the handbill on the desk in front of her were trembling, and the anxious eyes avoided hers.

'What ethics?' she asked more gently. 'What do you think about it? You're "out", you've made no secret of it, at least to your friends, but what if you'd been pushed? What if your parents had found out because someone else told them? What if you had a wife or children? What if I went in now and told Ted the truth about what at the moment he turns a blind eye to? Has anyone else got the right to make that decision for you?'

Rob looked away and shrugged.

'It's a good story,' he said again, less certainly.

'It's a good story,' Laura agreed. 'And one which Ted won't touch in his precious "family newspaper". How serious are the students anyway? Have they really got lists of people they're proposing to expose?'

'I think so, yes. They were talking about naming names

– councillors, doctors, someone high up in the freemasons, people in the university, I don't know who else. Maybe it's all just talk.'

'If it's not, we may get our story when they end up in court,' Laura said grimly. She glanced at the handbill again. The meeting it advertised to discuss the issue was being held at the university the following night.

'I might go up there just to listen in,' she said. Rob smiled uncertainly.

'Can I come with you?' he asked.

'You can be my guarantee of good faith, if you like,' she said, anticipating that she might have difficulty in talking her way into a gay and lesbian meeting. 'But seriously, if you want to get yourself into fearless exposés of this sort you're on the wrong paper. You'd better start applying for jobs on the Guardian.'

'What about you?' Rob asked. 'Don't you get pissed off too?'

She had not answered him. Oh yes, she thought, rubbing a space on her steamed up windscreen to get a better view of the station entrance from which a trickle of what looked like London travellers was at last beginning to emerge. Oh yes, she got pissed off, too. Young Rob was just too percipient by half.

Vince Newsom arrived at her flat with a bulging leather sports bag, a portable computer, a tape recorder and a bottle of vodka. He dumped his baggage in the middle of the living room, thrust the bottle into her hand without ceremony and looked round critically.

'You never did get those new curtains, doll,' he said. 'And no new man either?'

Laura dropped a bag of groceries on the kitchen table and put the kettle on, ignoring both questions.

'I've made up the bed in the spare room,' she said, without great warmth. Vince took off his coat and threw it on to the sofa, came into the kitchen and put his arms around her, sliding his hands under her sweater and around her breasts. He kissed her on the neck before she could wriggle free. She had not been sure that Vince's old attraction would not overcome her determination not to get involved again, but this direct assault provoked nothing but anger, followed quickly by relief at knowing so soon exactly where she stood. She removed herself to the far side of the kitchen table, out of his reach.

'I missed you, you know, doll? More than I thought I would,' Vince said, looking injured. He had, she thought, developed an even more petulant look than of old, a touch of permanent discontent around the mouth which marred his classic English good looks, fair-haired and fair-skinned, square-jawed and blue-eyed. He could have modelled for Bulldog Drummond, she thought irreverently.

'That's why you called so often?' she said, remembering only too well the first months of his absence when a call or a letter might have moved her to take the first train to London to see him. She had missed him at first, too, and had lain awake at night aching for his touch, although that was not a confession she proposed to make now.

'It's frantic down there,' he said lamely. 'You don't realise what the pace is like. Those first few months on the Review, our feet hardly touched the ground. And to see it all blown away like that, a letter delivered by hand to say thanks very much but don't bother coming in any more . . .' He shrugged bitterly and she realised that the last eighteen months must have been much rougher than Vince had allowed anyone in Bradfield to know.

'But the Globe looks hopeful?' she asked.

He shrugged again, more lightly.

'Could be,' he said. 'Certainly could be.'

'Right,' she said. 'Do you want to eat in or out?'

'Oh, out,' he said quickly. 'Where's it all at these days? Still the Lamb and Flag?'

FOUR

THE PLASTIC-COATED TICKET WHICH Harvey Lingard
had been issued for a left-luggage locker at Bradfield
Station had proved relatively impervious to damp and the
lively appetite of decay. It had been extricated from the
pocket of the dead man's jeans by the forensic scientists at
county HQ, and was the only item on the body which gave
any clue to his identity. If he had been carrying a wallet, or
the collection of credit cards most people have about their
person, then they had disappeared, leaving not one but
two mysteries surrounding his death. The first and most
urgent of those was to establish just who it was who had
lain in the rain and wind on the moor for the three weeks
since the ticket had been issued without anyone locally, as
far as police records showed, having reported him
missing.

The left-luggage card was better than nothing, Chief
Inspector Thackeray concluded thankfully, and it quickly
gave him access to the bulky sports bag which Lingard had
left at the station on what he guessed was the day of his
death. The locker should only have been available to
Lingard for twenty-four hours, the station manager had
guiltily confessed to Thackeray. But at a quiet station,
where the lockers were seldom used, no one had bothered
to remove the overdue baggage to store it as they should
have done.

'Don't noise it abroad in Belfast,' Thackeray muttered
sourly, but the irony was lost on the harassed official.

The contents of the bag lay scattered about Thackeray's office now, the used remnants of a life, all made pathetic by the bright sunshine which streamed through the grimy first-floor windows of Bradfield CID. Thackeray and Detective Sergeant Kevin Mower, who had just returned to the CID strength after a secondment to the drug squad, had sorted through the bag.

'So what does that lot tell you?' asked Thackeray, who had not yet warmed to this new arrival on his team any more than the Londoner had warmed to him.

The younger man shrugged and ran a hand across his short, dark, fashionably styled hair.

'It's all pretty ordinary stuff, guv,' he said, fingering the collection of T-shirts and sweat-shirts and underwear. 'Not cheap. Good names on the shirts and shoes. But not out of the way.' Mower himself affected an elegantly casual style of dress which encouraged Thackeray to take him seriously on questions of fashion, although his laid-back manner and the London vowels he found less appealing.

'Not looking to be businessman of the year, is he?' Thackeray asked, more sharply than he intended. 'No suit, no ties, all sports-wear, young man's gear, student's gear perhaps?'

'Could be, guv, but a bit pricey for most students. Someone just away for a break, perhaps. Not working, certainly.' Mower shrugged again non-committally. He was still feeling his way with the man he had hoped would not be his new boss. He had been bitterly disappointed when his application to remain with the drug squad at county HQ had been peremptorily turned down and he had been summoned back to Bradfield by Superintendent Jack Longley to resume his old duties with a new chief inspector in CID.

'So -- a short visit, because there's not much there. No formal clothes, so not expecting to work or go anywhere upmarket.'

Thackeray fingered the carefully sorted piles of

belongings again. What he had hoped to find – a wallet or some other source of personal information – was not there, lending strength to the theory that whoever had struck the victim down had also robbed him. Where those personal documents had gone was the second mystery, and one which could have dragged the identification process itself out for months if not years. Thankfully though, Thackeray thought, the bag did reveal the probable identity of the body. Tucked away at the side with a couple of paperback books which might, he supposed, have been the young man's final reading on the train to Bradfield, was a pad of plain blue notepaper and some envelopes, together with a bank statement in the name of Harvey Lingard, at an address in London.

'He wasn't skint, by all accounts,' Sergeant Mower said, glancing at the statement, which indicated a healthy balance in the account. 'A bloody sight less than I am, anyway.'

'And he intended to write some letters – an odd thing to be planning for a short visit, isn't it?' Thackeray asked. 'Do you ever write letters, Mower? Does anyone ever write letters any more?'

The detective sergeant shook his head.

'Not so's you'd notice, guv. If I can't give 'em a bell, I don't bother,' he said.

Thackeray nodded, unsurprised. He was tantalised by the case, but curiously not as excited now as he had expected to be by his first murder investigation since his arrival in Bradfield. There was something curiously depressing about the meticulous reports Amos Atherton had produced on the pathetically decayed body, the flesh of which, he had said, had almost fallen from its bones on his mortuary slab. Thackeray shuddered at the thought, although he guessed that Atherton might have been exaggerating to test his reaction, which he had controlled very carefully.

Why, Thackeray wondered, had no one come forward

to report a young man of that age – around thirty Atherton thought – missing. And why, even more mysteriously now the discovery of the body and the description of the young man who had once inhabited it had been widely publicised in the Gazette, had no one claimed him as their own or even volunteered having seen him in Bradfield, on the day three weeks earlier when he had stowed his travel bag in the left-luggage locker at the station, having just arrived in or perhaps just departing the town? There was no train ticket amongst the dead man's belongings so they still did not know whether he was at the beginning or the end of his visit to Bradfield.

But this was no drop-out or vagrant who had curled up to rest like a wild animal in a remote corner and fallen prey to a random killer. It would not be unusual for such a victim to go to his grave unmourned and unnamed, a brutal full-stop at the end of a life which had already trickled away into the anonymity of the back alleys and doss-houses, with little chance of the police ever finding the killer.

For while this death might well have been random, the victim was an obviously prosperous young man, well enough dressed, well enough organised, well enough funded indeed in London W9, not to have ended his life apparently unknown and unlamented in Bradfield. Thackeray, who was honest enough to admit to himself that he was a lonely man, found the circumstances of this young man's death frankly disturbing, but did not want to explore too deeply just why this should be. With an effort of will he pulled himself back to the matter in hand.

'So, do you fancy a trip to the Smoke, Sergeant?' he asked Mower, and was rewarded with a smile of almost boyish pleasure, the first unpremeditated expression Thackeray had seen break through the rather guarded reserve Kevin Mower had maintained since they had met two days previously.

'Sir,' he said enthusiastically.

*

Laura Ackroyd had woken that morning with a foul taste in her mouth and the sunshine falling warmly across her bed from the gap between curtains she had only half closed the night before. She stretched lazily and took a couple of minutes to orient herself. She was alone. She remembered insisting on that, in the teeth of Vince Newsom's amorous protests when they had returned from a heavy evening with present and former colleagues in the Gazette's local. The Lamb and Flag was a somewhat nondescript Victorian pub the main attractions of which were close proximity to the Gazette office on the fringe of a totally 'dry' industrial estate and a draught beer which suited Ted Grant.

Grant had been there, as he was most evenings, at his most beerily bonhomous, playing the knowing ex-Fleet Street hack on the strength of his couple of years of undistinguished London experience. It was a perform-ance he honed whenever national newspaper visitors were about. Frank Powers had made every joke there was to be made, and then more, about Vince Newsom's return to Laura's flat. Another couple of London reporters, up early for the by-election, had abetted Vince in his frenetic attempts to catch up on more than a year of Bradfield gossip and pin down what looked like being the key issues in the forthcoming battle.

Laura had watched the boys at play with amused detachment, ignoring their more chauvinist verbal assaults as beneath her dignity. She sat, short skirt hitched high and long legs swinging from a bar stool from which, by the end of the evening, she had begun to droop somewhat unsteadily as her glass was filled again and again.

'Oh, shit,' she said, lifting her head from the pillow and being rewarded with a wave of nausea. 'I should know better.'

She put on her dressing-gown and wandered into the

44

kitchen. She sliced a grapefruit in half with an unsteady knife and put coffee on to filter. The dormer windows on which she seldom closed the blinds gave a view through the branches of apple trees and a flowering cherry, on which the remnants of deep pink blossom still hung, across the shining slate roofs of the row of similar Victorian villas which backed on to the garden, to offer glimpses of the town in the valley below.

This morning the sunshine took the sharp edges off the industrial scene and gave it an almost rural softness. With the blossom and the fresh green of the new foliage in the garden and the hazy blue sky beyond they could almost be on the edge of the Mediterranean, she thought, instead of at the centre of the industrial Yorkshire heartlands from which her parents had been only too ready to run to the sun when the opportunity presented itself. It's not so bad, she thought affectionately. If you hung about long enough you could even learn to love the place, if not some of the obstinate breed who had always hewn a hard living amongst these precipitous hills.

She turned as Vincent came into the kitchen behind her. He was wearing a towelling robe of dark blue and cerise stripes above which his pale face, rather fleshier around the jowls this morning than she recalled noticing before, appeared to be tinged with a bilious green.

'You look rough,' she said unnecessarily, putting the grapefuit halves into bowls and shoving one across the table in his direction.

'Full of nourishing vitamin C,' she said, tasting a segment and pulling a wry face.

'I'd forgotten how much Ted and Frank can put away,' he said. 'Bloody Tetley's bitter.'

'Hollow legs,' she said dismissively, pouring coffee. 'So what are your plans for the day?'

'Check out the campaign headquarters, I suppose,' he said without enthusiasm, stirring three spoonfuls of sugar into his cup. 'And you?'

45

'Oh, I'm on the women's interest angle today, sweetie. I'm interviewing Angela Thurston at eleven.'

Vince grunted. If he had said what he was undoubtedly thinking about the pointlessness of women's pages, Laura thought, she would quite likely have hit him.

In fact it was after eleven when she parked the Beetle outside the Thurstons' house in Southwaite on the other side of the town. She was slightly surprised to see what was obviously Richard Thurston's campaign car, heavy with red and yellow posters, parked outside and Richard himself, accompanied by a couple of middle-aged men in dark suits, coming down the drive towards her.

Richard was aging, she thought with a sense of shock as he approached, his face thinner and his hair greyer than she remembered from the last time she had seen him a few months previously. His eyes lit up with genuine warmth as he recognised her. He took her shoulders and gave her a quick kiss on both cheeks. He had always been prone to these continental gestures, anathema to good Bradfielders, she thought with amusement, noting the looks of disapproval on the faces of his two companions.

'Laura,' Richard said warmly. 'It's good to see you. You won't give Angela a hard time, will you? She hates all this, you know.' He waved an all-encompassing arm at the car, the posters and his companions.

'This is Ron Skinner, from Amalgamated,' Richard went on rapidly, introducing the older and smaller of the two men, who nodded at Laura without warmth and passed on towards the car. 'And this is Jake Taylor, the member for Eckersley – my minder, for the duration. They don't let you out on your own, you know, when you're fighting a by-election these days.'

Taylor was younger than either of his companions, taller, slimmer and better dressed in a well-cut navy suit with his regulation red rose pinned to his lapel at an angle of precise alignment with the cut of the cloth. He gave Laura the benefit of a practised smile which did not extend to his eyes, which were neutral and appraising.

'Will you be covering the daily press conference, Ms Ackroyd?' Taylor asked and looked genuinely disappointed when Laura shook her head, smiling faintly at the politically correct address. He obviously knew of her connection with Richard Thurston and was hoping to capitalise on it, she thought cynically as she told him that her political colleagues would be covering that chore.

'Laura writes mainly features,' Richard explained slightly apologetically. 'But you did say you wanted to do a "day in the life of a candidate" type piece later in the campaign, didn't you? I'm sure we can arrange that for you.'

Laura nodded. She could see Angela Thurston standing at the window of the substantial stone house behind them watching the conversation. She raised a hand in greeting. She knew that Richard's gruelling schedule of daily press conferences started this morning and was not surprised when Taylor hurried the candidate away into his campaign car, a proprietorial hand on his arm.

Angela Thurston came to the door to greet Laura as she climbed the solid stone steps from the garden level. The house was a late Victorian villa, of a style and in a neighbourhood which had been quietly running to seed until the newly promoted university brought an influx of newcomers to the town twenty years before, newcomers who appreciated the spacious rooms and could make use of the substantial attics and cellars which had deterred more frugal local people from buying property in these genteelly decaying avenues.

Angela was already dressed to play the candidate's wife, Laura thought as she took her hand on the doorstep. She remembered Richard's wife as a rather lumbering but discreet presence around the house or, more often, the garden when Richard had invited groups of students for coffee or sherry and a mixture of academic and political chatter. She had seldom bothered to change out of her heavy gardening trousers and loose smocks in those days, dressing in a style which emphasised her already thickening figure as she pottered amiably but uncommunicatively from greenhouse and potting shed to large family kitchen where she was always happy enough to include a couple of visiting students in the filling meals she put on the scrubbed pine table for her own two teenagers.

But today she was wearing a dress of a rich Paisley pattern, dark stockings and even moderately high-heeled shoes, and had had her hair styled very recently. She's not nearly as frumpy as she pretends, Laura thought as she followed Angela into the sitting-room overlooking her beloved garden where a magnificent magnolia in full bloom dominated the lawns and flower beds.

'I understand you're doing the wives,' Angela said quietly, waving Laura into a comfortable armchair facing the window and pouring her a cup of coffee from a pot already in place on a tray on a low table.

Laura grinned, looking much younger than her thirty years, and feeling herself inexorably sucked back into the role of student in this house and under Angela Thurston's level gaze. She was uncertain how much disapproval she should read into Angela's question.

'I'm afraid so,' she said. 'You'll be appearing alongside Mrs Antonia Lennox, I'm afraid, and baby Justin too, I shouldn't wonder. And you can bet your life you'll get less space than they do. Have they been up to take your picture?' Angela nodded with a slight grimace. A photo session would not be something she would come anywhere near enjoying, Laura thought.

'Why do you stick with the Gazette?' Angela asked suddenly.

'Ah,' Laura said, reluctant to answer. 'I'm the one supposed to be asking the difficult questions.'

They spent half an hour discussing Angela's plans for the campaign and her approaching role, more certain with every opinion poll, as an MP's wife. Angela talked frankly about the campaign, non-comittally about Richard's ambitions, and tentatively about her interest in taking up her own research again. Her answers are not quite mechanical, Laura thought, but verging on it. There was no warmth in her carefully expressed hopes for her husband's success, no engagement, even, with the plans for her own future. It was as if she had rehearsed her replies carefully and, as the expected questions were forthcoming, was ticking them off in her mind with an element of self-congratulation over a task accomplished.

Laura switched her tape-recorder off with a sense of relief as soon as she knew she had enough material for her purpose. She leaned back slightly in her chair and watched Angela's discomfort visibly diminish as she put the recorder into her bag, her tense expression relax and her clenched fingers unwind from the folds of her dress.

'Off the record,' Laura said. 'You hate all this, don't you?'

Angela ran a hand across her carefully coiffed hair, ruffling it into its more normal semi-disarray, and gave a slightly rueful smile.

'I've led too domestic a life,' she said. 'Perhaps you despise that. You young women are so sure of yourselves. But when we married and had the children, looking after them and Richard seemed the normal, the natural thing to do. I was just a bit too old to burn my bra and get involved in women's lib, and all that excitement.'

'It's not that unusual even now,' Laura said, thinking of Vicky and her two boisterous little boys and a third baby on the way. 'I had two really close friends here at the university. One's now a contented wife and mother, and the other's some sort of whizz-kid for an international oil company in London. I envy both of them sometimes, depending which side of the bed I get out of.' She laughed. 'I don't think the choices have got any easier,' she said.

'Well, I sometimes think that some of Richard's female

students are contemptuous of me, I've led such an ordinary life,' Angela said, a hint of anger in her voice. 'But that was actually what I wanted, it was what I chose. Now here I am, talking about fighting a by-election when all that political in-fighting actually appals me, chattering on about going back to academic work when the prospect of academic bitching actually terrifies me.

'I'm at my best when I've got lots of people milling about here wanting to be looked after. I was in my element when the children were growing up and needed me. You become the centre of that little world, you know, the hub that holds the whole thing together as they all come and go. You don't realise that in the end the centre won't hold. They won't need you any more. Even husbands, it seems, can leave you in the lurch in the end. The children have gone and now Richard's planning to go too. What am I to do to fill the time if Richard is in London most of the week?'

She ended on a note of despair, and suddenly all her carefully constructed façade cracked. Her face sagged and aged before Laura's eyes, a single tear ran down her cheek and her pale eyes could no longer conceal the desperation within.

'So what will you do?' Laura asked quietly.

'Do? What will I do?' Angela's voice rose as she choked down her emotion. 'I'll do what I've always done, of course, for Richard and the children. Protect him, if he needs it. Keep quiet when I have to. Back him up when I have to. Stand by him – that dreadful cliché. Help him fight the election when I'd rather run and hide from all those dreadful insults that get hurled about in politics. Look ecstatic when he wins, even though I believe neither of us is equipped for the jungle he's decided to enter. What else are wives of my generation for?'

She stood up suddenly and determinedly, and smoothed down her hair and her dress, as if to restore the formality which had previously prevailed.

'I'm sorry,' she said. 'I shouldn't have said any of that. You won't breathe a word to anyone will you, Laura? I will get through the next three weeks, you know. I've got through things before.' Her face hardened and Laura had few doubts that she would succeed in the monumental dissimulation she was proposing.

'I'm sorry,' Laura said, feeling the inadequacy of the conventional phrase.

FIVE

SERGEANT MOWER HAD DRIVEN THE police Granada down the M1 with a controlled aggression which had seldom allowed them to drop more than a mile or so an hour below the legal limit. At his side, Chief Inspector Thackeray dozed for much of the journey, the ultimate compliment to his driving, Mower supposed, but still presenting an irritating impediment to his determination to get to know the senior officer better.

Thackeray filled him with curiosity. His two months away from CID at country headquarters meant that he had had little chance to get used even to the look of his new boss before he was precipitately catapulted into his role as his sergeant for the present enquiry. He did not know whether the appointment would extend further than that and he suspected his future might depend upon how he performed, His careful culling of canteen gossip over the last two days had not been reassuring: 'quiet', 'remote', 'a bit of a bastard' and, imparted incredulously, 'doesn't drink', had been the sum of the collective wisdom he had been able to glean.

No specific complaints about the new man had emerged from his colleagues, but neither had he apparently attracted much personal warmth during his first few weeks in Bradfield. Mower glanced at the totally oblivious figure in the seat next to him, grimaced and returned his eyes to the carriageway ahead as they approached Hendon. Harry Huddleston had been an irascible old beggar, he thought, but at least life with him had been exciting. With this one, he just did not know.

As they had swung into the grinding traffic of the North Circular road, he handed the now wakeful Thackeray a well thumbed copy of the A to Z, the travelling Londoner's bible.

'Somewhere near Warwick Road, I think,' he said perfunctorily. 'You know West London at all, guv?'

Thackeray shook his head and offered the younger man a slightly grim smile.

'Not if I can avoid it,' he said.

'When I was in the Met I was stationed at Paddington Green for a while,' Mower said. 'Knew that area well.'

'But not Harvey Lingard?'

Mower glanced at the older man sharply, picked up the glimmer of amusement in his eyes and relaxed at the wheel again. He wants watching, this one does, he thought to himself before turning his attention to negotiating the junction into the Edgeware Road.

'Not far now,' he said.

In fact it took him another half hour to inch the car through the congestion towards the centre of the city, and then into the broader, quieter streets of Maida Vale. Just beyond the last of the tall handsome blocks of mansion flats he pulled into a narrower street of older, more dilapidated houses, many with small nondescript shops on the ground floor and converted into flats above. Number 37 was one of a terrace, four storeys high and with a basement entrance in an area below, a bank of doorbells flanking its heavy front door, painted a fading purple. The name Lingard did not appear on any of the tattered bits of card and paper which identified the occupiers of some of the flats.

'Try the lot, that's usually the best bet,' said Mower enthusiastically, pushing all the bells in succession. When a thin voice responded on the crackling entry-phone they were grudgingly admitted and told to come to the top

53

floor. The dimly lit landing, covered with a brown material which might once have been carpet but which had been reduced by decades of accretion and compression into a felt which felt slightly sticky underfoot, and ending in a ramshackle-looking fire exit to the roof, did not prepare them for the interior of the apartment into which a shadowy figure waved them.

It apparently took up the whole of the top floor of the building and the living area was huge, formed from the amalgamation of several previous rooms and painted a dazzling white which made it seem even lighter and larger than it was. Against that background what little furniture there was stood out in stark chiaroscuro on a carpet of charcoal grey: a black leather sofa, a table of chrome and dark smoked glass surrounded by chrome and black leather chairs, a goat-skin rug of silky grey and white in front of a modernistic slate fireplace, and the walls decorated with a series of hugely inflated Picasso drawings. There were no curtains at the two large windows which overlooked the street and the two men screwed their eyes up against the glare of the blood-red sunshine which poured in through the gleaming panes.

The young man who had let them in stood poised in front of them, like a gangling bird about to take flight.

'Have you come about Harvey?' he asked, even before they could introduce themselves. His voice was soft, with a nervous tremor to it. He was dressed in baggy black jeans and a white sleeveless vest above which his neck rose like a fragile stalk to hold up a thin, pale face dominated by dark, sad eyes, heavily shadowed as if he had not slept for days.

Thackeray, evidently taken aback, showed the youth his warrant card and offered his name and rank with a gentleness which Mower found excessive – not the sort of approach which would have found favour at Paddington Green.

'I was expecting you,' the young man said in a dull

54

monotone. 'Is Harvey dead?' His whole body appeared taut, as if waiting for an executioner's blow, as the two policemen guessed that by now, in a sense, he was.

'We've found a body which we believe could be that of Harvey Lingard,' Thackeray said quietly, closing the door and taking the young man's arm and steering him towards a chair. 'We have reason to believe he lived here. Is that right?'

The young man nodded jerkily.

'Oh, yes,' he whispered. 'He lived here.'

'And you are . . .?'

'I'm Larry Beacon. I live here too.' The young man shrugged off Thackeray's guiding hand and turned away from the two policeman, although not before they glimpsed the tears in his eyes. He crossed the room. His body had relaxed now, his shoulders slumped, and he dropped wearily into the corner of the sofa, as if he could no longer find the strength to stand upright, and buried his face in his hands.

Mower shot a look of entreaty at Thackeray but got no response that he could identify as encouraging. He shrugged and pulled out his notebook and took a seat at the table. Another one determined to do it his way, Mower thought bitterly. Thackeray followed Beacon and sat down beside him on the sofa, his face concerned.

'Mr Beacon,' he said, 'I'm sorry to have to bring you what is obviously upsetting news for you, but I'm afraid that this is an enquiry into a suspicious death and I must ask you some questions. We have only identified the body that was found near Bradfield very tentatively as that of your flatmate, so I need your help. Did he have any close family?'

'Not that he'd been in touch with for years,' Beacon said dismissively. 'I'm his family.'

Accepting this claim with a non-committal nod, Thackeray dispassionately described what the body which had been found on the moor had been wearing, glossing over the fact that there had been little enough left of the young man's face to provide a convincing physical description. He would have to ask Beacon to come to Yorkshire to identify the body formally, but postponed that harrowing request for the moment. He described the bag which had been discovered at the station, and itemised its contents. As he went through each list, Beacon nodded dully, in dispirited confirmation of the identification in which they now all believed.

'That is your flatmate?' Thackeray concluded at last. 'You are quite sure that is your flatmate?'

Very reluctantly Beacon disentangled his long, slim fingers which had been locked across his eyes and looked at Thackeray with fierce contempt in his dark eyes.

'Flatmate?' he sneered. 'You must know better than that, Inspector. Harvey and I were lovers. You may like to mince words where you come from but down here we've given all that hypocrisy up. Your description fits that of my lover – in every detail.'

Thackeray nodded, faintly amused as a Yorkshireman to be accused of mincing words, but careful not to let it show.

'That makes my job easier. So I can ask you quite straightforwardly when you last saw your lover, Mr Beacon, can I not? And whether you know when and why he travelled to Bradfield? And whether you went with him?'

Beacon sat for a moment with his face in his hands again before taking a deep, audible breath and straightening his thin shoulders. He turned back to Thackeray with an obvious effort of will.

'Harvey went away three weeks ago,' he said. 'A Tuesday. I don't know if it was the twenty-sixth or the twenty-seventh – you can check. Tuesday morning, anyway. I'd gone to college early that morning – I'm a drama student and I had an extra rehearsal at eight – and when I came back at tea-time I found his note. He didn't

56

say where he was going, or how long he planned to be away, but I suspected that it might have been Bradfield. He used to talk about it a lot. He'd been happy there, he said.'

'But not here?' Thackeray asked, to Mower's surprise. It was not the next question he had expected.

'Oh, here too,' Beacon said quickly. 'Till recently.' Thackeray let a silence fall again as if he expected Beacon to elaborate on his last answer, but he did not. He sat twisting his hands together in an anguished knot before changing tack.

'How did he die?' he whispered. 'I didn't expect it to be so soon.'

'But you expected him to die?' Thackeray asked, carefully controlling the surprise in his voice.

'Of course,' Beacon said flatly. 'He had AIDS. He had the full-blown disease. He'd already had pneumonia once, just after Christmas. He was getting worse.'

'And you?' Thackeray prompted, intensely aware of the young man's own fragility. Beacon shrugged again.

'I'm HIV positive,' he said. 'We were both going to die sooner rather than later but I didn't expect it to be as soon as this.' His voice trailed away into silence again, and again Thackeray let the pause last while Beacon summoned up the reserves of strength he seemed to need to continue.

'Your friend didn't die of AIDS,' Thackeray said quietly at last. 'We believe he was murdered.'

Thackeray and Mower watched Beacon's reaction to that closely, but the shock seemed genuine enough, draining his pallid face to an even paler shade and replacing the grief in his eyes with a sort of stunned horror.

'Murdered?' he whispered, as if he had not fully absorbed what he had been told. 'That's sick. Who would want to murder Harvey?'

'That's what we hoped you would be able to help us find out,' Thackeray said. 'Did you go with Harvey Lingard to Bradfield, Mr Beacon?'

'Of course not,' Beacon came back quickly. 'I've never

57

been to Bradfield in my life. Harvey went on his own. He'd been talking about it on and off for months, saying he wanted to see some old friends. I didn't want him to go. I begged him not to, in fact. But he wouldn't listen. He was quite manic about it, determined, almost as if there was something he wanted to do, or someone he wanted to talk to up there, before it was too late. But he didn't warn me he was actually going. That Tuesday, he just went. The note just said going away for a while, nothing else – and then, for weeks, nothing at all . . .'

'You kept the note?' Thackeray asked. Beacon did not answer. He uncurled himself from the deep seat of the sofa, moving more with the elegance of a dancer than an actor, Thackeray thought, and went over to a small desk against the wall from which he produced a single handwritten sheet of blue notepaper, a match for the pad which the police had found in Harvey Lingard's travel bag. He handed the note to Thackeray, who quickly confirmed that it offered only the brief and uninformative farewell which Beacon had already described.

'Did he never give you any idea who he might have wanted to see in Bradfield?' Thackeray asked.

Beacon shook his head.

'He was at university there. He always used to talk about it as if it was a very happy time in his life. But he never mentioned names. I always assumed he'd had a boyfriend up there and he didn't want to upset me by talking about him.'

Thackeray found it hard to reconcile that sensitivity with the abruptness with which Lingard had abandoned his lover, but he made no comment. He glanced around the flat curiously. Although from the outside the house had appeared run-down, dilapidated even, no expense had apparently been spared to turn this particular apartment into a stylish home. The decor was stark but the furnishings and fittings, from the hi-fi to the latest stereo TV, were impressive.

'Where did he work, your friend?' he asked curiously.

Larry Beacon followed the policeman's gaze.

'Harvey was in advertising,' he said. 'He was doing very well. He'd only really begun to have time off this last six months, though that was worrying him, what with the recession and redundancies all over the place. He was scared he'd lose his job long before the disease finished him off. He couldn't have killed himself, could he? I sometimes thought he might.' The question was asked with such leaden despair that Thackeray winced.

'No,' he said firmly, although he did not elaborate on exactly how Lingard had been killed. 'He didn't kill himself. There's no doubt about that.'

Beacon nodded, obviously relieved.

'I'll need to talk to Mr Lingard's employers,' Thackeray went on. 'And perhaps you can recall where you were yourself on the twenty-sixth and the twenty-seventh of last month. Some corroboration of your movements would help, obviously, in eliminating you from any further enquiries.'

'I was here and at college,' Beacon said dully. 'You can check there with my tutor. I can remember quite clearly. You don't forget when a nightmare begins. I thought he'd just left me, at first. It was only later, when he didn't write or call, that I began to wonder if he was dead, if he'd gone away to kill himself.'

Thackeray hesitated for a moment, trying to find a kinder way of asking his next question but concluding there was none.

'Would it have been in character for Mr Lingard to have simply left you? For someone else, I mean?'

Beacon shook his head vehemently at that.

'Harvey was the kindest person I have ever known,' he said, the tears running down his cheeks unashamedly now. 'He was everything to me. I knew I was going to have to live without him soon, but now it's happened I'm not sure I can.'

*

The students' union bar was dimly lit, sweatily crowded and intensely noisy. Laura Ackroyd and Rob Stevens were sitting in cramped discomfort on stools at a corner table drinking half pints of lager in desultory and enforced silence. The blaring music system, overlaid by another couple of hundred laughing and animated conversations conducted at a high level of decibels, made normal speech almost impossible. And neither Laura nor Rob felt any inclination to shout about what had brought them to the university.

They had failed to gain access to the gay and lesbian meeting which was, at that very moment, discussing its 'outing' campaign.

'I don't see why we should trust her,' the small intense student on the door had said fiercely to Rob Stevens when they had arrived, seeking to gain admittance. She had switched her angry gaze to Laura, who had tried to follow Rob into the crowded meeting room and been prevented by an outstretched arm from the young woman who appeared to be vetting each arrival.

'We don't need the Gazette,' the student said. 'We don't need the straight press at all, come to that.' She was a slight figure in dark leggings and sweater and lace-up boots, her hair cropped extremely short and without make-up or adornment of any sort except for a pair of enormous hoop ear-rings which shook vehemently as she spoke.

'Look, I'm trying to get you some sympathetic coverage,' Rob said. 'Laura wants to write a feature about outing.' That was stretching a point, Laura thought, but she was not disposed to argue in front of the angry doorkeeper.

'We don't need sympathy. We need our rights,' the student said obstinately.

'But if you won't explain what you want to the rest of us, how can you possibly make any progress?' Laura asked mildly.

'The rest of you.' the doorkeeper flashed back. 'Where are the rest of you when gays get beaten to pulp in back alleys in this bloody town? The rest of you turn a blind eye, don't you? Where's the coverage in your precious Gazette when we have a march against discrimination? Five hundred people supported Gay Pride outside the town hall a month ago. Where were you then? Nowhere, that's where!'

Laura caught Rob Stevens's eye and shrugged almost imperceptibly. The student had a point which had been laboured hard at the Gazette's news conference on the day of the demonstration to no avail. Ted Grant had decided that a photographer would not be sent to cover the march. There were other more pressing assignments, he had said, and would not be budged.

'Look,' Rob said placatingly. 'If you won't let us into the meeting, at least ask someone to talk to us, to explain what the Front's plans are, what it's all about. Will you do that? Please?' With a great show of reluctance, the student agreed. They should wait in the bar, she said, and she would ask one of the officers to come and talk to them when the meeting finished. Two hours later they were still waiting, and Laura was increasingly convinced that they were wasting their time. She drained her glass impatiently.

'Shall we go?' she mouthed against the surrounding din.

Rob shook his head stubbornly and picked up their glasses.

'One more,' he said and launched himself into the crush in the general direction of the bar. Laura watched him thoughtfully. She liked Rob Stevens, knew he was good at his job, though not in the flamboyant way that Vince Newsom had been good when he had exuberantly play-acted his way around the office and the town.

If he kept his head down, she thought, Rob would survive Ted Grant's homophobia and move on to a safer haven elsewhere. But she suspected that Rob was no longer keen on keeping his head down, that the students' campaign had unsettled him and made him reconsider his own very partial openness about his sexual preferences. She had no faith at all that if he 'came out' the climate of the times would make that anything other than very uncomfortable for Rob at work – uncomfortable and quite possibly fatal to his career.

Bradfield was no metropolitan haven for non-conformists, she thought, in spite of the liberalising influence of the university. In her experience, quite the reverse. It was a community which adapted to change slowly, and very often with ill-grace. It put up with its immigrants, its poor and other assorted minorities with a sort of sullen acceptance which could erupt into ill-tempered intolerance at the first sign of self-assertion. 'Uppity' Muslims had led to ugly confrontation in the not too distant past. 'Uppity' gays, she thought, might get the same treatment. The students' campaign risked stirring some very murky waters, and they were waters in which an innocent like Rob Stevens might drown.

Rob appeared through the crowd with their drinks, closely followed by the young woman who had prevented them from attending the meeting earlier. She nodded that they should follow her and pushed ahead of them to the corridor outside the bar which was marginally quieter.

'I'm Dilly,' she said. 'Dilly Jenkins. Jason said he couldn't talk to you now, but I'm to tell you about the campaign.' The words came reluctantly from that pursed, unfriendly face, as if she were obeying orders which she disliked.

'Jason?' Laura said.

'Jason Carpenter,' Rob said knowledgeably. 'He's the chair of the Front. Comes from London. He's very active in the theatre group as well – that's how I first met him.' Met and how much else, Laura wondered, and then disliked herself for wondering. It was none of her business.

'So,' Laura said sharply, made jumpy by the hostility which radiated from Dilly. 'What is the Front going to do?

"Out" the mayor and half the town council or what?' She knew the question was offensive and disliked herself even more. Dilly flushed slightly and swung her ear-rings angrily.

'That's what Jason wants, but we're not going ahead yet,' she said, her voice brittle with distaste. 'We're a democratic organisation, and there's not a majority for that yet. We'd like some discussion of the principle of outing, which is why they agreed that we should talk to you. We'll cooperate on a feature, if you let us see what you're going to say before it's printed.' Laura glanced at Rob and shook her head.

'I can't do that,' she said. 'If my editor found out I'd lose my job. No one gets that sort of veto. All I can promise is to report what you say sympathetically. Beyond that you'll have to trust us.'

'You must be joking,' Dilly said flatly.

'I'll write the feature, Dilly,' Rob said quietly. 'You can trust me.' Both women looked at him for a moment, the younger one uncertain, Laura anxious. She was afraid that if Rob put his name to this particular article it would lead to the confrontation with Ted Grant that most of the younger staff at the paper had spent the last two years helping him avoid.

'Rob can write it, but I'd rather my name went on it,' she said impulsively. 'If it's going to get in the paper at all it stands a better chance of getting past the boss if it's my work.' Rob nodded to her, grateful for the let-out.

'But we talk to Rob?' Dilly asked. Laura nodded her assent.

'Fair enough,' Dilly said. 'Let's go somewhere quiet.'

SIX

'YOU'LL NOT LEARN HOW THIS town runs if you don't mix,' Superintendent Jack Longley said flatly as he ordered Michael Thackeray a drink from the attentive waiter in the bar of the Clarendon Hotel. 'That was Harry Huddleston's great strength. He'd grown up here, been to the grammar school when it was a grammar school, knew 'em all, villains and town councillors, man and boy.'

'But it didn't help him with the Asians, from what I hear,' Thackeray said mildly, raising his glass in acknowledgement of Longley's generosity.

'Nay, well, they're newcomers,' Longley conceded. 'Not the first mind, nor the last, I dare say. There've been immigrants in this part of Yorkshire since the Huguenots – Germans, Jews, Poles, Ukrainians, Italians – you name it and they've come here. Wool brought them in, and I dare say the lack of it'll drive some of them away in the end.' He cast a mellow eye round the bar which was packed with a prosperous-looking crowd of lunch-time drinkers, most of them male, white and middle-aged.

Longley had dragooned Thackeray away from police headquarters into the Clarendon after the chief inspector had reported back at noon on his trip to London the day before. Thackeray had returned to Bradfield late and by train, leaving Sergeant Mower to continue their inquiries into Harvey Lingard's work contacts and other associates in London and to check on his flatmate's movements on the day Harvey Lingard travelled north. He would bring

64

Larry Beacon back with him to Bradfield to make the formal identification of the body.

Not that Thackeray held out much hope that the answer to the mystery of Lingard's lonely death at Heyburn lay in the south. His conviction, which he forbore to share with Mower as he allotted him a not unwelcome day in the metropolis, was that the key to Lingard's murder would be found much closer to where he had been struck down by a single blow from, Amos Atherton now surmised, a chunk of rock picked up at the site where he fell. Fragments of the heavy local stone had been found embedded in the wound to the head which had killed Lingard, and a more careful search of the boggy area around the stream had unearthed a piece of boulder which was light enough to heft but still heavy enough to kill, although if it had once been blood-stained there was little enough chance of proving that now, long wet weeks after the event.

'Take Victor Mendelson over there,' Longley went on, sticking to the theme of Bradfield's cosmpolitan population and indicating a stocky figure in a formal pin-stripe, his dark hair grizzled at the sides, the long intelligent face absorbed in conversation. 'You'll meet him in court soon enough, I dare say. Partner in one of our leading firms of solicitors. Brought here as a baby by his family just before the war. Penniless refugees from the Nazis somewhere or other.'

'A relation of David Mendelson's, Crown Prosecution Service?' Thackeray asked.

'His father.'

'I'm invited to dinner with them tonight,' he said reflectively. 'Is this all part of a campaign to integrate me into the community?'

Longley grinned conspiratorially.

'I've had a few words,' he admitted. 'You're not on the square. You need to meet a few folk, learn how the place ticks.'

'Just so long as none of them expects me to help it tick

their way,' Thackeray muttered. Longley took a long sip of his Scotch and looked at the younger man coldly.

'If you think that's the way my division works, you'd best transfer out of it as fast as you transferred in,' he said. 'The Force may have had a bad press lately, but not in Bradfield, lad. Not now, not ever.'

Thackeray gave a smile which lit up his normally sombre face.

'I'm pleased to hear it,' he said, in conciliation. He sank back into his comfortable leather chair and cast a sharply intelligent eye around the bar. At the next table he watched with interest as two men in dark suits engaged in an animated conversation which threatened to degenerate from the purely social. The older, more heavily built of the two was beginning to raise his voice in anger, and Thackeray glanced at Longley in amused interrogation.

'Who are those two pillars of the community?' he asked quietly. 'They look likely to come to blows.' Longley glanced over his shoulder at the pair, who were now engaged in overt argument.

'Ted Grant,' he muttered. 'Editor of the Gazette. And the older one is councillor William Baxter – Bill to his friends – of the Conservative Party. It'll be the by-election getting him steamed up, I dare say. They look set to lose it. I expect the Gazette's not doing them quite as proud as Bill thinks is their due.'

Whatever the cause of the now heated dispute between the two men, Baxter ended it abruptly. He stood up, draining his glass at one gulp, and pushed his chair clumsily away from the small oak table at which he had been sitting. Seeing him from the front for the first time, Thackeray recognised all the signs of anger in a face which would normally be florid but was at that moment scarlet with emotion beneath a shock of iron-grey hair. Whatever degree of self-control had kept the argument muted until that point now evaporated.

'You keep that interfering lass of yours away from those

trouble-makers up the hill,' Baxter said, loudly enough not only for Longley and Thackeray to hear, but for a large section of the surrounding crowd of drinkers to notice as well. 'I'll have 'em in court if they carry on the road they're going much longer, and you and that redhead too, if that's what it takes to stamp on this nonsense.'

Ted Grant half stood up in his seat, clearly nonplussed by this assault.

'I've told you, Bill,' he said in a stage whisper which carried half way across the room, where a good proportion of the drinkers were now watching the drama open-mouthed, 'I'm having nowt to do with it. Nowt!'

'Well, you'd best make sure your staff know that, hadn't you? We've got our contacts up there, whatever they tell you about students, so don't imagine we haven't. I know what's going on, and I want it stopped,' Baxter came back sharply, before turning on his heel and pushing his way to the heavy glass swing-doors, which he shoved out of his way with such force that Thackeray and Longley could feel the draught on the other side of the crowded bar. Glancing around the room in confusion, Grant downed the remnants of his own drink and quickly followed.

'What on earth was all that about?' Thackeray asked, as the normal hubbub of the busy bar resumed, a few decibels higher than before as an avid discussion of the disturbance took hold.

Longley shook his head.

'At a guess, it's something to do with the gay and lesbian students up at the university,' he said. 'They've been threatening to name prominent folk they claim are closet queers, gays, whatever they choose to call themselves these days. Could cause some embarrassment, that could.' He smiled a knowing smile, as if nothing that the students could reveal would come as much of a surprise to him, as Thackeray guessed that indeed it would not.

' "Outing",' he said thoughtfully.

'You what?'

' "Outing". That's what they call it in the States. That's where the idea originated.'

'I might have guessed,' Longley said, snorting his contempt for all things transatlantic. 'What bothers me is that I can't work out what offence they might be committing if they go ahead with it.'

'There isn't one, is there?' Thackeray said mildly. 'Not if what they allege is true. The tabloid newspapers do it all the time. If it's not true, then they'll get taken to the cleaners in the libel courts – not that that's much cop if they're students and don't have two brass farthings to rub together anyway. You're not thinking it could embarrass us, are you?'

Longley snorted again.

'Don't you know we've got a policy now for making gay coppers feel at home in the force?' he asked. 'Haven't you seen the guff they've put out from County?'

Thackeray nodded, not daring to let his amusement show this time.

'But not in your division?' he asked softly. Longley looked at him hard, the pale blue eyes in the plump face suddenly very cold and alert.

'Personal interest, have you, lad?' he asked. 'That's not what I heard.' Thackeray met his gaze and shook his head slowly, wondering just what Longley had heard. The force was a large one but not so large that official records did not pass from division to division without a scorpion's talk of gossip. His face took on a cold and distant look as his thoughts took a lurch into an area of the past which he normally avoided with iron determination.

'I thought you knew everything there was to know about me in that department,' he said. 'My lusts are strictly heterosexual, and I don't seem to get much chance to satisfy them anyway in this job.' He broke the tension with that rare, slightly tentative smile.

'Marriage is no alibi, as far as I understand it,' Longley said. Thackeray nodded his acquiescence to that but did not reply directly.

68

'Not that I go along with persecuting the poor buggers,' Longley went on, and Thackeray could not decide whether he had chosen the epithet ironically or not. 'Staking out public lavatories, pretty coppers peering over cubicle doors, and all that nonsense. But in the force, I'm not so sure. Anyone with a secret is open to blackmail, in my book.'

Thackeray nodded non-commitally and changed tack.

'I seem to be on the edge of an investigation into Harvey Lingard's gay contacts in Bradfield, and I've never thought it made much sense to go blundering about asking intimate questions with our prejudices hanging out,' he said.

Longley nodded, suddenly looking old and tired.

'You're right,' he said. 'The world's changing too bloody fast for the likes of me. It's time they put me out to grass with Harry Huddleston.'

Laura Ackroyd pulled her only pure silk slip over her head and smoothed it down critically over her hips.

'You're distracting me,' she said to Vince Newsom who was lying in her bed watching her dress. 'I should have gone swimming tonight. I'm not getting enough exercise.'

'That's easily remedied,' he said, patting the duvet invitingly.

'No way,' she said. 'No more. I haven't got time.' She picked up a pair of dark stockings and slid her slim legs into them, to his evident enjoyment. She was half amused at Vince's presumption and half annoyed with herself for having succumbed to it once already.

She had come in from work in a fury, after a row with Ted Grant. He had called her into his office half way through the afternoon and asked her why she had been investigating gay and lesbian activities at the university. Thrown by the fact that he had discovered so quickly that she – although apparently he did not know about Rob –

had been at the meeting the previous night, she had argued fiercely for the subject to be covered in the Gazette. The suggestion had been greeted with a barrage of abuse and an outright ban on any coverage on her pages. She had come away from the office wondering how she could break the news to Rob and, not for the first time, whether she should resign.

When she arrived at the flat, after driving home in a state of high emotion, she found Vince already there and, for once, a willing listener to her bitter complaints about Grant, the Gazette and the general unfairness of life.

'Drink that, doll,' he had said, pressing a large vodka and tonic into her hand as she sat hunched with nervous tension on the sofa. He had sat beside her and pulled her towards him into a companionable embrace. Gradually the drink and the warmth and the familiar closeness did their work, as she guessed afterwards he had hoped they might, and when he gently turned her face towards him and kissed her she had responded with an acceptance which quickly turned to passion.

An hour later, after dozing for a while in the familiar crook of his arm, Laura had jerked herself awake.

'God,' she said. 'I'm due at Vicky's for dinner in three quarters of an hour.'

'Cry off,' Vince had said sleepily, putting a proprietorial hand on her thigh, but she had rolled away from him, out of bed and into the shower. He was still trying ineffectually to prevent her departure as she slid into a short black skirt, a shirt of heavy deep green satin and ear-rings of an identical green which she knew did wonders to set off her creamy skin and her hair, piled up in a swirl of copper curls.

'You look ravishing,' Vince said, getting out of bed naked and clutching the duvet around himself to cross the room and plant a long kiss on her neck. 'Good enough to eat.'

'I must go, Vince,' she said, pulling away, laughing. 'I

promised Vicky. You know what she's like about her dinner parties. She does it for her father-in-law as much as for David. Old Mrs Mendelson can't entertain in her condition. It's all heavy political stuff, as often as not, but I just have to go.'

David Mendelson's mother, who was the parent who had found it hardest to come to terms with the fact that her daughter-in-law was not Jewish, had had to swallow both her pride and her disappointment as a nervous disease slowed her down and she had to rely more and more on the younger woman. Vicky had stepped in to take over the entertaining which the Mendelsons, father and son, regarded as an essential part of their legal existence.

As Laura drove to Southwaite, where the younger Mendelsons had a house not far from where she herself had been brought up, she felt irritably conscious of the red mark on her neck where Vince had kissed her with, she suspected, deliberate over-enthusiasm. When David Mendelson took her coat she glanced in the hall mirror and pulled the collar of her shirt up partially to conceal the bruise. The soft material would not stay up for long, she knew, but would at least offer a respectable first impression.

When David showed her into the drawing-room, Vicky was the first to see her and push her way through a crush of half a dozen or more people to embrace her enthusiastically. She was wearing a loose dress of a rich, dark, oriental fabric which, with her flowing brown hair and glowing skin, gave her a Pre-Raphaelite radiance which quite distracted from her thickening waistline.

'I'm so glad you made it,' she said. 'Dad has really piled it on this evening. There's going to be eight of us all together.'

'You're obviously blooming,' Laura said, returning her embrace, and looking at her critically for a moment. 'I'm sorry I'm a bit late. I got held up. Am I the last?'

'No, no,' Vicky assured her. 'David's policeman hasn't

turned up yet. Come and meet the Treadwells. You don't know Councillor Stanley Treadwell, do you?'

Laura shook her head and permitted herself the tiniest grimace, which made Vicky smile guiltily. Laura nodded a greeting to David's parents, before being introduced to a well-built, grey-haired, pasty-faced, elderly man whose Dickensian jowls overhung his collar and whose old-fashioned watch-chain described a perfect loop across his expansive corporation. His wife was an equally imposing figure in a dinner dress of an over-confident floral print and some heavy jewellery which could only have been of solid gold. The party was already well into its second sherries and was becoming animated, with the forthcoming by-election the main focus of interest.

'I'm can't say I'm hopeful, it has to be said,' Councillor Treadwell said solemnly when Laura asked him politely how he rated his candidate's chances. 'I'm not sure we chose the right candidate in the circumstances, you know. I reckon we'd have stood a better chance with a local man. Bill Baxter wanted the nomination, you know. And so did young Barry Eastman.' The second name was mentioned with a slight look of distaste which Laura knew reflected the split in the Councillor's party between the older generation and a newer, brasher breed who had espoused a harsher politics than Treadwell could easily stomach.

'Barry Estman would have done your opponents a lot of good,' Laura said judiciously, and was not surprised when Treadwell nodded his agreement gloomily.

'We didn't make that mistake, any road,' he said.

'Ackroyd,' Mrs Treadwell said sharply, suddenly turning off the fixed smile with which she had been listening to Laura and her husband. 'Are you Jack Ackroyd's daughter?'

Laura confessed that she was, and in response to close, and in Mrs Treadwell's case, overtly envious questioning, provided the Treadwells with an up-date on her parents' well-being and whereabouts.

'And Councillor Joyce's granddaughter and all,' Stanley Treadwell broke in accusingly. There had clearly not been much love lost there, Laura thought, knowing how wickedly her grandmother would have pricked this large man's pomposity and enjoyed the pricking thoroughly.

Laura nodded again, this time with a brilliant smile.

'She's well too,' she said sweetly. 'And looking forward to the by-election.'

Some sixth sense must have informed Vicky that the conversation was veering on to dangerously thin ice, because at that moment she took Laura's elbow and drew her towards the door.

'Let me introduce you to Michael Thackeray,' she said. 'Chief Inspector Thackeray, who's just transferred to the local CID. Michael, this is Laura Ackroyd, who's features editor of the Gazette.'

Laura found herself face to face with a tall man whose strong, square, rather sombre face seemed at odds with his unruly dark hair. His smile of greeting was muted and his blue eyes remained non-committal as he and Laura looked at each other for a moment in silence. Laura's hand strayed to the neck of her shirt and she pushed it nervously up again to hide the tell-tale bruise on her neck.

'How do you like Bradfield?' she asked, feeling foolishly taken aback for a moment by the intensity of Thackeray's gaze. It was a politely conventional question but Thackeray seemed to give it a moment's serious consideration before he answered the young woman whose crowning attribute had been brought to his attention that lunchtime in the Clarendon bar. This, then, he thought with interest, was the redhead who had so annoyed Councillor Baxter. With those looks she would have difficulty in doing anything surreptitiously, he thought.

'In my job you tend to see the dark underside of places,' he said slowly. 'I expect you do in your job, too. I can't say I've really learned to enjoy Bradfield yet.'

'It has its lighter side too,' Laura said, defensive suddenly. 'The countryside . . .'

'Ah, yes,' Thackeray said ironically. 'The countryside. I inspected my first murder victim there this week, at one of your beauty spots. Not much of a tourist attraction.'

'Oh, yes, of course, at Heyburn,' Laura said, recalling the front page coverage. 'We've all done our share of courting up there.' She chose the old-fashioned phrase deliberately because it seemed to suit the style of this disconcertingly traditional-looking man who could not, she thought, be that much older than she was herself.

'So I gather,' Thackeray said drily. He had refused Vicky's offer of a drink and at that moment David joined them, holding the hand of a small pyjama-clad boy in each of his own. These dark, beautiful, precocious children, Laura thought, were delighted to be paraded before their grandparents and the rest of the company before they went to bed. Having allowed them to admire his sons, who in their turn allowed Laura to kiss them goodnight, David urged his guests to take their places at the dinner table in the next room.

Thackeray, she noticed, watched the two little boys with unusual intentness as their father led them out of the room. For his part, he hoped that the spasm of almost physical pain which had seized him as he came unexpectedly face-to-face with David's sons was as invisible tonight as he had learned to make it usually. He turned away abruptly from Laura Ackroyd, ostensibly to go in to dinner but in fact to avoid those sharply observant eyes.

Laura found herself seated at the table between David, her host, and Councillor Treadwell, whose dinner-table manners, it turned out, did not extend to making much effort to converse with the women on either side of him. He confined himself for most of the meal to discussing local and national politics with Victor Mendelson, who sat at the opposite end of the table to his son, and who made valiant efforts now and again to include Michael

Thackeray in the debate.

Thackeray had been seated across the oval table from Laura, at an angle which made conversation difficult. While she chatted to David and to his mother, who needed her son's help to cut up her food, she kept a surreptitious eye on the taciturn policeman who ate modestly, drank hardly at all and then only mineral water, and offered unexceptionable opinions, when pressed, on the town, the weather, and the likely result of the by-election. She was faintly amused by this determined neutrality and wondered whether it was genuine or came with the job. She was not unaware that her silent interest in him was reciprocated.

After the dessert she helped Vicky carry the dirty dishes into the kitchen where every mod con was available and every available surface covered with the deritus of the meal's preparation. Vicky and David's house, not ostentatious but quietly luxurious, had been a wedding present from David's father, who had been silently perturbed by the financial implications of his son's inexplicable refusal to join the family firm.

'You'd do just as well with a cardboard cut-out when you need a spare woman for your dinner parties,' Laura said grumpily as she stacked plates into the dishwasher and Vicky switched on the coffee percolator.

'Aren't you enjoying yourself?' Vicky asked sweetly. 'Better things to do at home, are there?' Laura felt her hand move towards her neck and swung it back to her side angrily. Vicky had never liked Vince Newsom and had never hesitated to say so.

'Bitch,' Laura said, softening the epithet with a slightly shamefaced grin. 'Is it that obvious?'

'Only to them as knows you as well as I do,' Vicky said lightly. 'You bruise easily, I recall. How long is he staying?'

'Not long, I hope,' Laura said, surprised at how serious that hope was.

'You're not planning to go back to London with him?'

'Nope,' Laura said. 'He's gorgeous, and sexy, and just as much of a self-centred pig as he ever was.'

Vicky looked at her friend seriously for a moment, her eyes clouded with concern.

'Don't say it,' Laura said softly. 'You know I envy you sometimes.'

'It wouldn't suit you, all this,' Vicky said, waving a proprietorial hand around the kitchen. 'You don't have the Jewish momma streak David spotted in me. But Vince is no good for you, either.'

'I know, I know,' Laura groaned. 'I'm through with him this time, I promise.'

Vicky nodded sceptically.

'So you say. Let's take the coffee in.'

'And can we liven the party up a bit?' Laura asked mischievously.

'So long as you don't give old Stan Treadwell a coronary,' Vicky said with a grin. 'The opinion polls seem to be pushing his blood pressure up something alarming.'

In fact it was the two women who were surprised by what followed, and the turn the conversation took needed no prompting on their part. Stanley Treadwell had turned his attention somewhat blearily to Michael Thackeray as the cigar smoke and brandy fumes thickened over Vicky's tiny bone china coffee cups. The older women had left the room to powder their noses, as they coyly put it, and had not returned. Laura suspected they had settled down in the drawing-room for their own brand of gossip out of ear-shot of their husbands.

'If they'd not taken the police committee away from us, I'd likely have been your boss,' Treadwell said suddenly to Thackeray. 'There was a lot to be said for the old watch committees, you know. Knew our officers, we did, which is more than can be said for the present lot at county.'

Thackeray nodded cautiously.

'A lot of the old boroughs were very small,' he said. 'There were six police forces in this part of the world just before I joined. It couldn't go on like that. Crime doesn't pay much heed to borough boundaries.'

'It's all a question of economies of scale these days, isn't it, Michael?' Victor Mendelson broke in. 'With all this high-tech equipment you have to invest in now, there's not much of a place for tiny police forces.'

'But local knowledge,' Treadwell persisted. 'That must help, wouldn't you say? You're not local yourself, are you?'

Thackeray smiled faintly and shook his head.

'It depends what you mean by local,' he said. 'I was born Arnedale way.'

'The right county, any road,' Treadwell said grudgingly. 'Went to the grammar school there, did you?'

'It was comprehensive by the time I got there,' Thackeray said, and Laura caught the faintest glint of amusement in his eyes.

'Ah,' Treadwell grunted, before returning thirstily to his brandy. There was a wealth of contempt in the sound. 'That was a fine school in the old days. Nearly as good as Bradfield Grammar. My lad went to Oxford University from BGS.'

'Really,' Thackeray said, his amusement deepening perceptibly. 'When was he up, Councillor? I was there myself in the early seventies.'

Treadwell made a choking sound into his brandy glass and Laura shot a delighted grin at Vicky across the table.

'A bit earlier than that, my lad were,' Treadwell muttered before subsiding again into his cigar smoke.

'Did you read law?' David Mendelson asked Thackeray, interested.

'No,' Thackeray said. 'History. I didn't really decide to join the police force until after I graduated.'

'It was quite tough then for a graduate in the police, wasn't it?' the older Mendelson asked. 'Not like now when they're advertising all over the place for graduate recruits.'

'We survived,' Thackeray said. 'Though no one went out of their way to smooth the path. We went straight on to the beat and took our chances just like the eighteen-year-olds. No special privileges.'

'But quick promotion? Obviously, in your case,' Victor Mendelson persisted.

Thackeray shrugged slightly.

'If you were any good,' he conceded evenly.

'So you're reckoned to be some good, are you?' Treadwell bulldozed back into the conversation, just the safe side of offensively. 'You'll have this murder case wrapped up pretty soon then, I dare say. Have you identified the body yet, that's what I'd like to know.'

Laura watched Thackeray with admiration as he looked speculatively at the enormous and increasingly hot and steamy bulk of Councillor Treadwell across the table, like a matador sizing up his opponent across the bullring. I'd have lost my temper by now, she thought, knowing her limitations only too well.

'We'll be telling the press who the victim was in the morning, as it happens,' Thackeray said with a sideways glance at Laura, who looked down quickly to hide the irrepressible gleam of interest in her eyes. 'So I don't suppose it matters if I tell you now. In fact, as I think you did your degree here at the university, didn't you David? – it's just possible you might have known him. His name was Harvey Lingard, and he was a student at Bradfield about ten years ago.'

David shook his head blankly at the name. It was Vicky and Laura who gasped slightly in recognition, and Laura alone who stared at Thackeray with a look of appalled shock on her face.

'Harvey?' she said, shivering slightly as if the room, which was stuffy, had suddenly become cold. 'I used to go to tutorials with Harvey Lingard. He wrote for the student paper when I did. Oh, God, poor Harvey.' The dinner table fell silent as they absorbed Laura's distress.

'I remember him vaguely,' Vicky said to Thackeray, speaking quickly, anxious to break the horrified silence.

'Laura and I were in the same department. That's how we met him. David did law of course, so probably never came across him. It's an unusual name. There couldn't be two Harvey Lingards.'

'I'm sorry,' Thackeray said. 'If I'd known the news would upset you I'd never have told you.' He looked in concern at Laura who was staring blankly at her empty coffee cup now, her face pale. Abruptly she stood up.

'I think I'll have to go home, Vicky, David,' she said. 'It's been a rough day.'

It was enough to break up the party. Vicky went with Laura to get her coat and the other guests began to make their excuses and prepare to depart with many thanks and promises to meet again soon.

In the hallway, with her coat collar turned up and Vicky's arm around her, Laura found herself face to face with Michael Thackeray again. After completing their farewells to Vicky they went out of the house together.

'I'm sorry,' he said slightly hesitantly as she stopped by her car. 'I'd no idea Lingard might be a friend. No idea that you and Vicky were even at the university here.'

'He wasn't close,' Laura said. 'But I knew him and liked him. It's not pleasant to think of him lying up on the moor for all that time.'

'I'll need to talk to you about him some time – officially, I mean,' Thackeray said. 'I'll need to talk to anyone who knew him when he was in Bradfield. He seems to have lived in London for a long time and I think he must have come back to see someone. An old friend, perhaps?'

Laura did not respond to the tentative question and glanced at her watch. It was half past eleven and she was dog tired. It had been an emotional roller-coaster of a day.

'I'll be pleased to help, of course, but not tonight, if you don't mind,' she said. 'I have a friend staying with me for a few days . . .'

'Of course,' Thackeray said. 'You mustn't keep him waiting. I'll contact you tomorrow if I may. Good-night.'

79

Laura looked hard at the policeman as she got into her car and switched on the engine, but she could not decide in the dim light from the street lamps whether he was smiling or not. How did he know her visitor was male, she thought irritably. And why, she asked herself, should she care anyway if all he had made was an accurate guess?

Thackeray, for his part, sat in his car for a few moments watching Laura's Beetle speed away down the street before he too drove off looking distinctly thoughtful. An excuse to see Laura Ackroyd again was definitely not unwelcome, he admitted to himself, though his pleasure at the thought was muted by the knowledge that it could lead him, not for the first time, down a road with a definitively dead end. And before that, he thought sombrely, he had to face the task he liked least in a profession with more than its share of grim chores. Next morning he and Mower had to visit the parents of the murdered man, before his name could be officially announced to the world at the press conference booked at police HQ for noon.

SEVEN

'IT WERE THE JUDGMENT OF God,' Harold Lingard said flatly and with no apparent sign of emotion. He was a stocky, grey-haired man well into middle age, his heavy face deeply lined from the base of his thin nose almost to the edge of his chin, offering to the world a look of such uncompromising grimness that his thin lips, clamped now in a straight line, looked almost soft in comparison. He had shown the two police officers into the austere and chilly front room of his unassuming semi-detached house on the outskirts of York. His wife, Enid was already sitting huddled in an armchair as close as she could apparently get to the single red bar of the small electric fire which was perched on the beige tiled hearth.

They were a pale couple, dressed in uniform greys and browns, and had accepted calmly enough Thackeray's clinical description of how the man he believed to be their son had died and the grounds upon which he had made the identification of the body. But Harold Lingard had become increasingly enraged as Thackeray told them cautiously about his son's terminal condition and his final trip from London to the North. It was the word Aids itself which had provoked Lingard's allusion to divine retribution.

'I beg your pardon?' Thackeray then said in surprise, glancing briefly at Mrs Lingard who had not spoken and was now rocking herself backwards and forwards in her chair in some evident distress. Lingard looked at him coldly.

'We knew our son were a pervert,' he said. 'We prayed with him for years without ceasing before he left home. We've gone on praying for him day and night, isn't that right, Enid? We've struggled with the Devil for that lad. We warned him that the Lord God would not be mocked. Evidently to no avail.'

Thackeray felt an unexpected surge of anger. He paused for a moment, not breathing, his jaw clamped tight to prevent the words which rushed to mind from escaping into the cold and musty atmosphere which smelt, he thought, of death and lack of charity.

'Was Harvey your only child?' he asked when he had himself under control again.

Lingard nodded.

'He broke his mother's heart,' he said.

'I'm sorry to be the bearer of such bad news,' Thackeray said, addressing himself now to Mrs Lingard, down whose cheek a single tear crept unremarked. 'But there are things I need to ask you if I'm to find who killed him.'

'We'll do what we can to help,' Lingard said unexpectedly. 'We render unto Caesar what is due in our Church. We're not exclusive brethren.' There was the contempt in that remark that one splinter group reserves for another. Sergeant Mower, who had been listening impassively to the exchanges so far, allowed himself the faintest of knowing smiles at that. The deeply curdled love which pervaded this house astonished him as much as it did Thackeray, but the rivalry of one small church for another he was familiar with from his days in London, south of the river, where he had grown up and trodden his first police beat.

'So you knew Harvey was gay before he left home, did you?' Thackeray asked, feeling his way tentatively through the maelstrom of conflicting and violent emotions which the Lingards evidently concealed beneath their superficial calm.

'We don't want to talk about that,' Enid Lingard muttered, speaking for the first time. 'Let the lad rest in peace now. It's all over. The Good Lord may be able to forgive him on the Judgment Day and God willing we may find it in our hearts to do the same, in time.'

Harold Lingard looked sceptical at that, Thackeray thought. He might pay lip-service to Christian charity but his God was in reality an avenging Old Testament deity who would neither forget nor forgive.

'What do you want to know, Chief Inspector,' Lingard said, ignoring his wife. 'Vengeance is mine, saith the Lord, but that's no reason to let a murderer run free on this earth, Enid.'

Haltingly the story came out of the much wanted only son, blond in looks and sunny in temperament, whom they strove not to spoil 'for his own good'. Thackeray could well imagine the texts which would have been summoned forth to justify a regime in which rods were not spared nor devotions neglected. He had heard many of them himself.

All had gone smoothly enough for the Lingards until the boy was in his teens: he was doing well at school, studious rather than sporty, but none the worse for that, and happy enough to fall in with their religious devotions at weekends, even to the extent of testifying, Bible in hand, on the little church's weekly forays into the main shopping streets to urge the impervious burghers of York to see the light and be saved.

At fifteen, tall and willowy now, and still startlingly fair, Harvey had been extricated from the apparently unsolicited clutches of a Sunday-school teacher, a young man some years older than himself. Passionate prayers had been said and public repentance offered by the lad for his potentially unchaste desires, and the incident had been almost forgotten when a more dramatic scandal broke in the close-knit church community. This time it had been Harvey who had been accused of making the advances, a younger boy regarded as the lamb led astray, and the family and public anger all the greater.

'We lost him then,' Enid Lingard broke in to her

husband's harsh monologue. 'We wrestled for his soul, but we lost him.'

'And that's when he went away to university in Bradfield?' Thackeray prompted.

'Aye. I wanted nowt to do with him after that. He made no secret of his perversion, I'm told, once he went away. Sodom, that place must be.' Lingard relapsed into an angry silence again, his eyes full of pain, while his wife twisted her hands in anguish towards the feeble heat of the electric fire.

'Have you never seen him since?' Thackeray asked, finding it hard to accept what he was hearing. Lingard shook his head vehemently, but Enid Lingard appeared to Thackeray to hesitate. She glanced nervously at her husband.

'I've seen him,' she whispered. 'I've seen him twice.'

'You never,' Lingard muttered in astonishment, but Thackeray raised a warning hand at him and urged Mrs Lingard on.

'I went to his graduation,' she said, more bravely now. 'I found out when it were going to be, and I went over to Bradfield for the day. I saw him and some of his friends. We had a cup of tea. He seemed very happy then, full of life . . .' Her voice trailed away miserably and another tear trickled down her pale, dry face.

'And the second time?' Thackeray asked gently.

Enid nodded, her faded blue eyes filled with more tears.

'I saw him two years ago. I went to London with my church women's group and I rang him up. I knew his address because he'd sent a postcard with it on. Harold never saw that, but I kept it in case . . . you know, just in case of anything happening. I met him in a place in Oxford Street, a pizza bar place. He said I'd be able to find it easily, and I did. He were waiting for me there at a table by the window.'

She stopped at that with a tremendous shudder as her face cracked open with the grief she had so far contained deep within herself. She seized a handful of paper tissues from the box on the settee at her side and buried herself in them. Her husband, looking nonplussed rather than concerned, watched impassively.

'Could you not make your wife a cup of tea?' Thackeray asked him, trying to keep the anger he felt out of his voice.

'It were the judgment of God, Enid,' Lingard said sharply, but he got up with ill-grace and went into the kitchen where they could hear him clattering around with kettle and cups.

When he had gone Enid Lingard composed herself enough to look at Thackeray again with red-rimmed, tragic eyes.

'He must have been ill by then,' she said. 'He were right pale and thinner than I'd ever seen him. He told me he were fine, told me about the lad he were living with, about his job, his flat and everything, but on t'coach coming back up t'motorway I guessed. When your policewoman came round yesterday I weren't surprised he'd gone, only at the way he went.'

She looked at Thackeray, almost pleading with him to understand.

'I know it were wrong, what he were doing. I know that,' she said fiercely. 'It's all in the Book. There's no escaping that. But he were my child, my only child, and now he's gone. How can I help grieving over that?'

The question, Thackeray knew, was not directed at him at all but at the man who stood behind them in the doorway, cup and saucer in hand, his face as unyielding now as when he had let them into the house half an hour before. This distraught woman would get no comfort there, Thackeray thought, for a pain which he knew was almost past bearing.

'I knew an old priest once,' he said quietly to Mrs Lingard. 'He used to say hate the sin but not the sinner. Maybe that's the answer you're looking for.' It was, he thought bitterly, like trying to cure cancer with an aspirin, but the need to comfort the inconsolable ran deep even when you knew it served no purpose.

Lingard handed his wife her tea with a snort of contempt, and resumed his seat opposite her while Thackeray took her gently over whatever else she could remember of her two meetings with her son that might be useful to their inquiries, which was not much. Of his friends and acquaintances she knew little and feared the worst.

'Jesus wept,' Kevin Mower said explosively as Lingard eventually shut his door firmly behind them and they walked back to their car, which was parked on the other side of the quiet suburban street.

'I'd guess he weeps more over religious nuts like that than over many of the lads we like to call villains,' Thackeray said. 'In many ways they do more harm.' There was an edge to his voice which made Mower look at him sharply, but Thackeray's expression gave nothing away. Mower shrugged.

'That bastard's the one who should roast in hell,' he said. 'If I'd had a father like that . . .' He broke off suddenly and gave Thackeray a slightly shamefaced grin. 'If I'd had a father,' he said, and laughed. They got into the car in silence, each locked in thoughts that neither would have dreamed of confiding in the other.

'Were you brought up religious then, guv? Priests and that?' Mower asked, cautiously giving in to his curiosity as he started the car, and resuming his intermittent and so far largely unproductive attempts to persuade Thackeray to tell him anything about himself. Thackeray glanced at him, the faintest flicker of amusement in his eyes again.

'A Catholic,' he said. 'But not now.' There was no invitation to probe further and Mower took the hint, driving as sedately as he was able back to Bradfield.

'Yes, of course I knew he was gay,' Laura Ackroyd said fiercely to the two police officers with whom she was closeted in Ted Grant's office. Thackeray and Sergeant Mower had turned up seeking an interview towards the end of the morning, immediately after the press conference which had made public the murder victim's identity. Fred Powers, who was in charge in Ted Grant's temporary absence, had looked askance but, with the front page still to finalise, had waved them into the privacy of the editor's suite with no more than a curt instruction to Laura to report to him when she had finished.

Thackeray had sympathetically taken up more or less where they had left their conversation the night before, while Mower, after an appreciative mental inventory of Laura's slim figure, clad this morning in a dark red suit over a cream shirt, had taken out his notebook and perched himself elegantly at the spacious conference table at the back of the editor's office.

'Have you seen Harvey Lingard recently?' Thackeray had asked first. Laura shook her head.

'I haven't seen him since we graduated,' she said. 'I remember him being there on graduation day. It rained, I remember, and Harvey had one of those huge golf umbrellas. They're fashionable now, but they were quite unusual then. After the ceremony he made quite a drama of escorting people from the main hall to the department where there was a sort of reception for graduates and their parents. I don't remember his parents being there, but I was with mine, and my grandmother – all dressed up in best bib and tucker, you know how it is, and me in my cap and gown – and we all sheltered under his umbrella. Harvey did everything with style,' she concluded sadly.

The inevitable question had come next, and Laura had responded angrily.

'He made no secret about his sexual preferences,' she said with some force. 'It was the beginning of gay liberation, gay pride, all that stuff. People of our generation weren't trying to hide the fact any more. Harvey was gay. So what? It really didn't signify.'

Thackeray looked at her for a moment. Her eyes were bright with emotion and her cheeks unusually pink. She had fastened her hair back from her face this morning, in a style which made her look far younger than she had done the night before. His face betrayed nothing of what he was thinking but Mower, who was tapping his pencil on the table in an irritating little rhythm, was gazing at her with open admiration in his eyes. Thackeray wondered which generation Laura Ackroyd assigned him to, and suspected that it was not her own.

'I was trying not to make any value judgements,' Thackeray said at last, the merest touch of asperity in his voice. 'We know Mr Lingard was gay. We've made contact with his partner in London, and we saw his parents this morning. What I need to discover is why he abandoned his job and what seems to have been a stable relationship to come to Bradfield without telling anyone about it. I guess – but I'm only guessing – that he came up here to see someone, and it seems likely that that has to be a friend from his time at the university. He wasn't brought up round here, so it's unlikely to be anyone he knew before that time. So I need to know about his student friends. In particular, I need to talk to anyone who's still in Bradfield who knew him then.'

There was no reason why he should have provided this sort of justification for his questions, he thought to himself irritably. Indeed, he was aware of Mower looking at him curiously from the other side of the room. Laura Ackroyd, on the other hand, seemed almost to accept the explanation as no more than her due and nodded gravely in acknowledgement.

'I didn't know him well,' she said, calm again now. 'He turned up from time to time with articles for the student paper. But he was very involved in gay politics. They set up an organisation which must have been the precursor of the Front which is making all the waves at the moment.'

'Which you've been investigating, I understand? As a reporter, I mean?'

Laura looked at the policeman for a moment in surprise, wondering how he had come by that piece of information.

'Not very seriously,' she said grudgingly. 'My editor isn't very interested in gay rights.' Thackeray nodded non-committally at that.

'But Lingard was in your department?'

'Closer than that. He was in my tutor group,' Laura said. 'we were with Richard Thurston: me, Harvey and a girl called Sally Wong Lee, who was Hong-Kong Chinese and who I think went back there when we graduated. I nit-picked over Harvey's essays and he nit-picked over mine. We came at things from different perspectives.'

She fell silent, unexpectedly moved by the memory of those long lost wrangles over Marxism and capitalism and half a dozen other isms which had seemed the very stuff of life at the time but had now faded like dreams. She had been Joyce's granddaughter with a fierce passion then, she thought sadly, but whose son had Harvey been, with his Thatcherite devotion to individualism and the free market? She had never asked then, and now would never know, though he would have suited her own father very well, she thought wryly. Better than she, who had never been more than a sub-standard substitute son to Jack Ackroyd. She jerked herself back with an effort to the measured gaze of Chief Inspector Thackeray.

'Thurston, the by-election candidate?' Thackeray asked, simultaneously trying to work out the political implications of interviewing a prospective MP as he listened to Laura's answer. If Longley wanted him to find his way around Bradfield, he thought grimly, this case looked set fair to give him a whirlwind tour of some of the town's main corridors of influence and power.

'Yes, that Richard Thurston. He's trying to put his academic interest in politics into practice, didn't you know?' Laura said. Her answer had an edge of cynicism to it which brought her up short. Am I really so far gone, she asked herself.

'So, Dr Thurston should remember him pretty well?'

'Tutors see a lot of students over the years, but, yes, I

guess Richard would remember Harvey as well as anyone on the university staff. He hasn't forgotten me, anyway,' Laura said with a half smile.

Mower grinned at that, but forbore to make the obvious comment. He did not yet know Thackeray well enough, he thought, to judge when or whether a cheeky remark would be tolerated. He would have been surprised to know that much the same thought passed through the Chief Inspector's mind, though he was far too wary to even consider uttering it. No one, the two men were unconsciously agreed, would be likely to forget Laura Ackroyd in a hurry.

'Right,' Thackeray said slowly. 'Now I want you to think back very carefully to the time when you and Mr Lingard were students together. You knew he was gay. Can you remember anyone who might have been his boyfriend? Or, failing that, anyone we could talk to who might have known him well enough to have that sort of information?'

Laura thought. It had been one of the happiest times of her life: Bradfield University, unfashionable, poorly housed on the western slopes of the town in a series of buildings which had almost without exception started life as something less illustrious – a technical college there, a former school here, even a redundant non-conformist chapel had been converted to accommodate a nascent department of education – and it was still one of the newer universities, regarded as poisoned pools of subversion in high places. Even so, Bradfield had been her own personal choice, made in the teeth of pressure at home and at school to opt for some more socially acceptable institution. And it was a choice she had never regretted.

She had come back to the university in her home town as a deliberate act of defiance after her bitterly resented years at boarding school and had immersed herself in work and in student politics. Her parents had paid her grant and born her post-adolescent enthusiasms with more tolerance than she expected or, she suspected now, deserved. Her grandmother had encouraged, advised and occasionally commiserated as campaigns waxed and waned, as idols were hoisted on to pedestals and eventually dashed to the ground, as rainbow coalitions were formed and dissolved, and as, ultimately, Laura grew up and Joyce grudgingly learned to accept that her granddaughter would not after all follow in her political footsteps.

Thackeray watched Laura's face, fascinated, as she cast her mind back to her turbulent student years, and her expression changed almost as if clouds were passing across the sun and away into the distance again. Eventually she came back to the present with a sigh and a shrug and a faint smile of defeat.

'He had friends in the gay liberation group,' she said. 'But no one I can remember very clearly. I don't think any of them were in my department. There was a tall boy called John something, and a black girl called Fiona, but again I can't recall her second name. Your best bet is the staff who taught him.'

'Do you think he could have come back to see anyone in the present gay group?' Thackeray cast around at random now.

Laura looked blank.

'I wouldn't have thought so,' she said. 'Student memories are very short because of the time-scale. It's ten years since we graduated. It's a long time ago. You don't get much continuity in student politics.'

Nor in much else, Thackeray thought, thrown back in spite of himself to his own situation ten years previously, when he might not have minded lying down on the bleak moors above Arnedale to die, as Harvey Lingard had died at Heyburn. He thought again of that body rotting quietly in the spring rain and shuddered.

'He might have wanted to come and talk to them anyway, without knowing them as individuals,' he said suddenly, seeking to get something out of his system and still, he realised, affected by that implacably unforgiving home which Harvey Lingard had abandoned. 'He might have

91

seen himself as some sort of dreadful warning to the next generation, an Old Testament prophet, perhaps. Apparently he had AIDS.'

Laura looked at Thackeray with unashamed sadness in her eyes.

'Poor Harvey,' she said, almost to herself. 'Old Testament he was not. He loved life, enjoyed every minute of it, lit up the room when he walked in. I can't really believe he's dead. He was one of those people who ought never to die. They should turn into trees or flowers like Greek gods and go on giving pleasure for ever.'

'Did you fancy him then?' Sergeant Mower asked bluntly, to Thackeray's obvious annoyance, but Laura just laughed.

'No,' she said. 'It wasn't anything sexual. I told you. We all knew his preferences. He was just a great person to be with – lively, warm, fun . . .'

'So who could have hated him enough to kill him?' Thackeray asked sombrely. Laura shook her head.

'I have no idea,' she said. 'No idea at all.'

The interview had clearly gone as far as it could to a conclusion, and Thackeray and Mower left with Laura's promise to contact them if anything else occurred to her which she thought might help their inquiries. Depressed, she sat on in Ted Grant's chair for a moment after the police had gone, trying to come to terms with the waste of a life which had touched her own at a time when impressions were vivid and would linger for a lifetime. Eventually Fred Powers put an inquisitive head around the door to ask what the police had wanted.

When she told him his eyes lit up.

'We'll be leading on the identification,' he said. 'Do me a nice quick 500 words on The Harvey Lingard I Remember, will you, love?'

92

EIGHT

RICHARD THURSTON HEARD THE REPORT of the police press conference on the local lunchtime news at his campaign headquarters, surrounded by the hubbub of half a dozen people trying to attract his attention at once with information on the latest canvass returns (encouraging), the latest unemployment figures (exploitable) and a fierce attack from the enemy camp on his own party's proposals for pensions (conceivably an own goal in a constituency with a high proportion of pensioners amongst the electorate).

No one in the crowd noticed the tightening of the candidate's face muscles as he concentrated on the news-reader through the surrounding clamour, nor could they have suspected the clenching of his suddenly nauseous stomach as he absorbed the full implications of what the broadcaster was saying. Thurston turned to Jake Taylor MP who was at his elbow, as he had been since the campaign began.

'We need a private word,' Thurston said. The younger man looked at him sharply and nodded, picking up his jacket which he had draped carefully over the back of a chair when they had returned to their HQ after a morning's tour of the town in the party's campaign bus. He led the way into the tiny office at the back of the community hall which was their nerve centre for the three weeks of the campaign, picking up a plate of slightly curled sandwiches and a couple of cans of soft drink as he went, and closing the door firmly behind them in the scowling face of Ron Skinner, Thurston's trade union driver and chief bottle washer for the duration.

'You look worried. What's the problem?' Taylor said, grimacing over his first mouthful of sandwich and washing it down with a swig from his can, which clearly proved equally unpalatable. He did not wait for an answer. 'This pension statement's just what we're looking for, isn't it? You can come straight back on that tonight at the meeting at the Heights, nail the lie that it would mean big tax increases, give the old folk something to come out and vote for. We could even think about a special leaflet if they keep on that tack. We can't lose.'

'No. no, that's fine,' Thurston said, pushing the plate of food away and ripping the seal off the second can with an anxious tug. 'It's nothing to do with that. It's this murder. You must have read about it. They've just announced the identity of the man they found up at Heyburn earlier in the week. It's an old student of mine. Graduated nine, ten years ago, something like that.'

Taylor put his can down on the cluttered office desk very carefully, his eyes narrowing and suddenly as cold as Pennine sleet.

'You taught him?' he asked. Thurston nodded.

'Is he local? Have you kept in touch?'

'No, I've never seen him since he finished his course,' Thurston said angrily. 'I didn't know he was back in Bradfield. I'd no idea.'

'So what's the problem?' Taylor asked.

'Well, they're asking anyone who knew him to talk to the police,' Thurston said, his mouth dry. He sipped unenthusiastically from his can again and put it down quickly to hide the fact that his hand was trembling. 'I'm not sure that's going to do the image much good, is it?'

'Helping the police with their inquiries?' Taylor said more lightly. 'I don't see why that should do you any harm. It's the least a public-spirited citizen could be expected to

94

do. And we can use it to play on your local connections. You were actually here ten years ago, getting the university off the ground, while your opponent was probably just out of some up-market boarding school in the Home Counties, still wet behind the ears. We can make something of that. Can't be bad.'

'You don't understand,' Thurston said quietly. 'Harvey Lingard was gay.'

'Ah,' Taylor said thoughtfully. He paused for a moment, thinking, his face cold and watchful now, his fingers drumming lightly on the table.

'In that case a low profile operation might be better. I shoudn't think the gay vote in Bradfield is one worth pursuing, is it? A bit on the shy side, perhaps?'

'Extremely,' Thurston said. 'They're likely to get a severe thumping down some back alley otherwise. The only ones who put their heads above the parapet are the students who are making a lot of noise just now about gay rights.'

'Yes, well, students do that, don't they, but it's generally all hot air,' Taylor said dismissively. He thought for a moment before continuing.

'So – you tell the fuzz what you know about this Lingard lad. We issue a statement saying you have been very happy to help, but that you haven't seen your former student for ten years or so, are very sorry to hear about his death etc etc. That'll do, won't it? Or do you want me to consult head office on this one? See how they think you should play it?'

'No, no, I'm sure you're right,' Thurston said unhappily.

He felt much less sure about that judgement when Chief Inspector Michael Thackeray, in dark trench-coat over rumpled suit, and a smartly dressed young detective sergeant turned up at the campaign headquarters later that afternoon. Thurston and Jake Taylor were stepping wearily off the campaign bus, which had just done a tour of a shopping centre on the outskirts of the town, when the police car drove up.

95

Thurston waved the policemen into the small private room at the back of the hall and asked one of the multitude of helpers milling about outside to bring them some tea.

'I need it even if you don't,' he said by way of explanation to Thackeray. He looked exhausted. He sat at the cluttered table, piled high with posters and leaflets and almost filling the small room, and spread his hands in what could have been taken for supplication.

'How can I help you, Chief Inspector?' he asked, with an attempt at a smile, although he knew the answer to his question and suspected that this tall dark policeman whom he had never met before knew that he knew the answer too. Thackeray did not speak at once, taking his time in appraising Thurston who exhibited every sign of nervous tension as he fiddled compulsively with one of the piles of paper in front of him.

'You know that the body which was found at Heyburn has been identified as that of Harvey Lingard?' he asked at last.

Thurston nodded non-committally. He looks tired out, Thackeray thought, and wondered why a man of his age, already successful in one career, should put himself through the gruelling process of trying to become an MP.

'I take it it's the Harvey Lingard whom I taught?' Thurston said, shrugging. 'It's an unusual name.'

'There's no doubt it's the same person,' Thackeray said. 'He talked to his partner about being a student in Bradfield and we've spoken to his parents, and to Laura Ackroyd, who says she was in tutorials with him. Can you tell me what you recall about his time here?'

Thurston did not respond at once. He looked past Thackeray with a far-away expression at the poster-bedecked wall behind the policeman where his own face, reproduced a dozen times, stared unhelpfully back at him. He looked as if he were trying physically to cast himself back ten years to the intense tutorials Laura Ackroyd had described.

'Bright, lively, gay – in the modern sense of the word, of

course, but in the old sense too – politically very active,' Thurston said at last. 'Tutorials with Harvey and Laura Ackroyd in them were always stimulating. They disagreed about most things.' He smiled faintly.

'Of course, I tended to sympathise with Laura's views,' he went on, 'so I had to be careful to give Harvey a fair hearing. But he could hold his own. He was a very bright lad.'

'We suspect that Lingard came back to Bradfield to see someone he knew. Could that have been you, do you think, Mr Thurston?' Thackeray asked.

Thurston shook his head.

'If he had that in mind he certainly never contacted me to let me know he was coming,' he said. 'I've heard nothing from Harvey since he graduated. Nothing at all.'

'You're quite sure?' Thackeray persisted, surprised by the note of vehemence which had crept into Thurston's voice.

'Quite sure,' Thurston insisted.

Nor was Thurston much more help when it came to identifying other friends, or boyfriends, of Harvey Lingard's. He knew little about his students' social lives, he said somewhat testily after turning away several urgent queries brought to him by helpers from the campaign which still bubbled and boiled away audibly in the hall outside the door. Harvey had come to his house once or twice for a drink or a meal, as many of his students did, but he had always come alone, as far as he could remember, or with Laura and Sally, the other members of the tutorial group. He regretted that he could not be more help to the police, but it was all a long time ago and students inevitably grow dim in the memory of their teachers as time passes.

'Did you believe him?' Thackeray asked Mower as they drove back to police HQ. Mower pulled a sceptical face.

'What reason could he have for lying?' he said. 'Do you reckon he might be gay?'

Thackeray thought about that for a moment.

97

'As far as we know he's a respectable married man with a couple of grown-up kids. That's what it says on his election address so it must be true, mustn't it?' He too felt uneasy about Thurston but could not put a finger on a reason why.

'If Thurston's got any sexual secrets, he's got a hell of a lot to lose right now,' he added thoughtfully. 'He's certainly under a lot of pressure, but it may be no more than the pressure the by-election is putting on him.'

He nodded out of the car window to a poster site where two of Thurston's supporters, colourful in red and gold rosettes, were putting up a notice announcing the visit of the leader of the opposition to support Richard Thurston at Bradfield Town Hall in less than a week's time.

'Politics! Why do people do it?' Mower asked, not seriously expecting an answer, but Thackeray looked at him with a grim half smile.

'For the same reason we do this job, I expect,' he said. 'Because they think it'll make a difference.'

'What's the matter with your friend Richard Thurston?' Vince Newsom asked Laura Ackroyd. He squinted at her through a raised glass of deep red wine which glittered in the candle flame of their dinner table at the new country house hotel near Arnedale she had recommended when he, to her surprise, had offered to fulfil his promise of a dinner date.

She could see the appreciation in his eyes, and knew it was for her as much as his careful choice of wine to accompany their meal. She had flattered him by choosing another of her heavy silky tops, in a rich aubergine this time, low enough cut at the neck to give a hint of cleavage, a fact which he had celebrated by planting a kiss as close to her breast as he could reach before they had left the flat, and which she had not failed to emphasise herself by wearing a heavy amethyst pendant on a gold chain which had been a present from her father.

'What's supposed to be the matter with him?' she countered. 'He seemed to be on good form at the press conference this morning.'

'Yeah?' Vince said, looking sceptical. 'I missed that. Got up too late – and who's fault was that, doll? But I saw him later on doing one of his walk-abouts and thought he was looking thoroughly shot at. The Tory yuppie is positively skipping about, in comparison.'

He turned his attention to the wine for a moment and she had time to wonder how Richard Thurston would have reacted to the news of Harvey Lingard's death and the desolate manner of it.

'You saw the press release they put out this evening?' she asked.

'About the murder victim? Yeah, I saw that. It didn't add anything to what you told me last night – too late. I may say, to add a par to my story.'

In fact she had found Vince asleep on her sofa when she had returned from the Mendelsons' dinner party and, to her considerable relief, in no fit state when she roused him to do anything more than listen bleary-eyed to her information about the murder and then fall desultorily into her spare bed to sleep off his evening in the Lamb and Flag.

'I'm not working for the Globe,' Laura said tartly. 'Dig for your own stories.'

'Is that all there is to it?' Vince came back. 'Thurston taught this Lingard fellow and hasn't seen him since?'

'As far as I know. I haven't seen Richard since the police announced the victim's name. You can ask him yourself at the press conference in the morning – if you get up in time,' Laura said. 'But from what I gathered from Chief Inspector Thackeray, Harvey Lingard hasn't been back to Bradfield for years, probably not since he graduated.'

'Yeah, well, it's not a place anyone would come back to for a holiday, is it, doll?'

'You seem to be doing quite well out of it again,' Laura

said. Vince's sharp, perceptive feature articles, with the
edge of cynicism which she knew so well, had found their
way into prominent positions in the Globe for three
mornings running now, and she knew he was well pleased
with his visit to the North.

'Yes, well, it's nice to be up here and able to afford a
place like this occasionally,' he said, glancing appreciatively round the busy restaurant with its individually lit
tables and snowy white table-cloths. 'You'll not get here
often on what the Gazette pays you.'

'We've had this conversation before,' Laura said. 'And
the answer's still no.'

'You'll get trapped,' Vince said, an edge of impatience to
his voice. 'When you decide you want to move you'll find
no one wants you. You'll be too old.'

'At thirty?' Laura asked, laughing incredulously.

'Thirty's old in this game,' Vince said. 'You're stuck in a
rut and you're too good for it, doll, you really are. Come to
London. You don't have to move in with me if you don't
want to. Get a place of your own, if you prefer. But come.
Get out of Bradfield before Bradfield gets you.'

Looking across the lamp-lit sparkle of the wine glasses
and silver, through a glow which softened the urgency of
Vince Newsom's face and lent a more kindly light to his
blue eyes, Laura was almost convinced that she could be
persuaded. There were times, she admitted to herself,
when she had to grit her teeth in the morning to get
herself to the Gazette and the arbitrary world of Ted
Grant's decision-making.

At her best, she knew, she could write like an angel. At
her worst, and too often these days she felt she was at her
worst, the grinding dullness of her assignments drove the
fluency from her mind and she had to drag out each word
as though squeezing the last slick from a mutilated tube of
toothpaste. She needed change. She needed new
excitements. Vince Newsom was playing a tune she craved
to dance to but was determined to ignore.

100

'This duck is tough,' she said angrily, pushing her plate away. 'This place is a rip-off.'

Vince's face hardened. He drained his wine glass and signalled to the waiter to bring the bill. She knew he would not beg, and was glad.

'I'm going to interview Thurston tomorrow,' he said. 'I think his recollections of Harvey Lingard might make a good piece – linking the murder and the by-election. Did he have political ambitions that far back, I wonder. What do you think, doll?'

'Terrific,' she said coldly, and walked out to the car alone, leaving Vince to settle the bill.

NINE

SUPERINTENDENT JACK LONGLEY WAS AN angry man. This was a new experience for Thackeray and he gave nothing away as he sat in the proffered chair to read the neatly typed report which Longley had thrust into his hand after summoning him preremptorily to his office at nine that morning. The superintendent's normally jovial features were grim, and there were unusual creases of anxiety about his eyes and forehead as he watched Thackeray open the buff folder. He looks quite ill, the chief inspector thought, puzzled.

The subject of the report was a suicide, not a matter which would normally have been passed to this level of CID once the fact of self-destruction had been firmly established by the duty officers. However, it was soon clear to Thackeray that this particular suicide was one which would send shock waves right across the town and one in which the suicide notes, for there had been two, implied criminal activity of a particularly unpleasant kind.

He read quietly through the file, ignoring Longley's impatient drumming of fingers on his desk. The facts of the case were not in dispute. Councillor Bill Baxter had been found by his wife less than two hours ago with a bullet in his brain and an old war-time service revolver still clutched firmly in his right hand. It was, the uniformed inspector who had attended the scene had written laconically, a miracle that the gun had fired, but it had done its job efficiently enough, killing the councillor instantly if somewhat messily in the front seat of his BMW.

The shot had been fired the previous night, according to the estimate of Amos Atherton, who had been summoned straight from his hearty breakfast to inspect somewhat dyspeptically the body of an old acquaintance. Baxter's overnight absence had not been noticed by a wife who slept in a separate room and retired early and his body must have lain inside the car inside his garage for the better part of ten hours before being discovered. The potential embarrassment in the case, and that was what Thackeray guessed was causing Superintendent Longley such obvious concern, lay in the duplicated suicide notes which offered two quite different explanations as to why Bill Baxter had decided to depart this earth with such efficient precipitateness.

The first note, addressed to his wife and obviously intended for public consumption, was a brief and sketchy affair asking for her forgiveness. It was handwritten in language which was stilted enough to carry little enough emotional weight, and offered no explanation for his departure beyond 'financial problems weighing on my mind'.

It was the second note which had arrived by hand at police headquarters addressed to Jack Longley himself which had caused the urgently convened conference in the superintendent's office and, Thackeray surmised, Longley's expression of extreme unease. Baxter was an old friend, Longley had said curtly, in response to Thackeray's barely expressed question – not close, but they had been members of the same masonic lodge, active in charitable affairs, drinking partners occasionally in the Clarendon bar.

'God, man, I've known Bill Baxter for as long as I can remember, he goes way back,' Longley muttered, as though that explained everything. His irritable reluctance to say anything further to this newcomer to the town was equally apparent. Thackeray could feel the drawbridge of reticence being raised against the outsider, the defensive portcullis rattling down to keep even the most oblique and tentative questions out.

Thackeray glanced down at the letter Baxter had written to his old friend the previous evening and marked portentously 'For Your Eyes Only', a naive and vain hope in the circumstances, he thought sourly.

'Did he deliver the note himself?' he asked.

'So it seems,' Longley snapped, his customary composure evidently shattered by the unprecedented nature of the letter and its presumptuous appeal. Thackeray still held the single sheet of high-quality cream notepaper, the address printed in an old-fashioned gothic type, unwaveringly over the file on the desk in front of him, the upward tilt of the paper almost an interrogation in itself as he waited patiently for Longley to continue.

'The desk sergeant says it was dropped in at about ten last night,' Longley went on, as if grudging every word. 'Bill delivered it himself. He must have gone straight home and . . . and done it, soon after. He didn't tell the desk who he was but the description tallies. Frazer was on duty. He's a good lad, reliable. Bill isn't . . . wasn't the sort of man who could disguise himself very easily. You didn't meet him, did you?'

Thackeray shook his head almost imperceptibly.

'You pointed him out once in the Clarendon,' he said, recalling the occasion clearly enough but not wanting to remind Longley at this moment of the context. 'Overweight, iron grey, not very tall, looked like he owned the place?'

'Aye, that was Bill.' Longley slumped into a heavy silence, his head seeming to sink into his own fleshy neck, his pale eyes watery and distant.

'It must be forty years,' he said at last, running a hand wearily over his brow and his own almost bald head. Thackeray dropped Baxter's letter gently back into the file and watched his boss warily, unsure quite what was expected of him.

'Did you know he had tastes which laid him open to blackmail?' he asked quietly at length.

'No I bloody didn't,' Longley said, jerking back to attention, his colour rising. 'What do you think I am? Another bloody pansy?'

'From what he says it's been going on for some time,' Thackeray said, rereading Baxter's staccato description of several years of small demands which had culminated in one final twist of the screw so excessive that even such a relatively wealthy man as Baxter, whose chain of clothing shops had outridden a series of take-over bids and, so far, the latest recession, could not comply.

'So why didn't I know about it?' Longley asked himself as much as Thackeray. He was clearly finding it difficulty to digest the fact that his local knowledge did not, after all, extend as far as he thought it did, that there were aspects of a lifelong friend's behaviour which had been kept from his private as well as his official gaze. 'The crafty beggar,' he said, half to himself.

'But why risk killing the golden goose?' Thackeray asked, more interested in recent crimes than old secrets. 'And why now, when any fool knows that businesses are short of liquid cash? Why make modest demands in the boom and ask for thousands when the bottom's fallen out of the market? It makes no sense.'

'Unless it's political,' Longley said. 'He damn near got the Tory nomination for this by-election, Baxter did. Fancied himself at Westminster, apparently, but they reckoned he was too old. He's high up in the party, been out with their man on the doorsteps, at the press conferences, quoted in the Gazette, on the box, the lot. He and Treadwell are the Conservative Party in this town, in spite of the efforts of the sharp young estate agents and car salesmen to take it over. A scandal just now before the by-election would be bound to do them a lot of damage.'

'You think that's why he wrote a note to his wife which

says nothing, and one to you which says everything? Is the first intended for the inquest? For public consumption? And the second for what? To make sure the blackmailer gets done later? He doesn't ask you to keep the second note quiet though.'

'He doesn't need to ask,' Longley said scornfully. 'He doesn't need to spell it out. He knows me well enough, and I know him – knew him, I should say. He knew that I could work it out for myself.

Thackeray looked at Longley, an unspoken question in his eyes, his face impassive, only a slight tightening of the lips indicating the tension within. Longley looked down at his desk, his fingers still continuing their nervous tattoo on the pile of unopened files in front of him – the day's work, Thackeray assumed, not started. Still Longley avoided the issue which preoccupied Thackeray. Just how far, he wondered, would Longley go to protect his friend, and how far down that rocky road would he expect his subordinate to follow him?

'The daft thing is that if he were alive and he'd come to me we'd go out of our way to keep his name out of it,' Longley said angrily. 'He'd have been Mr X if it ever came to court. He's a bloody sight worse off dead. You can't defame the dead. The papers can say owt they like if it gets out.'

'If it gets out,' Thackeray said. 'In a sense he's gone a long way towards protecting his political friends, for the time being at least, probably long enough for the by-election to be out of the way. He must have been convinced that he was about to be exposed and that would do the maximum damage this next week. He'd guess that even if we launch an investigation nothing much will come of it in public before the inquest. It's hardly likely to lead to a quick arrest. And anyone who was thinking of outing him will keep their heads down if they think we're involved and looking for a blackmailer who's driven a man to kill himself.'

Thackeray was conscious that his words gave Longley the opening he needed, if he should choose to take it. The silence lengthened and Thackeray grew restive, shifting uneasily in his chair.

'I'll take advice on this one,' Longley said thickly at last, as if forcing the words out through a mouthful of treacle. 'I've got a meeting with the Chief at noon at county. It's not a decision I want owt to do with, in the circumstances.'

Thackeray nodded.

'I can understand that,' he said, hiding his immense relief behind a careful re-ordering of the file, which he replaced on Longley's desk.

'Aye, well, I expect the Chief will want a full investigation, by-election or no by-election,' Longley said. 'And he'll want it launched now, not in a week's time when the votes are counted. All I'll say about it is this, Mike: if you can keep a low profile until this political thing is out of the way, then for Christ's sake keep a low profile. If it turns into a political row, we'll never hear the end of it. And if it damages anyone's chance of getting elected, I wouldn't put odds on either of us still being in our jobs when the new MP for Bradfield takes the train to Westminster, would you?'

'What's with this town, guv?' Sergeant Mower had asked in disbelief when Thackeray had explained their new assignment to him later that afternoon. 'One gay corpse you stumble across now and again in the normal line of duty, generally bashed on the head by a rejected lover. Two gay corpses, plus all the ranting and raving that's going on up at the university, is more than a joke. Do you think Harvey Lingard could have killed himself after all, then?'

'Amos Atherton says that's impossible,' Thackeray came back grimly as they drove into the gravelled driveway of a large detached stone house in Southwaite. They parked

107

behind a couple of expensive small cars and the sober black saloon which hardly needed to advertise the fact that it belonged to the undertaker. A tall man in the traditional weeds of his trade was taking his leave of a young woman in the substantial stone porch. The two policemen watched in silence as she closed the door and her visitor got into the black car and drove away.

'Uniformed's report on Baxter doesn't leave much room for doubt that it was suicide in this case,' Thackeray said. 'Atherton thinks the same. The shot was fired at point-blank range, the gun still firmly clasped in his hand, and according to his wife and Jack Longley the notes are in his handwriting. So what we see is apparently what we've got. One murder, one suicide and one blackmailer. Which doesn't for a minute mean that the deaths may not be connected.'

'Lingard came to Bradfield to see Baxter, perhaps,' Mower suggested, his dark eyes bright with the excitement of the chase. 'Lingard came to Bradfield to blackmail Baxter? And Baxter shut him up?'

'Softly, Sergeant,' Thackeray said. 'You're jumping ten steps ahead of yourself. And we've got a delicate bit of manoeuvring to do here. Judging by the separate notes Baxter left, his family can't have a clue what he'd been up to in the way of extra-marital affairs. They've had one shock today already. Let's watch our step, shall we?'

'Right, guv,' Mower said more soberly.

They were let into the house by the same young woman who had shown out the undertaker a few minutes previously. She was about thirty, of medium height and build, pale faced and dressed in a grey dress of nondescript style which even Thackeray, who seldom gave female fashion a moment's thought, guessed that she must have felt appropriate to the occasion as it did so little to flatter her. Mower gave her his customary sharp-eyed appraisal and did not bother to disguise the dismissive expression which quickly followed. With her fair hair hanging in a loose and untidy veil around a face almost devoid of expression, the woman showed no sign of particular distress or surprise as she asked their business and cast a cursory eye over Thackeray's warrant card. She introduced herself as Marcia Baxter, the dead man's daughter-in-law.

'My mother-in-law's in the drawing-room,' she said briefly, waving them through a thickly carpeted hallway furnished, like the rest of the house, with heavy and undoubtedly expensive reproduction furniture and a series of Constable prints in gilt frames which continued into the drawing-room itself. Three people were sitting round the gas log fire which flickered in the ornate fireplace, although the day was not cold. There was no mistaking Mrs Baxter, who nodded without curiosity at the newcomers. She was a heavy woman in late middle age whose careful make-up could not disguise the sagging folds around the jaw and neck or the puffy signs of recent tears around her pale blue eyes. She was dressed in a dark blue wool dress adorned with a brooch of gold and precious stones which, if genuine, was worth at least a month of his salary.

One of Mower's pleasures in life as a young constable had been to handle the occasionally retrieved proceeds of burglaries on his London patch as they were being restored to their grateful owners. He did not covet them so much as simply appreciate the look and feel of money made manifest, and he had developed a canny judgement for what it could buy.

Baxter, he thought, must have done well out of the family business and he wondered just what exorbitant sum the blackmailer had demanded to make him despair of meeting the bill and persuade him that death was a more attractive option. Or perhaps, he thought, glancing round at the man's family – each in their own way a solid pillar of unimaginative bourgeois respectability – the threat of outing was the more potent. There was no one here, he thought, who would obviously take a charitable view of the dead man's particular tastes in philandering.

Mrs Baxter was flanked by a woman of similar age and similar style, her hair perhaps a suggestion more elegantly coiffed, her patterned wool dress from a designer of marginally more flair, and her make-up more effective at presenting to the world the face of an attractive woman of a certain age and uncertain weight. The younger Mrs Baxter introduced her vaguely as her mother-in-law's friend Mrs Moor, and the younger man in a suit on her other side, his fleshy face almost as grey as the good local worsted he wore, as her husband, Ian.

The introductions over, all four looked expectantly at the two policemen. Thackeray addressed himself to Ian Baxter, not out of any old-fashioned conviction that the women present should be protected from discussion of the family's bereavement but because Mrs Moor quickly and prohibitively informed him that Mrs Baxter had been given tranquillisers by her doctor. Looking closely at the widow Thackeray could see in her eyes the dazed expression of drugged shock. He would gain little coherent help there at the moment, he was ready enough to admit.

'I'm sorry to have to trouble you at a time like this,' he said. 'Perhaps if Mrs Baxter is not feeling up to answering questions we could have a private word with you, Mr Baxter. I understand you worked with your father in the business.'

Ian Baxter nodded and, with an almost furtive glance at his mother and his wife, stood up quickly.

'We can use my father's study,' he said non-commitally, leading the way out of the drawing-room and across the hall into a not much smaller room at the back of the house, where the tall window gave a view onto extensive lawns and an incongruously garishly tiled swimming pool, not yet filled but still glaring in the deceptively bright spring sunshine. Baxter closed the door behind Thackeray and

Mower and waved them into the solid green leather armchairs beside the stone fireplace, sitting himself behind the mahogany desk which stood in the window bay.

Ian Baxter was some way off forty, Thackeray guessed, probably younger than he was himself, but he had already developed the heavy build and jowls, verging on the overweight, of a much older man, and a ponderous style of speech and movement which gave the impression of accepted if not positively welcomed middle age. His hair was that sandy in-between colour, neither red nor brown, and his pale eyes were partly masked by old-fashioned tortoiseshell glasses with thick lenses. Even his suit, a dark grey worsted three-piece worn with mandatory black tie, and carefully cut to accommodate the already noticeable paunch, seemed several weights too heavy for him and for the time of year. Within a few years he would be the image of his lately deceased father, Thackeray thought, although perhaps lacking the bullying style which he had witnessed in public on his sole encounter with the dead man.

'Do suicides always merit the attention of the CID, Chief Inspector?' Baxter asked, a touch of aggression in his tone. He offered both policemen a cigarette from the heavy silver box on his father's desk and, when the offer was refused, took one himself and lit it appreciatively with the matching lighter. He gave every impression of a man trying out the study and its accoutrements for size.

'Not usually,' Thackeray said neutrally. 'But in the light of your father's note – and other information received – there are a couple of things we would like to ask you about.'

'Go ahead, Chief Inspector,' Baxter said expansively. 'If I can help, I will.' He settled himself more comfortably in the green swivel chair and swung it as if to put his feet on the desk, then hesitated as if thinking better of it and swung back to face Thackeray again.

'The gun,' Thackeray said. 'That was definitely your father's? That's what your mother told the uniformed inspector this morning.'

111

'Oh, yes, that was dad's all right,' Ian Baxter said dismissively. 'He used to show it to me when I was a lad. He just made it into the army before the war ended, fought in Normandy, was always going on about it. I'm amazed it fired after all these years.'

'Did you know he had ammunition for it?'

Baxter shrugged non-committally, the pale eyes behind the glasses giving nothing away.

'I don't remember ever seeing any, but then he might not have told me about that when I was a boy for fear that I'd be tempted to try and load it. It's not something I'd take much interest in, to be perfectly honest. All that memorabilia – not really my cup of tea.'

'Have you seen the gun recently, Mr Baxter?' Sergeant Mower asked. Thackeray picked up the note of annoyance in his voice and smiled to himself. There was something in Baxter's manner of incipient condescension which he too found intensely irritating. Young Mower will not be patronised, Thackeray thought, and found himself pleased by that.

'I've not seen it for years,' Baxter said. 'I'm amazed he still had it, actually. But as I say, he had this thing about the war, so I expect he'd be reluctant to throw his souvenir away.'

'In his note your father mentioned financial problems,' Thackeray said. 'Could you tell us what those might have been?'

Baxter's face hardened perceptibly at that and he shook his head emphatically.

'It was nothing to do with the business, that I can tell you,' he said, an edge of anger to his voice. 'Times haven't been easy these last two years, but that's true of pretty well any business you can name. But we've kept our heads above water. We didn't take the daft road that so many retailers did and move further up market than our customers could afford. Good, reliable, economical clothing: that's what Baxter's have always dealt in and that's what's seen us through. None of these designer labels at fancy prices that they can't shift for love nor money now.'

'So the business is on a sound footing?'

'Sound enough,' Baxter said in a tone which brooked no contradiction.

'Personal financial problems then?' Thackeray asked.

'Nothing he's told me about.' Baxter said. 'Not that he would be likely to confide in me. We were not that close.' There was just the faintest hint of resentment in that last remark, Thackeray thought, and he wondered if there had been some disagreement between father and son.

'But perhaps something he might have told your mother about?' Thackeray persisted. 'Would he have shared his worries with her?'

Baxter looked at the chief inspector appraisingly.

'I don't know if you're married, Inspector,' he said. He ignored Thackeray's brief shake of the head, which Mower, looking up with interest from his note-taking, filed away for future reference. With his eyes fixed on a point somewhere near the top of the bookshelves which were crammed with volumes apparently chosen more for their gilded leather bindings than their contents, Baxter hurried on in a strangled voice with a speech he would clearly have preferred not to make.

'My father was a very busy man,' he said. 'There was the business, although he was leaving more of that to me these days, and not before time, I may say. And there was the Tory Party. He'd been on the council – mayor, magistrate, active in the masons – you know the sort of life men like that lead. Meetings every night. Lunches and dinners out. Now, of course, the by-election . . .' He hesitated and Thackeray waited, aware that there was more to come.

'I don't really know what marriage meant to him,' Baxter said eventually. 'I never discussed it with him, if you really want to know. But I'd guess that he thought himself a good husband and in the sense that he provided

113

all this . . .' Baxter waved a proprietorial hand to take in the opulently furnished study and the expansive and well-manicured garden beyond. 'In that sense, he was a good husband. My mother, and my brother and I never wanted for anything.'

'Materially, you mean?' Thackeray said.

Baxter shrugged.

'Materially, certainly. In other ways we lived our own lives. My mother has her bridge, her charities, the house and garden. She's always seemed perfectly content. My older brother is a solicitor and moved away when he qualified. He was never interested in joining the business. He visits once or twice a year, but we're not close. Monica and I have the children, our own interests . . .'

'So if there was something troubling your father, troubling him enough to persuade him to blow his brains out, your mother might not have known?'

The question was brutal and Mower's pencil hung motionless in the air over his notebook as if waiting for an explosion which did not come. Ian Baxter merely looked rather harder at Thackeray than he had done previously, as if attempting anew to assess what made him tick, before he responded.

'I've been with her all morning,' he said. 'I don't think she has a clue. She's completely overwhelmed by it. It seems to have come out of a clear blue sky.'

'Could the problem have been personal?' Thackeray persisted. 'Did he go in for extra-marital adventures to your knowledge?' Again Baxter looked hard at Thackeray before replying, but again the hesitation seemed to have more to do with surprise or resentment at the question than a guilty preparation of his answer.

'Not to my knowledge,' he said. 'Nor, as far as I know, to my mother's. I should think if anyone wanted a quick bit of how's-your-father with my father they'd need to make an appointment three months in advance.'

Baxter allowed himself a brief snort at his own joke and

114

settled himself more comfortably into the leather chair. Thackeray gave him a moment to compose himself again before terminally disturbing his self-satisfaction, as he knew he must, not so much with his next revelation as with the price tag which he guessed Baxter would instantly put upon it.

'We have reason to think he might have been blackmailed,' he said at last. Baxter's colour rose as he took this in, and expressions of shock and outrage passed across his heavy features before they settled into a look of almost comical disbelief which Thackeray did not feel was wholly genuine. 'Whatever for?' Baxter spluttered, although Thackeray was sure that he would much rather have asked, if he had dared, how much? 'I can't believe he could have done anything to be blackmailed about. Or have been so stupid as to pay up!'

'You know of nothing at all, in his business dealings or his private life?' Thackeray asked mildly. 'There's not many of us lead such blameless lives that someone couldn't find something we'd rather our nearest and dearest didn't find out about us.' Baxter did not take the opportunity the question offered.

'Nothing I know of,' he said flatly. 'Nothing at all.' His eyes narrowed. 'Is there something you've been told that I don't know about?' he asked.

'Nothing definite,' Thackeray said carefully. 'There is no hard evidence. But we are pretty sure that he was paying someone to keep quiet about something.' Baxter contained his indignation at that with difficulty, clearly deciding that bluster would not get him far with Thackeray. He changed tack.

'Do you know who was doing the blackmailing? Or how much he paid them?' Baxter forced the most important question out from between pursed and constipated lips.

'No, to both questions,' Thackeray said. 'But we'll be working on it.'

Baxter looked at him speculatively for a moment,

working out the implications of that.

'Do you have to?' he asked at length. 'Now he's dead I mean. Is there any point picking at old scabs? It won't bring him back, will it? And it's bound to upset my mother, whatever it was. Isn't this a case for letting sleeping dogs lie, Chief Inspector?'

It was a moment when old Harry Huddleston would likely have hit the elegantly corniced ceiling in a fit of only partially contrived outrage, Mower thought, but when Michael Thackeray was more likely to lapse into one of the moods of chilly, contained anger with which the sergeant was becoming familiar.

'Do you think that would be in the public interest, Mr Baxter?' Thackeray asked. The other man looked flustered and did not reply.

'We'll need to look at your father's papers, although I'd guess that he has taken the trouble to destroy any record of the transactions we're talking about.' Thackeray said, getting to his feet. 'And I'll need to speak to your mother when she's feeling up to it. Whether you tell her about this conversation yourself or leave it to us when we see her again, I'll leave to your judgement. But I have no doubt that she will have to know what has been going on, if she doesn't already. I'm sorry.'

'Did you believe him, guv?' Mower asked when they had taken their leave of Baxter and his now almost comatose mother and returned to the car. Thackeray shrugged.

'I think our Mr Baxter isn't as upset at his father's death as he'd like us to think,' he said. 'Whether that's simply because he's got control of the business at last, or because he hopes he can cover up his father's less than salubrious sex life once and for all, I wouldn't like to guess.'

'You think he knew about it?' Mower asked.

'Oh, yes, I think he knew. Given a few hints like that, wouldn't you be desperate to find out exactly what had been going on? He wasn't even remotely curious enough. He knew all right.'

'And now he knows you won't let it lie?' Mower asked, giving the chief inspector a sideways glance.

'Oh, I expect he'll go over my head to see if he can find someone who will over-rule me,' Thackeray said evenly, recalling Longley's equivocation that morning.

With Harry Huddleston, Mower might have risked a small wager on the outcome of Baxter's efforts, but the grim profile Thackeray offered did not tempt him into such foolhardy flippancy and he contented himself with a knowing grunt, concealing his irritation. One day, he thought, he would get himself back to the Smoke where villains were villains and the righteous middle classes knew their place, which was well away from the paths of the ungodly and those who hunted them down. These lifetime loyalties confused him. Where he came from you were lucky if you met anyone who had known anyone for longer than six months, he thought. And that made life much simpler all round.

TEN

RICHARD THURSTON STOOD LOOKING OUT of the window of his university room with an expression on his face as bleak as the urban landscape he scanned. He appeared to be searching for some secret refuge in which to conceal himself like a wounded animal. Nothing in his demeanour nor his posture – shoulders sagging beneath the jacket of his dark suit, hands clutching the window ledge as if for support – gave any indication that he spied the lair he sought on Bradfield's crowded canvas of streets, buildings and derelict sites spread out three storeys below. Even his red rose buttonhole looked dejected and askew on his lapel.

Behind him Laura Ackroyd sat in the same familiar low, red upholstered chair, rather more worn and faded now, in the same familiar book-cluttered room in which she had delivered so many student certainties what seemed like so very few years ago. Richard had rung her at the Gazette earlier that morning and asked her to meet him urgently for coffee at the university. He could escape from his minders, he had told her ironically but with an unexpected catch in his voice which alarmed her, on the pretext of dealing with some urgent academic business for an hour.

Finding the lift out of order, she had climbed the three familiar flights of stairs to the sociology corridor with a growing sense of foreboding and was not surprised when Thurston had opened the door to her knock and almost dragged her into the room by the arm. But she was shocked by the unmistakable look of panic in his eyes and the desperation on his face. This, she thought at once, is more than just the pressure of the campaign. Vince had been right.

'I need your help,' he said. 'I don't know who else to turn to, Laura. You must help me, as a friend, not a reporter.'

'Of course,' she said, without hesitation, but after he had waved her into that familiar chair he had turned away to the window, unable or unwilling to say any more.

'Is it Angela?' she offered tentatively at last, recalling his wife's desperation at the prospect of the changes he was about to inflict upon her life. Thurston turned in apparent surprise.

'Angela? No, why should I need help with Angela? Angela knows nothing about this, this . . .' He stopped again, waving a hand helplessly in Laura's direction.

He really doesn't know how unhappy she is, Laura thought, with a feeling of slight shock. Or perhaps he does not want to know. The labyrinths of the married state never failed to mystify her. If you took account of the fierce, single-minded determination Richard seemed to have acquired as his political ambitions moved closer to realisation, his insensitivity to Angela's plight became understandable if not, she thought sadly, forgivable.

Thurston stood with his back to the window now, a sagging silhouette against the grey daylight of a cloudy morning, his face in shadow. He took a deep shuddering breath and appeared at last to come to a decision. He spoke slowly and quietly and so hesitantly that Laura hardly recognised this as the confident teacher who had shaped her thinking so definitively not so very long ago.

'For about three years now,' Thurston began, 'perhaps a bit longer, I can't remember, I've been blackmailed. Fairly small amounts, fairly regularly . . .'

The look of horror in her eyes gave him fresh pause for a moment, although it was quickly replaced by a fierce flash of anger.

'You've paid up?' she asked, outraged.

Thurston nodded sombrely.

'I paid up. It seemed the simplest thing at the time, better than a scandal with the last general election and everything . . . so much to lose.' He hesitated again, fiddling obsessively with a pen he had taken from his breast pocket and avoiding Laura's eyes.

'Will you . . .?' Laura unusually hesitant now, not knowing quite how to ask what she wanted to know. 'Can you?' she corrected herself. 'Can you tell me why? Or doesn't it matter?'

'Oh, it matters,' Thurston said bitterly. 'Now, at this particular time, it matters a very great deal.' He looked squarely at her for a moment across the paper-strewn desk. He had never, Laura thought inconsequentially, been a tidy man. Then he dropped his gaze again and went on in a barely audible voice.

'I've had, over the years, three, four times, affairs with students,' he said.

'And that's what the blackmail's about?'

'The latest demand is much bigger. Far bigger than I can possibly pay. And the threat is to expose me now, in the middle of the by-election campaign, when it can do the maximum damage – to me, to my career, to the party . . .' Thurston shrugged helplessly. 'I can't possibly pay what they're asking, Laura,' he said.

'Then defy them, Richard,' Laura said angrily. 'Go to the police. It can't do you that much damage, can it? Lots of married men have affairs. I thought it was par for the course in politics: ministers and their secretaries, lecturers and their students, what's the difference? The voters will just think you're a bit of a lad.'

'Not if the students were young men, and one of them was Harvey Lingard,' Thurston said so quietly that Laura wondered for a moment if she had misheard him but knew she could not have done. She drew a sharp breath as

120

the full implications of what he had just said sank in and her stomach tightened in real fear for him. Oh Harvey, she thought bitterly, remembering the lithe, blithe figure who had sat opposite her in this very room, his arguments taking off at times into fantasy as he talked, almost drunk on the sound of his own voice and the quicksilver darting of his mind. Harvey could have charmed the birds out of the trees, she thought, and no doubt anyone he wanted into his bed.

'I didn't know you were gay, Richard,' she said quietly. 'I had no idea.' Yet when she thought back to those hours of exuberant cut and thrust she should have known, she thought. On reflection, there had been an obvious bond between Harvey and Richard, an enjoyment of the battle even as they disagreed most violently on some point or other, a clash of personalities which was as much sexual as intellectual, had she not been too self-absorbed herself to pin it down.

'I should have guessed,' she said. 'I knew Harvey was gay.'

'Gay? What's gay?' Richard asked. 'Sometimes I think I am, sometimes I just get on quietly with my marriage. I love Angela. I've always loved Angela and most of the time I've been faithful to her – till the next time I meet some beautiful young man and become obsessed. Harvey was the first I got seriously involved with. Before that I'd pretended that my inclinations weren't real, suppressed them, I suppose, but Harvey – you remember Harvey? – he was so alive, so . . . so radiant, and somehow he knew how I felt. He just knew. And he took me by the hand and showed me what to do and it was beautiful and innocent while it lasted, although that sounds a perverse way to describe what many would describe as simple lust. After that, when it happened again, I knew too, and I wanted it as much as they did.'

'They?' Laura asked.

'A boy called David, about seven years ago. He's in the

States now. And Rod Griffiths, big Rod, captain of the rugby team no less. And then Jason. Jason and his revolution, Jason and his passionate arguments, Jason who looks as though he'll be my undoing.'

'Jason Carpenter, the gay lib leader?'

'That's my Jason,' Thurston said bitterly. 'I succumbed to his charms last year, last spring to be precise, you know what they say about spring and thoughts of love? I think now that I went to bed with a boy who was already blackmailing me, Laura. He must have already known about David and Rod. How could I have been so stupid?'

'You think Jason is threatening you? It couldn't have been Harvey?' Laura asked, surprised at how automatically she had jumped to the latter conclusion.

'I'm sure Jason has me at the top of his list of people to be "outed",' Thurston said flatly. 'He more or less told me so when our ardour had cooled a bit. He is, and I should have seen this months ago, an evil, manipulative little bastard. God knows how many other people he's blackmailing on that list of his. They talk enough about people in high places. It could be half the town, for all I know. Or it could just be talk.'

Laura ran a hand distractedly through her hair.

'Richard,' she said, 'Harvey was murdered. Did you tell the police about your relationship with him?'

'Harvey's not relevant to all this,' Thurston said, his face taking on an obstinate look, like a small boy deprived of a treat. 'No one knows about me and Harvey, no one at all, not even the blackmailer. He hasn't been mentioned. It's ten years ago and I haven't seen him since. I haven't seen him and I haven't heard from him since he graduated. That's what I told the police and that's the truth, I promise you, Laura.'

Laura still looked doubtful, a vivid image of Chief Inspector Thackeray's watchful eyes flashing across her mind. She believed Richard but very much doubted that anyone else would, least of all Michael Thackeray, and she

122

was quite sure that in his professional mode the chief inspector could be very searching indeed.

'It may be the truth, but that's not to say the police won't think it very suspicious that you failed to tell them if they find out later. Angela's no fool, either,' she said quietly. 'Are you sure she hasn't any idea what's been going on?'

'Angela knows nothing about any of this – the boys, the blackmail, nothing at all. I've made sure of that, at least.'

'So what did you think I could do to help?' Laura asked, at a loss. Thurston stood up abruptly and came round his desk towards her, taking her hands in his. She had found him an attractive man in her student days, nurturing an occasional fantasy about going to bed with him herself, and she was slightly surprised to find that her new-found understanding that he was unlikely to have looked at her with similar interest made no difference to the warmth with which she clasped his hands in return.

'A scandal like this will lose us the election,' he said. 'It's all very well for these kids to advocate coming out for everyone, let's all call ourselves queer and all that radical stuff. You can get away with being openly gay in some fields, if you're an actor or a musician or a fashion designer. You can even get a knighthood. But how many openly gay MPs are there? Not a lot, and for a very good reason. It has to be a vote loser, even in the allegedly liberal south-east. Up here it'd finish my chances. Poofs don't win elections here.'

'So what can I do?' Laura asked again, wanting to argue with his analysis but reluctantly forced to agree. Bradfield, with its traditional working class and its devout Muslim minority, was hardly fertile ground for an experiment in gay politics even in the hurly-burly of a general election. With the national spotlight on the by-election, the 'outing' of Richard Thurston would turn into a case of political assassination by tabloid newspaper. There would be no quarter given or expected.

'See if you can find Jason for me,' Thurston said. 'With

this campaign going on I can't get away from the endless canvassing and meetings and the rest of it. I never get a minute to myself. Find him and persuade him to leave me alone. You can do it, Laura. Please see if you can get him off my back. You can charm the birds off the trees if you turn your mind to it.' Just like Harvey, Laura thought ironically as, with a reluctance she did not fully understand, she agreed.

Back at the office Laura sat at her desk, unable to concentrate on the women's page feature she had outlined on the computer screen in front of her. Her mind returned constantly to Richard Thurston, who had hurried away to meet his campaign car, leaving her to absorb his message and close up his office behind him. She had sat in the battered old red armchair, lost in memories of her student life there and grieving both for Harvey Lingard, his laughing presence gone for ever now, and for Richard, haunted and quite as likely, she feared, to be destroyed by Harvey's ghost as by Harvey's successors in his regard.

She had once asked Richard why, on top of his teaching, he spent so much of his free time nursing his ungrateful constituency, apparently determined to exchange his lecture theatre for the larger stage of the House of Commons at an age when many men might have been looking forward to a quieter life. She had asked the question lightly, in the thick of the last general election campaign, but Thurston, who had been entertaining local journalists to drinks in the Clarendon bar, had taken it seriously.

'I seem to have been talking about politics all my life,' he had said quietly, drawing her away from the crush around the bar with a friendly arm around her shoulder. 'Talking, teaching and lately getting increasingly angry and frustrated. They say there are people who do things and people who teach. For a long time I was happy enough with the latter. But for years now I've been watching the destruction of so much of what my generation believed in. I suppose we'd begun to take it all for granted. We thought we didn't have to argue for decent standards any more, that the battles were won long ago. But we were wrong, and suddenly it didn't seem enough just to talk, or even to try to show you clever kids that there is an acceptable alternative to naked greed. I want to do more now. I want to get in there and help rebuild what I believe in, mend the gaping holes in the safety nets, pick the mad and the sad off the streets again. Does that make sense?'

It was Joyce Ackroyd's granddaughter who had nodded fiercely in return. To Joyce, Laura had thought, it would make perfect sense, and even now she sometimes regretted that she had lost the certainty with which, during her school holidays, she had once tagged along behind Joyce on her political crusades. There was a comfort in that sort of conviction which she doubted she would ever share again, although that was a thought she had not felt like troubling Richard Thurston with, resplendent in his party colours and his convictions, as she had sipped his Martini that evening towards the end of an election campaign in which old Charles Mortenson triumphed for the fourth and final time.

She might, she thought now, have been much more alarmed by his idealism if she had known then how vulnerable his private life was to the beasts who stalk the political jungle and who would regard tearing him apart and spitting him out as all part of a well justified day's work if it gained them some advantage. In the light of what she knew now, she thought, Richard Thurston's belated activism was based on a naivety which verged on the suicidal.

Today she had sat on in his red chair for half an hour before she had felt sufficiently recovered to go back to work, torn by conflicting emotions, not the least of which was fear for Richard and herself if the conspiracy they had entered into should ever be made public. She had agreed to his request to seek out Jason Carpenter, as she guessed that he had guessed she would, out of a mixture of old loyalty and new anxiety for a man she both respected and liked. But she had no idea then, and still had no idea hours later, how she might be able to fulfil his request even if she were able to track down the elusive campaigner, Jason.

The phone at her elbow rang peremptorily. She picked it up in a daze and took in the voice of the Gazette's chief receptionist informing her that there was someone at her desk with 'a story'. It was not an unusual message. Most newspaper offices receive a regular stream of unsolicited callers with some obsessive tale to tell, most of them too defamatory, vague or plain mad to be of any interest.

But amongst the dross there was always the possibility of gold, and someone usually spent a little time listening to whoever had taken the trouble to drop by. Laura glanced around the newsroom and took in the fact that those few of her colleagues who were in the office during the busy pre-lunch period were occupied with their own phones.

'I'll come down,' she said wearily, glad to get away from the pretence of concentrating on her work. She stuck a notebook in her shoulderbag and took the lift to the reception area two floors below. To her surprise the young woman the receptionist indicated as she approached was familiar. It was the student Dilly Jenkins, the girl from the university gay group, dressed this morning even more sombrely than when Laura had last seen her in tight dark leggings and buttoned boots beneath a very short black skirt and an attenuated green duffel coat. Her long metallic ear-rings jangling aggressively as she stood up at Laura's approach, her face as pale and uncompromising as ever.

'It's you,' she said in recognition. 'Good.'

'How's the feature going with Rob Stevens?' Laura asked.

'Oh, that,' the girl said dismissively. 'I shouldn't think we'll bother with that now. We've decided to be more pro-active. We're going ahead with the outing. We had a meeting last night and decided that this is the ideal time, with the by-election and everything. It'll make the maximum impact.'

Laura looked at the girl sharply, guessing where the challenge was about to lead.

'Come over the road to the pub,' she said. 'I was just on my way out for an early lunch. You can tell me all about it while I grab a sandwich.'

Reluctantly the girl followed her into the Lamb and Flag, still almost empty, the smell of polish and air-freshener just disguising the tang of stale beer, with the clock above the bar not yet showing noon. Dilly consented to Laura's buying her a tomato juice and sat poised on a low stool at a corner table, as if ready to take flight at the least provocation. Laura came back with drinks and a plate of pale ham sandwiches, curling at the edges: her colleagues patronised the Lamb for its beer, not its cuisine, and in reality she hardly ever came into the place at lunchtime.

'So?' Laura asked non-commitally after taking the first sip of her vodka and tonic. 'Who are you intending to out, then?'

The answer came back with brutal directness and was what Laura expected, but to hear Richard Thurston's name uttered with Dilly's brand of venomous contempt still shook her.

'He sleeps with boys,' Dilly said.

'But you don't object to that,' Laura returned with as much calmness as she could muster.

'Of course not,' Dilly said. 'What we object to is his keeping quiet about it.'

'Isn't that his choice?'

'Not when other people who've come out are being harassed. If people like him stay in the closet it damages

127

the rest of us. We'd like a gay MP. We'll campaign for him once it's out in the open. He owes it to us.'

'I doubt if he will see it quite like that,' Laura objected. 'In reality it will lose him the election. You can't go round the Heights, or up Aysgarth Lane wearing a green carnation. It's not realistic.'

Dilly shrugged slightly at that, her face pale and closed to any persuasion, her ear-rings swinging with an angry life of their own.

'It's a pity the Tory's not gay too. That'd really put them on the spot, wouldn't it, she said without humour. 'We did try to suss him out, but without any luck so far. We're working on it.' Laura believed her. There was a deadly seriousness about the girl which was chilling in its total absence of human sympathy.

'You won't find anyone who will publish allegations like this without evidence,' Laura said slowly. 'There are laws of libel.'

'We can give you evidence,' Dilly said. 'He slept with Jason Carpenter. Jason will tell you anything you want to know.'

'I'll need to talk to him,' Laura said firmly, deciding to play for time. 'I don't think you realise what a stir this will cause if the Gazette decides to print anything – which I'm not sure it will. But just supposing: I'll need to talk to Jason and anyone else who can substantiate what you say.'

'He's not around this afternoon,' Dilly said evasively. 'I won't see him before this evening. Can I call you?'

Laura finished her drink and pushed the plate of sandwiches away disgustedly. If she could see Carpenter on her own, she thought, she just might be able to use those powers of persuasion on which Richard Thurston had pinned so much hope, but she was not confident. At best, she thought, she might be able slightly to delay the inevitable as these young Jacobins pursued their objective with all the implacability of a revolutionary tribunal. The best she could hope for was to buy Richard a little time to prepare the ground for a revelation which she did not doubt for a moment would end his political career.

She gave Dilly her home phone number and warned her not to speak to anyone else.

'You're already laying yourself open to an action for slander,' she said grimly. 'If you've not already got a law student on your committee I should see if you can find one to advise you. You might need it.'

The girl looked at her, her dark eyes expressionless.

'We've thought of all that,' she said, getting to her feet and preparing to leave. 'I'll be in touch. But don't take too long with your research, will you. If the Gazette won't print the story, there's plenty of national papers that will.'

And that, Laura thought grimly, as she watched the girl weave her way out of the bar through the gathering crowd of lunchtime drinkers, was probably only too true. They would print it, and pay good money for the privilege.

At ten o'clock that evening Laura was standing outside the Blue Lagoon Club shivering and watching a couple of tall, black-leather clad young men make their way towards her along the ill-lit back street. In different circumstances she might have been made nervous by their approach down the deserted pavement to where she was standing beneath a streetlight which had failed. But not here. As she expected, they turned past her and took the steep steps down to the club two at a time, talking animatedly to each other over a jangle of metal chains and ear-rings, and giving Laura not even the most cursory glance.

She had heard nothing further from Dilly Jenkins that afternoon or evening in spite of waiting with growing impatience by her phone after work and refusing Vince Newsom's pressing invitation to join him for a drink at the Clarendon after he had been to the big Conservative meeting which was scheduled at the town hall that night. Pleading the beginnings of a cold, she had told Vince that

129

she would stay at home and have an early night. By nine o'clock, after several fruitless attempts to reach Richard Thurston by phone at his campaign headquarters and at home, where she had left what she hoped was an uninformative message with an obviously curious Angela Thurston, anxiety had got the better of her.

She had snatched up the phone again, rung Rob Stevens and explained as vaguely as she had dared, trying to keep the inner panic out of her voice, that she needed to find Jason Carpenter urgently. It was Rob's suggestion that they glance in at the Blue Lagoon before going up to the students' union. It was, Rob said shyly as they walked down the narrow alley which housed two of Bradfield's limited range of nightspots, a favourite meeting place for gay men. If Jason was there, he would find him, Rob had said, before diving into the cellar bar with every appearance of familiarity.

After ten minutes of waiting she felt both cold and irritable.

'Sod this,' she said aloud and plunged down the narrow cellar steps herself. The atmosphere below was dim and smoky, the bar lit only by small blue and pink spotlights which cast unexpected shadows on the walls and ceiling and gave the whole place, deliberately she supposed, the appearance of some fairytale grotto wreathed in mist. She stood a couple of steps above the packed room waiting for her eyes to grow accustomed to the darkness, unable to spot Rob and aware that she was the focus of some interest. The room below was exclusively male, although there the sameness ended. There were all sorts and colours and conditions of men below her, some conventionally dressed, some as outrageously clad as she guessed they thought they could get away with on the unwelcoming streets of Bradfield, all talking animatedly in couples or small groups. Someone pushed past her down the steps, glacing at her curiously from under heavily made-up black lashes as he passed.

130

'I think you've got the wrong bar, love,' he said as he plunged into the throng below. At last she caught a glimpse of Rod deep in conversation with the black leather duo who had recently arrived. She caught his eye, and he gave a wave to indicate that she should wait. After another minute's conversation he pushed his way through the crowd and led her back up the stairs.

'He was in there earlier looking very pleased with himself, the barman said. He was with another guy and they went off together looking fairly lovey-dovey so I'd guess he's gone home. Do you know where he lives?' Rob asked.

Laura thrust her hands into her jacket pockets and shrugged dispiritedly.

'No,' she said. 'And I don't suppose Dilly will tell us.'

Rob looked at her hard in the uncertain light cast by the only working streetlight further down the alley.

'Are you going to tell me what it's all about?' he asked in a carefully neutral voice. 'Or is it exclusive?'

'I'm trying to stop Jason doing someone enormous damage,' she said slowly. 'I can't tell you any more than that. I was told in confidence,' she said.

'Something to do with the outing?' Rob asked, as if he did not expect a reply. 'They have no right, have they, to try to destroy people like this?' His voice was strained with an emotion he could barely keep in check. Laura did not answer. She could not reassure Rob that the threat he felt from these implacable campaigners was not a real one for him too. There was no way of telling where the outing would end.

They were passing Bradfield's only strip club, the Copocabana, on the way back to her car. The alley narrowed here and the roadway sparkled in the multi-coloured light which spilled from the club entrance and speech was drowned by the recorded samba which was relayed into the street from the doorway.

It was the music, Laura concluded later, which had

131

made it impossible to hear the car which came up quickly behind them from the less well-lit end of the street. It did not slow, she firmly told the police who interviewed her in the hospital casualty department, even though it would have had difficulty negotiating its way around them both in the narrow bottle-neck of street where the Copacabana's entrance jutted beyond the building line and obliterated the pavement on which they had been safely standing minutes before.

With a shriek of tyres the car hit them both, catching Rob Stevens full in the back and tossing him like a half empty sack across the street and into a waist-high iron bollard which protected the jutting corner of the building from just such eventualities as recklessly speeding cars. Laura herself was struck a more glancing blow which threw her to one side to land, bruised and winded, in a heap on the opposite side of the road against an overflowing litter bin which crumpled under the impact of her body. She was sufficiently conscious seconds after the impact to be aware of the car speeding away round the corner of the street with a squeal of tortured tyres and into the busy thoroughfare beyond without apparently slackening its speed at all.

'Rob,' she said hoarsely, looking towards the ill-lit corner where she had seen him fall even as she had been flung in the opposite direction. She dragged herself to her knees, conscious of her stockings in shreds around her ankles, and of blood on her hands. Painfully she crawled across the incongruously glittering pink and gold roadway, half aware that someone else was running towards them from the Blue Lagoon end of the street.

She and the stranger reached Rob Stevens's crumpled body at the same time and together they turned his face gently away from the wall against which it lay. There was no sign of injury, except a trace of blood in the fair hair which glistened wetly in the garish flickering neon light from the club. But nor was there any sign of life. The leather-clad young man who had run the length of the street to help felt Rob's neck gently.

'That bastard never even braked,' he said. 'I'll phone for an ambulance, but I think he's dead.'

'Oh no,' Laura said. 'Dear God, no.' And she put her arms around Rob and her head on his unmoving chest, spilling a cloud of soft red hair across his jacket as she wept.

ELEVEN

LAURA LAY IN BED RIGID with shock and grief. She had lain awake for most of the night going over and over the split seconds in which tragedy had struck as if to unravel them in her mind and create a different outcome. Eventually the cold grey light of dawn crept in at the dormer window and picked out the familiar shapes and lineaments of her bedroom, none of which offered any comfort this morning. A single silent tear ran down her cheek as she came to terms with the fact that nothing that had happened the previous night could now be changed.

As the kindly stranger who had come to her aid had intimated, Rob Stevens had been killed instantly, not so much, the ambulance man thought, by the blow from the car but by the brutal force with which his body had been flung against the iron bollard which had been erected on that corner for pedestrians' protection.

She had travelled with Rob to the hospital, holding his hand in a vain attempt to will a response from his limp fingers. She had stood rigidly at his side, refusing to let anyone look at her own injuries, as the casualty doctor examined him and quickly confirmed the verdict she already knew in her heart was true.

'It must have been instantaneous,' the tall, harassed-looking Asian had said kindly. 'He wouldn't have known what hit him. Now you really must let us have a look at you.'

They had stripped her, examined her, X-rayed her and

told her what she already knew: that she was bruised and shaken by the accident but not seriously hurt. Not externally at least, she had thought as the casualty doctor pronounced her fit to go home. She had clenched her fists in her coat pockets to ward off the waves of panic which had threatened to overwhelm her. Somehow she had held herself together through the formalities of sudden death. She had confirmed Rob's identity, described what she could recall of the accident, which was very little, to an efficient-seeming policewoman who inveighed against hit-and-run drivers with subdued fury, and had rung Ted Grant to break the news to him and ask him to talk to the police so that they could make arrangements to contact Rob's family.

At last she had been free to go and took a taxi home. Closing her front door behind her and leaning against it wearily for a moment, she was aware of a strange noise. In the living-room she had found Vince Newsom slumped in an armchair fast asleep with the TV giving out a high-pitched whine of which he was apparently quite oblivious. Angrily she switched the set off and stood as if transfixed, gazing at him. He had taken off his shoes and tie and was spread-eagled across the chair in total alcoholic abandonment.

She had looked down at him, one hand outstretched in the abruptly aborted instant of shaking him awake, absorbing the dark smudges under his eyes and the petulant mouth hanging slackly half-open as he snored. Not for the first time she asked herself why she had found him so attractive for so long. Whatever that attraction had been in the past, as she stood there desperate for comfort in body and spirit, she knew deep within herself that it was not this man's help she needed. Wordlessly she had dropped her hand and, with a sense of desolation, had turned out the living-room light and closed her bedroom door on Vince, leaving him undisturbed.

The harsh morning light hurt her eyes and she ached all

over. Gingerly she felt her right side, where the car had apparently struck her a glancing blow, and her left shoulder which, she guessed, had hit the ground, and experimentally flexed her muscles. The sharp stabbing pain in her shoulder this induced was not encouraging, but did not deter her from rolling slowly out of bed and shrugging herself awkwardly into a dressing-gown. Her house-guest, she noticed, had removed himself from his armchair during the night without disturbing her and the spare bedroom door was tightly closed.

In the kitchen she poured herself orange juice and made toast and coffee, as she did every morning, hardly aware of what she was doing. She buttered her toast, took a single bite and pushed the plate away as she almost choked on the mouthful she had taken. She desperately needed to talk to someone but felt a profound unwillingness, undimmed by her fitful night's sleep, to confide in Vincent. She carried her coffee to the bathroom where she undressed gingerly and inspected her bruises, grimacing in pain as she twisted to inspect the darkening area of bruised and scraped flesh across her hip and buttock. She would be nobody's playmate for a while, she thought grimly, feeling a sense of relief that she had the perfect excuse to keep Vince out of her bed.

She washed and dressed in jeans and a loose sweatshirt, did not rouse her guest and left the flat before nine o'clock to meet the taxi she had ordered. She had told Ted Grant the previous night that she would not be at work for a day or so and her first priority was to collect her car which had been left parked the previous evening close to the Blue Lagoon. Paying off the taxi-driver she walked reluctantly to the corner of the narrow side street and looked down it. In the bright light of day, the nightclub and bars closed and silent, there was nothing to indicate what had happened there so recently. The crumpled litter bin still lay on its side where she had fallen, and the wind blew its detritus aimlessly around the narrowest part of the street.

136

On the other side of the entrance to what became at its narrowest little more than an alley-way, there was absolutely nothing to indicate the spot where Rob had died: if the police had marked the place where Rob had fallen with chalk, as she knew they sometimes did, all sign had been washed away by the overnight rain. The narrow, uneven pavement, the grimy brick wall and the rusting iron bollard were as innocent of blood as any other urban street-corner. Only Laura's mind could invest the place with the guilt of the death-trap they had combined to provide.

She shuddered convulsively and turned her back on the scene. Her car was waiting a hundred yards down the main road where she had left it the previous evening. She got in and had started the engine before she noticed that Rob's scarf lay on the passenger seat beside her. She picked it up and buried her face in the soft wool which still held the familiar scent of his aftershave.

'The bastard, the bastard,' she cried. You never understand until it happens to you, a distraught mother had once said to her years ago when she had interviewed her about the death of her child in a hit-and-run accident. She had been right, Laura knew now. She wished she could return to that grief-sticken suburban house that she could no longer precisely place to assure the woman that truly, now, she did understand, and that now she knew that none of the conventional words of sympathy she had uttered then had done anything like justice to the anger and pain which attended upon such wickedly culpable negligence.

She drove slowly across the town and out up the steep hill to the Heights. Joyce Ackroyd answered her door slowly, took one look at her granddaughter and took her wordlessly into her arms.

'What is it, pet?' she asked at last, when she had drawn her into her tiny living room, cluttered with piles of foolscap envelopes and gaudy election literature. 'Whatever's wrong?'

Laura told her everything that had happened since

137

Richard Thurston had made his confession to her the previous day. Joyce listened impassively, handing over a paper tissue when tears threatened to overwhelm Laura. When she had finished, Joyce sat silently for a moment, hands clapsed on her lap, her finely-lined face bleak, lips pursed.

'Our Mr Thurston's campaign committee won't be too chuffed if that gets out,' she said at last. Laura managed the faintest of smiles. It was typical of Joyce that, having mopped up the tears, she should turn promptly to the political implications of what she had been told.

'The tabloids will crucify him,' she said. Her grandmother nodded.

'Can you stop these daft students?' she asked.

Laura shrugged dispiritedly.

'I really don't know,' she said. 'They're a determined bunch and believe what they're doing is right. It's a sort of crusade with them.'

'And did your friend Rob believe what they're doing is right?' Joyce asked sharply.

'No, he didn't. He was as appalled as I was at the damage it could do – although I didn't tell him about Richard specifically.'

Joyce nodded and looked at her granddaughter shrewdly. She could see the pain of the previous night, physical as well as mental, etched in her pale face. But she knew Laura was a fighter and, since a child, usually a fighter for causes of which she had approved. She had always refrained from interfering in the girl's many arguments with her father, but had been ever ready to provide comfort and reassurance when the battle got bloody. This fight was more serious, its outcome unclear and unlikely to be painless. She could tell that Laura already blamed herself for Rob's death, and would take the destruction of Richard Thurston just as personally. But when it was over she would not forgive herself for giving up now.

'Your friend was killed helping you to look for this Jason lad,' she said at last. 'Hadn't you better keep on looking?'

Laura did not answer immediately. She looked around the cluttered room with another of her tentative smiles.

'What are you doing with all these?' she asked, waving a hand at the piles of envelopes.

'Addressing them and stuffing them with the election address,' Joyce said.

'Do you want some help?' Laura asked.

'If you like,' Joyce said, not hiding her pleasure. 'Happen I'll make a convert of you yet.'

'What's all this then?' Chief Inspector Thackeray asked suspiciously as Sergeant Mower dropped a buff file on to his desk.

'I just thought you'd be interested, guv,' Mower said with a disingenuousness which was ill-suited to his sharply intelligent face. 'I could have sworn you fancied Ms Laura Ackroyd.'

Thackeray looked at the sergeant with a distaste which took Mower aback. He had been tentatively testing out the line beyond which Thackeray would not let him step for days now without evident reaction. Now he had crossed it there was no mistaking exactly where it was drawn.

'I should restrict your fancies to the job, Sergeant, if I were you,' Thackeray said, a breath of the Arctic in his voice. 'Otherwise I might begin to believe the canteen gossip.'

Mower's expression froze at that. He had been away from the division on secondment to the drugs squad when Thackeray's predecessor and his former boss, Harry Huddleston, handed over the reins to his successor. He had no idea how much or how little of Huddleston's briefing might have touched on his own short career in the Yorkshire force, or his rather longer and more chequered stint with the Met. It was not a question which he could put to Thackeray or which Thackeray would be prepared to answer. Discretion, he concluded, was now urgently called for.

'It just seemed like a coincidence that she should crop up again so soon,' he said. 'I was chatting to a bloke in traffic and heard she was involved in a fatal hit and run last night. She's lucky to be alive, by the sound of it. The guy she was with bought it.'

Michael Thackeray looked down at the file and flicked it open quickly, determined that Mower should not see the concern which gripped him at the sergeant's laconic description of the previous night's events. He did not, he told himself angrily, 'fancy' Laura Ackroyd but he knew her well enough not to be indifferent to her undoubted charms or her fate. Further than that he was not prepared to probe.

He read the file, which was thin enough, quickly.

'There seems to be a witness missing,' he said. 'A young man ran to help the victims and then disappeared before anyone bothered to take his name.'

'I noticed,' Mower said. 'I expect traffic are trying to trace him. Do you want me to find out if they've turned him up?'

'Just ask them – tactfully, mind, it's not a CID case – to keep us informed,' Thackeray said thoughtfully. 'And then I think perhaps I would like another word with Miss Ackroyd, if she's up to it, before we go talking to the lesbian and gay radicals up at the university. She's already had a go at them and may have a few ideas about Councillor Baxter's little difficulty. Can you track her down for me? We'll go to her if she's not fit to come in here. Play it by ear.'

'Right, guv,' Mower said, with just the faintest hint of satisfaction in his eyes. 'All part of the service.'

They did not find Laura Ackroyd that afternoon although Mower, having discovered she was away from work, rang her flat at regular intervals without success. Thackeray had spent the afternoon talking to political and commercial colleagues of Bill Baxter's, in a largely vain attempt to discover who knew what about his extra-marital affairs. If any of the pillars of Bradfield society with whom he made contact knew of any reason why he might have become the victim of blackmail, they were not saying.

Thackeray went back to CID headquarters frustrated and with the distinct impression that ranks had been deliberately closed against him. The financial explanation for Baxter's suicide was the only one which his friends and colleagues seemed prepared to countenance, although they were vague about just what money troubles might have persuaded him to take out his service revolver and prove to a sceptical world that it still worked.

'They're not prepared to wash any dirty linen,' Thackeray said to Mower, who was tidying up his desk preparatory to leaving.

'They'll want to keep the lid on anything which might upset the by-election,' Mower said. 'They'll all be party members, you can bet your life.' He picked up the phone and dialled an outside number.

'I'll give the lovely Laura one more go, guv,' he said. 'I've already got a date tonight,' he added disarmingly, knowing that the remark could only be taken amiss by someone prepared to acknowledge sensitivity on that score, which he would take long odds that Thackeray would never do. The chief inspector contented himself with a chilly glance in Mower's direction before bending his head over his files again.

This time, though, Mower's persistence was rewarded, but as he made to speak Thackeray crossed the room and took the receiver out of his hand.

'Miss Ackroyd?' he said. 'It's Michael Thackeray here. I was very sorry to hear about your accident. I've been trying to contact you all day to see if you were OK.'

Mower stepped back and listened to this performance impassively, merely nodding as the chief inspector waved him out of the office and mouthed his good-night. He picked up his leather jacket and closed the office door quietly behind him, giving vent to his feelings only as he took the stairs to the main entrance two at a time.

'You cunning sod,' he said aloud as he went. 'I bloody knew you fancied her.'

TWELVE

LAURA HAD ALREADY ARRIVED AT the Malt Shovel in Broadley village when Thackeray arrived. Her VW was in the car park and when he entered the bar, still relatively empty at six-thirty in the evening, he saw her sitting at a corner table near the crackling log fire. In the flickering light her hair, loose around her shoulders this evening, glowed and shone with a warmth of its own but he saw with a sense of shock that she looked ethereally pale, beneath the mass of curls her face strained and slightly pinched and a bruise clearly visible above the left eye. She already had a drink in front of her and Thackeray bought his own and went across to join her.

'I hear you've been having a rough time,' he said quietly, taking a seat across the table from her, making no attempt to conceal his concern. 'I was sorry about your friend. I'm sure they'll pull out all the stops to find the car.'

'It's a sort of murder,' Laura said bitterly, swirling the ice around in her glass with a nervous tension which seemed to Thackeray to make her whole body taut enough to snap.

'Yes, it must seem like that.'

He watched her gravely for a moment, aware that she needed to talk about the previous evening far more urgently than she needed to help him with his inquiries, which was ostensibly why she had agreed to meet him at what she had described as a quiet country pub on the edge of the moors above the Maze valley. In fact it was a favourite meeting place for young people from Bradfield and Milford and many of the suburban villages between and the bar soon began to fill up with happy, laughing groups whose determined cheerfulness as they began their night out grated on Thackeray's nerves.

'Was he a very close friend?' he asked at last. Laura looked at him in a puzzled way.

'Rob?' she asked. 'Not close. Not close that way, not a boyfriend,' she said patiently, as if explaining to a child. 'But close enough, yes. I liked him a lot, was fond of him, I suppose, the way you are when you work with someone for a while. I'll miss him.' Thackeray filed those fresh snippets of information away in his mind while Laura gazed into her glass for a moment, where the ice picked up sparks of light from the fire. She suddenly drained her drink convulsively and put the glass down again with an angry movement.

'God, it's so unfair,' she said, loudly enough to attract some curious glances. 'One stupid drunken moment is all it takes!' She broke off, on the verge of tears.

'Do you think the driver was drunk?' Thackeray asked. That suggestion had not appeared in the reports he had read. Laura shrugged helplessly.

'The man who came to help,' she said, 'he said the car never even seemed to brake. It came straight at us without slowing down. It is a narrow gap to get through stone cold sober. But it wasn't dark. Not so dark that he wouldn't have seen us, anyway. We must have been easy to pick out against the lights in the main road. He must have been drunk, mustn't he, to have driven through at that speed?'

Thackeray nodded non-committally. There were inconsistencies here which puzzled him.

'The witness didn't leave his name. Do you know who he was?'

'I've no idea,' Laura said. 'I told your uniformed people. I think he must have come out of the bar after us. He was all in leather and chains, you know the sort of thing some of them wear in the Blue Lagoon. He was very kind.'

144

'Gay as well?' Thackeray asked sharply, surprised out of his determination not to push Laura, but she obviously took the situation as read and did not understand the significance of his question.

'We'd been to the Blue Lagoon,' she said. 'Haven't you come across the Blue Lagoon yet? It's a gay bar. We were looking for someone who might have been there. Rob came with me because – oh, because he was feeling protective, I suppose, that's all. He was trying to help.' She stared at her empty glass in desolation.

'Do you want another drink?' Thackeray asked, but Laura stood up abruptly, slim in her tight jeans and loose top and moving with a grace that made Thackeray draw an admiring breath in spite of himself. Damn Mower for putting ideas into my head, he thought to himself as he perforce accepted her abrupt offer to get him another.

'Tonic,' he said. 'With ice and lemon.' If she was surprised at his request she did not show it as she turned to head towards the counter. Thackeray watched her as she dodged between the growing crowd of customers to place her order. Several of the young men clustered around the bar glanced with more than passing admiration at her as she squeezed past them, but Laura seemed oblivious to their sharpened interest. It didn't take Mower to put ideas in his head, Thackeray admitted to himself. That was the trouble.

He turned away from the bar deliberately, apparently staring hard at the hunting prints on the wall behind their table, but in fact his eyes were blank and unseeing, his mind's eye focused on another face which had once been as beautiful, until Laura caught his attention again on her return. He took his drink and sipped it slowly, and she knew that something had happened in her absence which had made him wary of her.

'Was it the accident you wanted to talk about?' she asked, her own voice carefully neutral. He shook his head.

'I wanted to pick your brains about the gay and lesbian

145

scene,' he said. 'I need to talk to the students and I thought that as you had already had contact with them you might be able to give me the benefit of your advice.'

'What do you want to know?' she asked, suddenly wary herself as Richard Thurston's desperation, which had been overshadowed by the previous evening's tragedy, came flooding back.

'I didn't get very far with the Front,' she went on carefully. 'I told you, Ted Grant wasn't interested in running anything on outing. He's not averse to a bit of bum and tit in his family newspaper if he can get away with it – beauty contests, Miss Bradfield Supersave 1993, that sort of thing – but we're apparently not allowed to acknowledge that quite a lot of people prefer to go to bed with their own sex. Why are you interested anyway? Has the outing thing become a police investigation now?'

'Not as such,' Thackeray said. 'It's still essentially the Harvey Lingard case I'm working on.' He looked at her speculatively.

'Can I talk to you off the record?' he asked. She smiled, her face taking on something of its normal liveliness for a moment, with a hint of mockery in her eyes.

'I've left my notebook at home, Chief Inspector,' she said. He gave her a tentative half-smile and took a sip of his drink before apparently making up his mind to continue.

'It seems to me that the whole gay community in Bradfield is in turmoil, but it's not just the threat of outing that's causing anxiety. There's been a suggestion that someone has been screwing some covert homosexuals into the ground financially,' he said slowly, still unsure whether he was wise to trust Laura. If he had misjudged her and this sort of speculation appeared in the Gazette, it would be his career on the line, he thought grimly.

'Blackmail?' she said, without surprise.

'Blackmail, which has pushed one victim to suicide,' he confirmed.

Laura looked at Thackeray consideringly.

146

'Councillor Baxter?' she asked at last and seemed unsurprised when he nodded his assent.

'Was it generally known he was gay?' he asked, surprised himself at her response. Laura shook her head.

'Not generally known, but known,' she said, smiling faintly. 'You're forgetting my grandmother is an old political war-horse in this town. There's very little she doesn't know about what's gone on at the town hall for the last fifty years. I was with her this morning and we heard about Baxter's death on the local radio . . .'

'And?' Thackeray prompted.

'Her exact words were: 'One of the old bugger's boyfriends must have shopped him at last.'

'How old is your grandmother?' Thackeray asked, laughing in spite of himself.

'Seventy-five,' Laura said. 'She may not sound very politically correct but her heart's in the right place. I don't think she gives a damn who Baxter was going to bed with. It was his politics she couldn't stand. On those grounds she'd be happy to dance on his grave.'

'That might be a public order offence,' Thackeray said drily. 'But Baxter's tastes hadn't hurt his political career? So why should he be so worried about exposure now?'

'Bill Baxter's tastes were known to some people,' Laura said patiently. 'Certainly to some of the older generation. But they weren't publicly known. There's a difference. It's the old story. You can do what you like in private, but you mustn't upset the natives – or in this case, the voters. Bill Baxter and Stanley Treadwell were pretty well running the campaign for the Tory candidate and they'd fought off the young Turks in their own party to do it. Like most politicians, they were fighting on two fronts – against the opposition outside the party and the opposition inside it as well. A scandal now would have been a disaster for them in all sorts of ways.'

And how much more of a disaster for Richard, she thought, wishing for a single desperate moment that she

147

could confide everything to Thackeray but instantly pushing the temptation to the back of her mind. Thackeray wondered why her face suddenly lost its animation again and resumed its former look of bruised anguish.

'I happen to know that Baxter was furious about your plans to write about the outing campaign. He must have been terrified that the Gazette would blow his cover,' Thackeray said thoughtfully, and described the angry conversation he had overheard in the Clarendon bar.

'That figures,' she said. 'That must have been the day my esteemed editor told me to leave it alone. He'd been got at by Baxter. What a hypocritical bastard that man is. They're in all the same clubs, middle-aged men who never go home to their wives.' With Jack Longley one of their number, Thackeray thought to himself, wondering again just how hard a decision it had been for the superintendent to include Baxter's second and more damning suicide note in the case file.

'So, why were you and Rob at the Blue Lagoon last night if you'd been told to drop the story?' he asked, switching tack.

Laura looked innocently into Thackeray's deep blue eyes and lied.

'We thought the story might break anyway if the students went ahead with their plans,' she said. 'Rob is – was – very keen to carry on with some research, so I went along with him. We were supposed to be meeting Jason Carpenter there but he didn't turn up.' Rob, she thought with a shudder, would not be able to contradict this version of events.

'That's the lad who's chairman of the Gay and Lesbian Front?' Thackeray confirmed. She nodded.

'I haven't actually caught up with him yet,' she said, trying to keep her voice neutral.

'No? Well, I think perhaps I'd better catch up with him officially,' Thackeray said thoughtfully. 'So far Sergeant

Mower has talked to a girl – Dilly Jenkins, is it? – and not got much out of her except a lot of self-righteous claptrap about a more open and honest society.'

'Is it claptrap?' Laura asked.

'Your profession wouldn't do very well if there was less hypocrisy about sex, would it?' Thackeray said. 'Half the tabloid newspapers would be out of business.'

'Ouch,' she said, indignantly. 'I don't work for the tabloids. It's as fair to tar me with that brush as it would be for me to assume that you regularly write your suspects' confessions for them just because some of your colleagues are famous for it.'

'But your friend Vince Newsom works for a well-known tabloid,' Thackeray suggested, aware that the ice was paper-thin beneath his feet.

'You're too well-informed,' Laura said coldly.

Thackeray had the grace to look discomforted.

'It's my sergeant,' he said. 'He takes a lot of trouble to be well-informed and . . .' He hesitated long enough to arouse her curiosity to fever pitch, as she guessed later he must have known he would.

'And?' she asked. Thackeray rewarded her with his rare smile.

'Let's just say you seem to have bowled him over,' he said. 'He's a bit susceptible, I'm told.'

'Perhaps you should have sent him to buy me a drink,' she said tartly, remembering that look of appraisal in the dark young sergeant's eyes and finding that it still annoyed her. And what about you, Mr Thackeray, she wondered. Are you not susceptible at all? It was a question she found quite impossible to answer.

Her face had regained a little colour during this exchange but Thackeray had to admit that teasing her had not erased the wounded look from her eyes as he had hoped it might. She gathered up her jacket from the seat beside her and made as if ready to go.

'Can I buy you a meal?' he asked abruptly, but she shook

her head tiredly.

'I'm not hungry and I must go home,' she said. 'I want to go back to work tomorrow. I'm supposed to be doing a sort of "day-in-the-life-of" feature about Richard Thurston's campaign and I really don't want to fall down on that.'

'You really want him to win, don't you?' Thackeray, who took little interest in politics, said wonderingly.

'Professionally I'm completely neutral,' she said with an attempt at a smile. 'Personally, I'm enough of my grandmother's daughter to want him to win – passionately.'

He followed her out of the bar and into the car park. The pub stood on the edge of the village of Broadley, where the steep winding road which led to the rugged country to the north made a final right-angled bend before it was interrupted by a grid to keep the moorland sheep from invading the village gardens. Laura hugged her jacket around her and instead of going to her car she walked into the road and through the pedestrian gate beside the grid and onto the unfenced road beyond.

'If you come up here,' she said, 'you can see for miles. Look.' She turned, the sharp wind blowing her hair about her face, as she gazed past Thackeray to the dark valley below the village, criss-crossed by shimmering skeins of lights. Over the hills to the west it was still light enough to see the jagged edge of clouds being blown towards them across the valley, the edge of the hills broken here and there by the thin silhouetted finger of a surviving mill chimney. The darkness hid the scars of urban development below them and the air was full of the smell of peat and heather.

'Vince keeps asking me to go to London with him,' she said, 'but I would miss all this. I love this country.' Thackeray stood beside her, fiercely resisting the temptation to put his arm around her.

'When you stand above my father's farm like this,' he said, 'it's almost completely black. All you can see are the

150

lights from one or two cottages, tiny squares in the darkness. That's real country up there beyond Arnedale, not suburban country like this.'

'Is that why you came back?' she asked. 'You said at Vicky's dinner party that you'd been at Oxford. Not many people come back after that.'

'There were reasons why I had to come home,' he said. 'And one police force is much like another. And you? Will you go to London with Vince Newsom?'

Laura gave a thin laugh, very conscious of his evasiveness but unwilling to force herself where she was obviously unwelcome.

'Certainly not with Vince,' she said. 'Alone, maybe. But not yet.'

She shivered convulsively as the wind took her jacket and cut through her thin sweatshirt.

'I must go,' she said. Thackeray walked with her back to the car park and closed her car door on her gently. She wound down the window and smiled up at him.

'Thank you for letting me talk about Rob,' she said.

'Thank you for your help,' he said formally.

'It was nothing,' she said, only too conscious of what she had failed to tell him.

Back at her flat she flung herself into a manic session of cleaning and tidying, something she never did with enthusiasm unless she needed an excuse to forget some more pressing problem. Tonight the therapy worked and as she scrubbed the kitchen from floor to ceiling the vivid memory of Rob's inert body receded to the back of her mind. There was no sign of Vince, although he had left some of his shirts in the washing machine. Irritably she hung them up to dry in the bathroom and wondered how she could find a way to get rid of him. A few days, he had said. It was now only a week to polling day and she suspected he intended to hang on until the bitter end.

Exhausted by her efforts, she had a shower, wincing as the water lanced into the bruises and scrapes down one side of her body, and slumped into an armchair in her pyjamas and robe, flicking on the late-night news as she did so. She watched desultorily as the programme wound its way through the situation in the former Soviet Union and the prospects for the British economy. It was almost eleven before the presenter began to wind up and a disembodied hand passed him a bundle of the first editions of the next morning's national newspapers. At this point his eyes lit up and he waved what Laura at once recognised as the Globe in the direction of the camera and announced almost lasciviously what he suggested would be the by-election sensation of the decade if not the century. The Globe, he said, was leading its front-page on a story about the Labour candidate in Bradfield and his gay relationship with one of his university students.

Laura sat up, thrust into wakefulness, as she twisted her neck to read the banner headline.

'Oh, Vince!' she cried out aloud. 'Vince, you complete and utter shit! What have you done?'

THIRTEEN

LAURA COULD NOT REMEMBER WHEN she had ever been so angry. She had flicked the television to teletext to find a brief summary of the Globe's story, which told her little more than she knew already. She switched off and rushed into her tiny spare bedroom, where all the signs of Vince Newsom's occupation had been spread about with the abandon of one who feels perfectly at home. His portable computer stood open on the dressing table and beside it a pile of discarded sheets of notes. It took no more than five minutes to read, in draft at least, the twenty brief paragraphs which she guessed would end Richard Thurston's political career.

Vince had quoted 'Thurston's former lover' Jason Carpenter at some length. Times, places and a few more explicit details were not spared. The whole exposure was justified by Carpenter's claim that it was to the benefit of the whole gay community that openness should prevail. Vince had ended the story with Jason's pious hope that Richard Thurston would be elected triumphantly to Parliament as the North of England's first openly gay MP.

Laura picked up the papers carefully, as if they were infected with the plague bacillus, and carried them into the kitchen where she consigned them to the rubbish bin. She returned to the bedroom, switched off the computer, closed it and and hurled it heavily out of the bedroom door into the narrow hallway. Looking around her wildly she discovered Vince's leather sportsbag tucked ineffectually half under the bed and bundled the rest of his possessions into it. Dragging the bag behind her she went into the bathroom and crammed his personal gear and his wet shirts on top and zipped the bag up viciously before going to her front door and flinging it and the computer on to the landing outside.

Panting slightly, she went into her own room and threw herself on the bed, still shaking with suppressed emotion. She picked up the bedside telephone and punched in Richard's number, only to find it engaged. He had probably take it off the hook by now, she thought grimly, but as a ploy that would not last longer than the morning. By then the national press would be camped on his doorstep, and the national Party would be demanding explanations, while locally there were likely to be even more bitter and hurtful accusations of bad faith.

'Oh, Richard, you fool, you bloody fool,' she said to herself bitterly. 'You were never going to get away with it.'

As she lay on the bed, her head whirling, the telephone rang. As she picked it up she was aware that her hand was shaking. It was Ted Grant and he sounded as angry as she felt herself, although his reasons were very different.

'Did you hear about Vince Newsom's story in tomorrow morning's Globe?' he asked without preamble. She admitted that she had in a voice which sounded strangled to her although it did not apparently attract Grant's attention.

'So why the hell has he got it when we haven't?' Grant went on, so loudly that she had to hold the receiver further away from her ear in self-defence. She could think of no answer to that.

'Did you not have any idea what he was working on?' Ted went on. 'I thought he was your bloody boyfriend. What's he doing with an exclusive about the bloody candidate you're supposed to be covering for us? Why didn't we know about this Jason character? What've you been doing for the last two weeks girl, to miss this one? It's

154

the biggest thing to hit Bradfield since the mine disaster in '58.'

Laura looked at the telephone receiver with distaste and wondered whether to hang up, knowing that if she did she would probably be hanging up on her job as well as this particular conversation.

'Ted,' she said experimentally, as if trying out her voice to see whether it still worked. 'I haven't seen Vince all day. I only saw him very briefly yesterday. Last night I almost got killed, remember?' Grant was not a man whom an appeal for sympathy would normally give pause for breath but even he was brought up short by this reminder of the previous night's tragedy. He grunted explosively and followed this with a silence of, for him, unparalleled sensitivity.

'Blast,' he said. 'Are you going to be able to work tomorrow?'

Laura allowed herself a wan smile at that. In the circumstances, she thought, she would work tomorrow if she had to be carried into the office on a stretcher.

'I was due to shadow Richard Thurston for a day,' she said tentatively. 'I don't suppose he'll want to go ahead with that now. There'll be all hell let loose.'

This brought another grunt of deep concentration from Grant.

'Get down there as arranged and see if you can hold them to it,' he said eventually. 'You never know your luck. We're certainly due some after this cock-up. And if they won't let you in as arranged, then just see what you can get from the outside. We'll be looking for yards of copy on the man tomorrow. Call me by nine and let me know what gives. Right?'

'Right,' she agreed faintly.

'Oh, and by the way,' Grant went on by way of farewell, 'if you do see that bastard Newsom, buy him a drink from me. It's a cracker of a story. And if the Globe are fool enough not to offer him a staff job, tell him to get in touch.

155

He can come back here at double the money!'

Laura hung up with a groan. Reinforcements to the media circus in which, unless she resigned now, she could not avoid playing a part, would already be roaring up the M1 to Bradfield ready to begin the ritual sacrifice of Richard Thurston on breakfast TV and radio. She tried his number again, and again found it engaged, but she knew that he would not be able to keep silent for long.

Had he been culpably naive or wildly over-confident to think that he could get away with it, she wondered. There were, she knew, dozens of sharpened knives waiting for almost anyone who was bold enough to stick their heads above the political parapet. The chances of Richard's keeping his sexual adventures secret would not have been good at the best of times. With the furore being stirred up by the gay and lesbian students to coincide with the by-election, he had been led like the proverbial lamb to the slaughter.

It had been, she thought, the worst twenty-four hours of her life, and when she heard the sound of a key in the front-door lock she knew that it was not over yet. Wearily she rolled off the bed and went out into the hallway to meet Vince Newsom, who was standing half in and half out of the front door, his leather bag in his arms and an expression of bemused puzzlement on his face. He was quite evidently drunk.

'What's going on, doll?' he asked, with the look of boyish charm which she knew well but to which she now knew she was immune.

'You're leaving, Vince,' she said, taking the front-door key out of his hand and giving him a gentle shove out on to the landing again. 'It's over, you're finished, you're out. Understood?'

He rocked back on to his heels and put the bag down with exaggerated care on the floor.

'But why, doll? Just when things were going so well. Did you see TV tonight? They're following up my story already. Great stuff. It'll be the splash in every national in the morning. Didn't you see it?'

'I saw that someone had decided to ruin a good man,' she said softly. 'You could have told that little bastard Jason to get lost. It wouldn't have been that difficult.'

Vince looked at her, uncertainty apparent now through the alcoholic amiability with which he had tried to enter the flat.

'You're joking, doll,' he said hesitantly. 'It's a great story.'

'I know Richard Thurston too well to go along with that,' she said.

The self-satisfaction with which he had come up the stairs was disintegrating now into irritability in the face of her unexpected hostility. He looked at her with disbelief in his eyes, his colour rising.

'Oh, come on,' Vince said. 'You're just ratty because you didn't get to my boy Jason yourself. Don't tell me you wouldn't have written it if he'd come to you. I don't believe that. You don't walk away from a story like that, doll. No one does!'

'I do. I did,' Laura said, although afterwards she did not think that Vince had really heard her. 'Get out!' she added more fiercely. 'Richard was a friend. What you've done will finish him. He's a good man and didn't deserve it.'

Vince took this in slowly, and his face hardened. He pushed his floppy hair out of his eyes and his normally bland features curled into a sneer.

'You silly bitch,' he said. 'You silly sentimental bitch. You won't last in this game, you know, if you've got such a delicate conscience. You're in the wrong trade, doll. You should be a bloody social worker, not a reporter. You're too bloody sensitive by half.'

'Get out,' she said again and as he turned to pick up his belongings she closed the door on him and pressed her head wearily against the hard woodwork with a feeling very close to despair.

157

Laura arrived outside Richard Thurston's campaign headquarters before eight o'clock the next morning to find that she was already a latecomer. A couple of television crews, a radio car from the local station, assorted photographers, some with metal stepladders to give themselves a better view, Vince Newsom and more than a dozen other reporters, tape-recorders at the ready, were already camped outside the community centre, the doors of which appeared to be still firmly locked. Vince nodded at her briefly and turned away deliberately to continue his conversation with a plump, camel-coated colleague whose face looked vaguely familiar. After a moment's thought Laura recognised a television reporter, famous for his coverage of by-elections, looking paler and considerably older in the harsh morning light than he normally did on screen.

Some of the other journalists she recognised as the political specialists who had been covering the by-election for the last week; others were strangers with the bleary-eyed look of those who had travelled overnight, as she supposed they must have done. The atmosphere was excited, jovial even, as gossip and jokes were exchanged, bacon sandwiches and the occasional swig from a flask consumed, and incessant questions asked.

Vince Newsom was inevitably the centre of attention, a position he clearly relished, and was turning away constant questions about where he had hidden his informant, Jason Carpenter, with a self-satisfied smile and an occasional smug glance in Laura's direction.

Laura recognised Jim Crossley, a Gazette photographer, on the far side of the crowd, and moved to join him.

'What's happening?' she asked.

'God knows,' Jim said. He was a tall, taciturn man who undertook daily news photography on sufferance, as he freely admitted, for the chance to station himself once a week behind the goal at Bradfield United's football games. If Jim had dreams, and looking at that familiar craggy face Laura thought that unlikely, they would be of following United to Wembley and on to further glories in Munich, Rome or Madrid, fantasies which most eleven-year-olds were too realistic to entertain for the distinctly uninspired local team.

'Is anyone in there?' Laura asked, indicating the battered double doors with their array of red and yellow posters.

Jim shrugged. He never wasted words where an expressive gesture would do. 'If there is they must have gone in before first light. I was here at six.'

'Nothing on whether the press conference is on or off?'

'Nowt said,' Jim said. The town's most modern hotel had been the scene of regular morning press conferences for the last four days as the campaign had hotted up, but this delapidated building in a run-down area just outside the town centre was the nerve centre of Thurston's campaign and would be the source of any announcements on this most unusual of mornings. Laura winced mentally at the idea of Richard Thurston having to face the barrage of intimate questions which would come from this crowd if he consented to be grilled this morning. Perhaps Vince was right, she thought bleakly. Perhaps she just wasn't cut out for this job when push came to shove and her emotions were involved.

Introspection was interrupted by a shout from one of the photographers on the edge of the crowd.

'There they are,' he shouted, pointing to the corner where three cars had stopped briefly. The whole pack of journalists set off at a trot towards the far end of the street, photographers and television crew cursing freely as they hurriedly tried to gather up their bulky equipment to keep up with the more mobile reporters with their tiny tape-recorders. But the cars did not stop at the end of the road. They all pulled away round the corner, out of sight

159

long before their pursuers had caught up with them. Laura pulled an irritable Jim Crossley back towards the rear of the perspiring and now angry mob.

'Isn't there a back way in?' she asked quietly. Jim hesitated.

'Aye, you're right,' he said.

'Come on,' Laura said, tugging him back towards the main doors. 'That'll be where they've gone. It's in the alley off Commercial Street. They'll be inside long before that lot catch up with them.' As the rest of the press turned the corner of the street a hundred yards away, she listened at the community centre's main doors until she heard movement inside and then she rapped sharply. A muffled voice asked her business.

'It's Laura Ackroyd,' she shouted. 'Ask Richard Thurston if I can come in.'

There was a long silence, and Laura anxiously watched the street corner, aware that the rest of the pack would be back as soon as they discovered that they had been outwitted and the back door had been closed against them as firmly as the front.

'They'll not wear it,' Jim muttered lugubriously. But he was wrong. They heard the bolts being withdrawn and a key turning in the lock before the door was opened an inch by Ron Skinner, Thurston's union driver, a small, belligerent figure with an extremely unfriendly gleam in his eye.

'Five minutes,' Skinner said flatly. 'And no pictures.' Laura hesitated and glanced at Jim.

'Let him in,' she said quickly. 'You can take his camera if you like, but if he stays out here they'll lynch him when they get back and find we've tricked them.' Skinner's eyes flickered towards Jim Crossley and his look thawed half a degree.

'As it's him,' he said.

Jim's own features were split by the thin crack which passed with him for a smile.

160

'That were a right nice shot your lad got in for United last Saturday,' he said to Skinner, who nodded appreciatively in response.

'It were that,' he said as he hustled them through the doors, locked them again securely and took Jim's equipment off him.

'They're in theer,' Skinner said, indicating the small room at the back of the main hall which had been turned into Richard Thurston's semi-private sanctum for the duration. Laura and Crossley picked their way across the hall, weaving their way between the cluttered tables waiting for the day's influx of campaign workers, and the piled up boxes of campaign literature, many of them empty and discarded now, which littered the floor.

The office door stood ajar and as they approached Thurston himself pulled it fully open and confronted them. He looked, Laura thought, as if he had not slept for a week. His shirt and tie were evidently fresh, but his grey suit was crumpled and his lapel boasted a dangling pin but no campaigner's red rose. But it was his face which made Laura really draw in her breath in distress. His normally thin features had become almost cadaverous overnight. There were dark circles under his eyes, which appeared to be screwed up against the light, and the lines of strain around his mouth turned the smile he gave Laura into a near grimace.

Over his shoulder Laura saw the darkly suspicious face of Jake Taylor MP. Early as it was he had not skimped on his toilet: his face was freshly shaved, his navy suit impeccable, his red rose-bud fresh and at a jaunty angle. Only his cold grey eyes and the uncompromising line of his mouth gave any indication that this was not a normal morning in a campaign which his protégé had seemed to stand every chance of winning. It was Taylor who spoke.

'Come in,' he said curtly. 'We've got a proposition for you.'

As Laura followed the men into the room she impul-

161

sively put a hand on Richard's arm.

'I'm sorry. I never found Jason,' she said quietly. 'Vince must have got to him first.'

Thurston shrugged listlessly.

'It wouldn't have made any difference,' he said. 'They were determined to get me, one way or another.'

Jake Taylor waved everyone into seats and took the chair at the top of the table himself. Laura slid into a chair next to Thurston. Beyond him was the party agent, Bert Barraclough, a plump, ineffectual man who this morning had the bemused look of an accident victim waiting for help at the side of the road. Ron Skinner squeezed awkwardly into a corner seat, which left Jim Crossley, looking naked without his equipment, to stand by the door which Taylor had firmly closed.

'Right,' Taylor said aggressively. 'Ms Ackroyd, I want your assurance that nothing you hear discussed here will be used without our say-so. You're here because Richard wants you here. He thinks that if we're to save anything from this mess the Gazette is going to be crucial to us and, not to put too find a point on it, you're our best friend on the Gazette. By chance we had a date with you today anyway, but until I say so this is so far off the record it's out of sight, deepest background. Understood?'

Laura nodded cautiously. 'This story is going to run and run,' she said. 'And there's no way I can control what Ted Grant decides to use. The only way I can get stuff in the paper is if it's genuinely newsworthy, better still exclusive. Then it'll get used.'

'We're not asking you to compromise yourself,' Richard Thurston said quietly. 'I'll give you an exclusive interview for today's paper. Will that get used?'

'You bet,' Laura said, unable to suppress a gleam of excitement in her eyes. The circumstances might be dire, but as usual there was something in it for the well-placed reporter, the one who could get closest to the carcase, she thought wryly – more a case of jackals than weasels. And

162

this morning at least she seemed to be the jackal a nose ahead of the rest.

'Right,' Taylor said again. 'Now let's think about some damage limitation.'

Half an hour later Laura and Richard Thurston found themselves alone in the hot and stuffy little office. Jim Crossley had taken a series of photographs of the candidate and returned to the office to have them processed for the first edition and to tell Ted Grant what Laura would be bringing back. Jake Taylor and the rest of the committee had retired to the outer hall to let in the party workers to reassure them that the campaign would continue in spite of the night's setback and to try to restore battered morale. The combination of activity and a hefty dose of calculated reassurance had left the candidate still visibly crumpled but with a touch more self-possession now his campaign committee had pledged itself to seeing the election through to what Laura assumed would be an inevitably bitter end. Laura was also committed to writing up an interview for that afternoon's paper.

With an efficiency she did not feel she got out her tape-recorder and put it on the table. But before she switched it on she sat for a moment looking at Richard, who was leaning against the radiator under the high window of frosted glass which let so little light into the room that the flickering fluorescent strip had to be kept on constantly. He met her gaze and attempted a rueful smile which did not reach his eyes.

'I thought last night of withdrawing, but Jake persuaded me that we couldn't let the other lot take the seat by default,' he said.

'But you'll lose votes,' Laura said. It was a statement rather than a question and he nodded.

'We've already had phone calls from one of our Muslim supporters' groups. They won't be available for any more

163

canvassing or leafleting. There are Christians who'll feel the same. It runs very deep, you know, with some people, the idea of sin. I don't think we can win now.'

'How has Angela taken it?' Laura ventured carefully. A look of pain crossed Richard's face and he ran a hand through his hair.

'Badly,' he said. 'She . . .' He hesitated for a moment, looking almost puzzled. 'She was quite distraught last night. She seemed to be blaming herself somehow, as if she should have known, or could have done anything about it if she had.'

'Will your marriage survive?' Laura asked gently. He shrugged again.

'In public, till after the election anyway. She's coming to the press conference later to say that. I didn't want her to, but she insisted. After that I don't know. It's a lot to ask anyone to forgive. I've been deceiving her for a long time.'

'She'll stand by her man, will she?' Laura asked, a touch of irony in her voice. 'That's what usually happens in this sort of situation. But it doesn't always last, you know.'

'I know.'

Thurston's acceptance of the situation was painfully raw. It was as if exposure had stripped away every last shred of a mental hiding place and taken some of the normal everyday skin of polite prevarication with it, leaving him naked and flayed in front of her. If he faced a wider audience at his press conference like this, she thought, even with Angela at this side he would be publicly humiliated.

At that moment there was a tap on the door and Jake Taylor put his head in, looking even grimmer than he had done previously.

'More bad news,' he said. 'We've just had a call from London. The leader won't be coming to the town hall meeting after all. Sudden urgent shadow cabinet business.' He laughed mirthlessly. 'Like hell!' he said and slammed the door closed again.

'Rats – they can recognise a sinking ship at two hundred miles,' Thurston said. 'You know if members of Parliament reflect the population as a whole there must be fifty or sixty gay MPs down there. I know of two who admit it.' He held his hands out in despairing supplication. 'What shall I do, Laura?'

'Fight the bastards,' Laura said angrily. 'You can't just lie down and let them walk all over you. What you do in your private life shouldn't affect the election. What you did wasn't loyal to Angela, but if she'll stand by you, how can anyone else complain? You haven't done anyone else any harm.'

'There's a lot of people wouldn't agree with you. All those innocent young boys? Now Jason's talked it won't be long before the rest comes out.'

'Yes, I was surprised Vince's story only mentioned Jason, not the others.'

'Perhaps that's being kept for the next instalment,' Thurston said bitterly.

'Were they innocent?' Laura asked.

Thurston hesitated for a moment and then shook his head with a faint smile.

'No,' he said. 'They were not. With Harvey Lingard I was the innocent one, though I was twice his age. He knew precisely what he wanted, while I was still only half aware of it. He seduced me, though no one's going to believe that. With the rest – it was six of one and half a dozen of the other, I suppose. We all knew exactly what we were doing. But tell that to a jury – or the voters – and they won't believe it for a moment. I was the older man so I must be to blame.'

'I thought you said no one knew about Harvey,' Laura said. 'At least he won't be giving evidence against you. If I were you I'd be very wary of dragging Harvey Lingard into this, if you can possibly avoid it.'

'Oh, I expect after this morning's headlines our new model chief inspector will be round putting two and two together and making five,' Thurston said.

165

'Promise me there's not five to make,' Laura said lightly, but not lightly enough to hide the real fear that his words engendered. 'I always had a soft spot for Oliver Cromwell.'

'You?' Thurston said. 'You're a cavalier at heart, Laura my love. Follower of lost causes, like me. But I promise. I plead guilty to being gay, promiscuous even, though not very, and mercifully free of AIDS, I may add. I've had the test, for Angela's sake if not my own. But I'm not a murderer, God help me.'

'So fight the bastards then,' she said. 'Go to your press conference and face them down. Take the students' point. If ten per cent of the population are gay where are they all hiding? It's out in the open for you now, so make the best of it.'

Thurston looked at her without speaking for a moment, feeling infinitely old as he looked at her bright eyes and fierce expression. Then he shrugged and gave her a smile which for the first time that morning had some genuine warmth in it.

'We can't win, you know. The seat's too marginal. We'll lose too many votes over this. But you're right. It's better to go down fighting.'

'Good,' Laura said, switching on her tape-recorder at last. 'So let's do your coming-out interview. And then you can go and tell Vince Newsom and the Globe and the rest of the reptiles where to go.'

FOURTEEN

'YOU HAVE TO HAND IT to him, he's got guts, guv,' Sergeant Mower said, turning off the television in Superintendent Longley's office where he and Chief Inspector Thackeray had been watching live coverage of Richard Thurston's press conference.

'He also tells lies – at least by omission,' Thackeray said.

The two men had watched Thurston's performance in silence. In spite of the ingrained scepticism of the professional policeman, each had been impressed by the dignity with which the candidate, flanked by Jake Taylor on one side and his wife, Angela, pale-faced and unsmiling, on the other, had faced the assembled media.

Thurston had read a brief statement admitting that the main facts of the Globe's story that morning about his affair with Jason Carpenter were true and that in his view and that of his campaign committee his private life had no bearing on his fitness to become a Member of Parliament. He would, he said, make no more statements and answer no questions about the affair. He would fight as vigorously as he was able to win the Bradfield seat for his party and he trusted that the voters would listen to his political message, not to newspaper gossip about his private life.

Vince Newsom had been prominent amongst the audience of avid questioners who disputed Thurston's ban on personal questions vigorously, seeking to know his views on the morality of gay sex, the future prospects for his marriage and his estimate of the voters' reaction to the

167

overnight disclosures. A small man at the back had asked bluntly whether or not the candidate had AIDS, at which Thurston had given an anguished glance at his wife and shaken his head, but said nothing. The television camera had also given them a brief glimpse of Laura Ackroyd, whose red hair stood out like a beacon amongst the journalistic throng, but who apparently asked no questions, personal or political.

After ten minutes of mayhem Thurston, growing visibly more tense, had refused to take any more questions at all and Taylor, who was chairing the meeting with a face like stone, allowed Angela Thurston the briefest opportunity to speak. In a strained voice scarcely strong enough to register with the bank of microphones in front of her, she confirmed that she had forgiven her husband and would support him fully during the rest of the campaign.

'He's not going to get away with it, is he?' Mower asked sceptically. Thackeray shrugged.

'That's an interesting question,' he said. 'I don't know how tolerant the voters of Bradfield will turn out to be. But from our point of view it's not half as interesting as the questions I want to ask him about his relationship with Harvey Lingard.'

'You reckon Lingard did come up here to see Thurston after all, then?'

'Taking account of what we now about Thurston's tastes, it has to be a possibility. I want a new publicity campaign to find our more about Lingard's movements while he was in Bradfield. I must know what he did between the time he put his luggage in the left-luggage locker and the time he got to Heyburn village. I don't believe no one saw him in that couple of hours.'

Appeals for help in the Gazette and other local papers to trace Lingard's movements had so far brought forth only one witness: another elderly inhabitant of Heyburn who had been shopping in the town and got off the village bus with Lingard that day as it had arrived on schedule at ten minutes past two. Burdened with shopping and anxious for a cup of tea, Alice Brown had hurried home without paying much attention to where the young man who had given her a helping hand off the high bus platform had gone after that, but Thackeray was working on the assumption that as no one remembered him calling in the Fleece for a drink he had headed straight off up the rocky track which led to the moor where he probably met his death soon afterwards.

Thackeray sat thoughtfully for a moment in Jack Longley's chair, hands clasped under his chin and his blue eyes remote, while Mower waited patiently for further instructions. Mower had still not succeeded in gaining any real understanding of how the chief inspector's mind worked, although he knew, with an anxiety that occasionally knotted up his stomach, that in some respects his career depended on it. Irascible old Huddleston had been a doddle compared with this inscrutable beggar, he thought irritably.

Mower, consumed with ambition and with few scruples about how that ambition might be fulfilled, would have been shocked if he had known just what was going through the chief inspector's mind as he sat bleakly at the superintendent's desk. As the morning's events had unfolded, Thackeray had been seized with a deep disinclination to pursue his investigations further, although he accepted that there was no question that ultimately he must. The simple murder inquiry which had been launched in the bracing moorland breeze at Heyburn now looked like twisting away down tortuous, foetid corridors of illicit sex, blackmail, suicide, and messily disintegrating public reputations, in a case which he doubted that Bradfield would give him much thanks for solving. Too much mud would stick, he thought with deep distaste, soiling the innocent as well as the guilty.

Blackmail was like that, contaminating everything it touched in a way that murder, more often than not a crime of swiftly erupting and often bitterly regretted anger, less often did. And if the crime of blackmail led, as he was now convinced it would, to his playing a leading part in the destruction of Richard Thurston, then he would in a sense become its aider and abetter, the inevitable accomplice of whoever had driven Bill Baxter to despair and – he guessed – had thrown Thurston to the media wolves as well.

'Sir,' Mower ventured at last, breaking into Thackeray's reverie. 'Was there something else?'

'Yes,' Thackeray said, forcing himself back into action with a heavy sigh. 'The other person I want to talk to urgently is Jason Carpenter, the other star of the Globe's front-page story. He has to be in the frame as our gay community blackmailer. If it wasn't him, then it must be someone else with access to the same nasty little blacklist they compiled for their outing campaign, and he should be able to tell us who that might be.'

'I guess the Globe have got him stashed away somewhere quiet so's the other hacks can't get at him,' Mower said.

'Then find their man Vince Newsom and tell him that I'll have him for obstructing the police with their inquiries if he doesn't produce the little shit by tea-time. He can't have taken him far. There hasn't been time.' Thackeray spoke with a quiet fury which no longer surprised Mower.

'Right, guv,' the sergeant said placatingly. The two men walked slowly back to their own office in silence and Mower picked up his phone to begin his inquiries. But before he could make his call, the door opened to admit a uniformed sergeant who nodded to Thackeray and dropped a buff file on to Mower's desk.

'You asked about the witness to the hit and run the other night,' he said. 'We're running an appeal for him to come forward in the Gazette tonight. We guess he came out of the Blue Lagoon so he's likely a respectable citizen into a bit of shirtlifting by night, so he may be a bit shy.'

170

'Thanks, sarge,' Mower said, with a quick glance at Thackeray to gauge his reaction to the casual abuse, but the chief inspector gave no indication of having even registered the insult to the Blue Lagoon's clientele.

'I think Laura Ackroyd's friend, the one who was killed, was gay too,' Thackeray said when the uniformed officer had left. 'She didn't let on herself, but when I spoke to the barman he said he knew him, had seen him in there before. Did I tell you?' Thackeray had not told Mower and the sergeant looked startled.

'Christ,' he said, shocked out of his habitual caution with Thackeray. 'What have we got here? Some sort of holy war against gays?'

'You wouldn't approve of that?' Thackeray asked.

'No way,' Mower said, without hesitation. 'I don't have any hang-ups in that direction. Do you?'

Thackeray smiled thinly.

'I didn't see much difference between Larry Beacon and the average widow we break bad news to, if that's what you mean,' he said. 'But the way I was brought up was not that remote from Mr and Mrs Lingard. Plant the idea of sin in a child and it's not easy to throw off later . . .' He shrugged, unwilling to explore his own prejudices and quelling, with a frosty look, any idea of pursuing the subject that Mower might have entertained.

'As for your holy war,' Thackeray continued, 'I think the sort of people you're thinking about believe AIDS will wreak the vengeance of the Lord quite nicely, without their having to lift a finger. Still, it's a theory we could pursue if the more obvious one falls down. You could go and listen to a few sermons in the more fundamentalist tabernacles. I've no doubt that would be good for your soul.'

'The more obvious theory, guv?' Mower asked, wondering if Thackeray intended him to fail to follow his reasoning for the purposes of some put-down he did not understand.

'Think about it,' Thackeray said, an edge of impatience in his voice. 'We have a murder, a suicide, and a fatal accident – which I suppose could be something else. All the victims are gay, though only Harvey Lingard was openly so. We know Bill Baxter was being blackmailed. We now know Richard Thurston was open to blackmail, at the very least. We also know that the gay students were threatening prominent members of the community with outing – which in itself is a sort of blackmail. I don't think we really need to run around the fundamentalist sects looking for someone playing avenging angels, do we? I think the answer's there in the gay community, where the tension's been quietly building itself up to an explosion for months now.'

'And the by-election blew the lid off?' Mower said.

'Well, it certainly made Councillor Baxter and Richard Thurston vulnerable to exposure in a way they wouldn't normally be, yes. Neither political party wanted that sort of scandal. The blackmailer knew that. He turned the screw on Baxter to the point where he broke.'

'And Thurston, guv?'

'Perhaps he broke too,' Thackeray said, with the chill in his voice of a man who had seen all too many men and women break.

'Get me Richard Thurston first,' Thackeray went on. 'And then Jason Carpenter. And don't take no for an answer with either of them. I'm going to fill Jack Longley in on the latest developments. He wants all this kept under wraps until after polling day but I think that's a bit of wishful thinking on his part.'

He picked up the files on his desk and left the office without another glance in the sergeant's direction. Mower shivered as the cold draught from the door cut through his thin, well-cut primrose shirt. He did not envy anyone Thackeray chose to interrogate to breaking point.

*

'Yes,' Richard Thurston said in a voice devoid of emotion. 'I was being blackmailed.'

He was sitting in his cramped campaign office again, facing Chief Inspector Thackeray and Sergeant Mower across the conference table. Mower had located Thurston at home after his gruelling press conference and had been surprised at how readily the candidate had accepted his polite invitation to talk to Chief Inspector Thackeray again later in the day. Not at home, had been Thurston's only mild condition and not, for the sake of what was left of his reputation, at police headquarters.

They had agreed on the campaign office later in the afternoon, and Thackeray had himself equably offered to arrive in an unmarked car by the back entrance, to avoid the sharp eyes of the still hovering reporters. Settled now, with the office door tightly shut and a grim-faced Ron Skinner set to keep out interlopers, the three men eyed each other warily as they absorbed the implications of Thackerey's first blunt question and Thurston's unequivocal answer.

'Do you know who the extortionist was?' Thackeray went on. Thurston shook his head wearily.

'I've no proof,' he said.

'But a good idea?'

Thurston shrugged. He slumped rather than sat in his chair, as if dogged by intense weariness, his face grey and strained and his eyes empty of emotion.

'I think it was probably Jason Carpenter,' he said. 'Although the blackmailer seems to have known more about my affairs than he's told the Globe, so perhaps it wasn't him after all. I just don't know.'

With a patience which surprised Mower, Thackeray coaxed the whole painful story out of Thurston: nearly three years of gradually increasing demands, culminating in a final letter claiming so outrageous a price for silence in the febrile atmosphere of the by-election that Thurston had resigned himself to exposure before polling day.

173

'Did you know Councillor Baxter, Bill Baxter?' Thackeray asked. Thurston nodded slowly.

'Yes, I've met him once or twice. He was leader of the council when I was first adopted as a candidate. I was invited to a few events at the town hall.'

'Did you know he was gay?' Thackeray asked.

'Good God, no,' Thurston said, clearly surprised. 'He was always with his wife when I met him, all dolled up in their best suits and chains of office. I had no idea.' The full implication of what Thackeray had said sank in slowly, and Thurston seemed to shrink further into his chair, shock overcoming for a moment his apparently desperate fatigue.

'That's why he shot himself?' he asked in little more than a whisper. 'He was being blackmailed too?' Thackeray did not answer the question but his silence was answer enough for Thurston, who shuddered.

'Do we deserve this, Chief Inspector?' he asked with an unexpected flash of anger. 'We're supposed to have progressed since the days of Oscar Wilde, but all this makes you wonder.'

'I'll be very happy to arrest whoever was blackmailing you, Dr Thurston, but you will have to give evidence . . .'

'After today perhaps I'll do that,' Thurston said, his voice tight with suppressed emotion. 'After today, I've very little to lose.'

'Did you keep the blackmail letters?' Thackeray asked, and was surprised when Thurston nodded. They were the sort of evidence that was all too often destroyed by distraught victims.

'I don't think they'll be much help, though,' Thurston added hastily, in response to the gleam of interest in the policemen's eyes. 'They were done on a word processor. Not much chance of tracing that, I shouldn't think.'

'No, but it narrows it down to people who have access to one, and who know how to use one,' Thackeray said. 'Did you tell anyone else about what was going on. Did your

174

wife know, for instance?'

Thurston shook his head.

'Not Angela,' he said. 'She didn't know anything until last night. Nothing at all.'

'But you told someone,' Thackeray said, picking up the slight hesitation in Thurston's voice. 'Who was it?' Quiet as Thackeray's questioning was, it left no doubt that to each and every question he required an answer, Mower thought.

'I told Laura Ackroyd,' Thurston said reluctantly. 'I asked her if she could find Jason for me, as it was too difficult for me to get away from my minders.' His face was anguished again now. 'I think she must have been looking for him when her friend was killed the other night,' he said.

'Ah,' Thackeray said, understanding Laura's reticence now. 'She said she had been to the Blue Lagoon. You are not part of the gay scene, then, Dr Thurston? Not a regular at the Blue Lagoon yourself? I believe that's where all the gay contacts are made and the gossip goes down. Where you might have heard about Bill Baxter, for instance?'

The questions could have been insulting, prurient even, but were offered in the same flat, uninflected voice that Thackeray had adopted for the whole of the interview. No offence was offered and none taken.

'No, mine were very private affairs. Or so I thought,' Thurston said bitterly, as if it had not really sunk in yet that his affairs were now very public property indeed.

'Affairs?' Thackeray said softly. 'There was more than one, then?'

Now we're getting to it, Mower thought, turning over a page of his notebook and watching Thackeray at work with undisguised admiration. He'll have him eating out of his hand in a minute, he thought.

Thurston looked down for a moment at his own hands, which were clasped in front of him on the table, and

Mower noticed the knuckles whiten perceptibly. Then Thurston suddenly unlocked his clenched fingers and spread both hands out to Thackeray in supplication.

'There were others,' he said, facing his interrogator squarely now. 'The blackmailer knew about two others.' And he told him the names of the students he had slept with.

'And Harvey Lingard?' Thackeray said, without emphasis. 'Aren't you forgetting Harvey Lingard?'

Thurston shrugged again and gave a half-hearted smile of defeat.

'Harvey was the first,' he said. 'Ten years ago. The blackmailer never mentioned him. I assumed he didn't know about him.'

'And Harvey came to see you on the twenty-fifth?' Thackeray continued with only the faintest hint of satisfaction in his voice. But Thurston shook his head angrily at that.

'No,' he said. 'I didn't see him. Everything I told you about that day was the truth. If Harvey came looking for me that day, he never found me. I haven't seen Harvey Lingard since the day he left the university.'

Thackeray did not press him further and for a moment the two men looked at each other appraisingly.

'Do you know Heyburn moor?' Thackeray asked, at length.

'Yes, I do,' Thurston said. 'Like most people in Bradfield, I've walked up there often enough. I went there more than once with Harvey. Since you identified the body I've wondered whether that was why he went there that day, or whether he'd been there with other lovers too. The thought made me quite jealous after all these years. A foolish, adolescent reaction, I know, but Harvey had that effect on people. But if he went to meet someone there on the twenty-fifth, it wasn't me, Inspector. That is the truth.'

'I think, Dr Thurston, we had better go over the events of that day very carefully now,' Thackeray said. 'We

176

believe Harvey Lingard arrived in Bradfield on the eleven fifty-eight train from Leeds. He put his luggage in the left-luggage locker at four minutes past twelve – the time is printed on the ticket – and he was seen getting off a bus in Heyburn just after two. We will never know exactly when he was killed but as no one ever saw him alive again we suppose it was that afternoon. I'd like to know where you were and who you were with that afternoon and evening, Dr Thurston.'

Thurston did not answer. He was very still, staring at Thackeray from eyes which had sunk into their sockets, but his expression was more one of resignation than fear.

'You really believe I killed him,' he said at last. 'But you're wrong, Chief Inspector. I loved Harvey, in my way. I know some people don't think homosexual love counts for anything. Perhaps you're one of those, but I assure you that's not right, either. I could no more have killed Harvey than I could have killed my wife or child.'

Thackeray unexpectedly shook his head as if to dissociate himself from Thurston's accusation.

'I need to eliminate you from my inquiries, Dr Thurston,' he said.

Thurston shrugged helplessly and pulled a diary from his inside pocket and flicked back through the pages. He had been in a tutorial until noon, he said, and gave them the names of the students he had been teaching. He had had lunch with a colleague, and had been teaching again from two until four. He had stayed in his room marking until five-thirty and then gone home. It had been, he said, a normal and unremarkable Tuesday. Nothing had happened that he could remember to disturb either its rhythm or his peace of mind.

'Check out his alibi,' Thackeray said to Mower as they got back into their unmarked car at the back of the community centre a quarter of an hour later.

'Do you believe him, guv?' Mower asked, his scepticism showing. Thackeray slipped the car into gear and drew away from the curb, heading slowly down the narrow alley at the back of the building and out into the main road where they could see a small group of people still gathered desultorily around the main entrance to the campaign headquarters. Eventually the chief inspector glanced in Mower's direction, taking in those cold bright eyes in the dark, good-looking face with its expression of knowing disbelief.

'I'd be surprised if Richard Thurston turned out to be a murderer,' he said. 'Though God knows he had a powerful enough motive, if he thought Lingard was the blackmailer . . .' He hesitated and gave Mower a crooked half-smile. 'But I've been surprised before,' he said.

Vince Newsom had not wanted to reveal the whereabouts of Jason Carpenter, but when it came to a clash of wills, even down a telephone line, he was no match for Kevin Mower, who feared the likely close-range consequences of not tracing the student far more than Newsom feared his editor's displeasure at a distance of two hundred miles. Carpenter was staying at the Globe's expense, at the new country house hotel on the Arnedale road, Newsom eventually admitted.

Having entirely failed to elicit from Mower the reason for police interest in his protégé, Newsom had flung the phone down angrily, promising that he too would be at the hotel at the appointed time with a solicitor, in case legal advice was needed.

'Your privilege, Mr Newsom,' Mower had said with a grin, but he thought the reporter had not heard. It was no skin off his nose, he thought, if the Globe wasted its money.

He and Thackeray drove out of town towards Arnedale just ahead of the late afternoon build-up of traffic. The fast dual-carriageway followed the valley of the Maze, by-passing Milford and moving into open country beyond

Eckersley, where the hills began to close in and the valley walls rose more steeply above the road. An occasional straggle of stone cottages and wragged birch trees followed each narrow lane as it headed off up towards the high country to west and east of the river.

'It must be pretty bleak up here in winter,' Mower said as the road narrowed and took a series of sharp turns fifty feet above the tumbling water where the Maze threaded its way through a precipitous tree-lined gorge before the valley widened again into the flat water-meadows which surrounded Arnedale itself.

'Not half as bleak as it gets ten miles further up the dale,' Thackeray said. 'This is my home ground you're coming to now. I spent the first eighteen years of my life on those fells up there.' He waved towards the hazy line of blue hills beyond the town.

'A lot of sheep up there, are there?' the sergeant asked, curiously. He found it hard to envisage the urban Thackeray he knew as the country boy he seemed once to have been. There was a steely core to the man which Mower did not associate with farmers, still less with sheep. He held a low opinion of both.

'A damn sight more sheep than folk,' Thackeray said. 'My father still runs a flock up there. It'll be mine one day, I suppose, for what that's worth.'

'But you'd not go back?' Mower asked, unable to keep the incredulity out of his voice. Thackeray glanced at him with a suspicion of amusement in his eyes at the question but he shook his head emphatically.

'No, I'd not go back,' he said. Mower wondered if he was imagining the hint of regret in the words.

The hotel where Vince Newsom had brought Laura Ackroyd for dinner three days before stood well back from the main road. Mower swung the car through a wide stone gateway and followed a broad gravelled drive to parking spaces in front of the low stone manor-house which had recently been converted from family home to

179

country hotel.

'Very nice, too,' the sergeant said, relaxing slightly as he switched the engine off and took time to admire the sweep of well-kempt lawns and the glass of leaded windows in the pale gold afternoon light. 'Kiss and tell obviously pays dividends.'

'And here's our cheque-book journalist,' Thackeray said, nodding to Vince Newsom, who had got out of an opulent-looking BMW parked several bays away as soon as they had arrived. Another man, heavy and prosperous-looking in a dark overcoat, got out of the driver's side of the car and as Mower locked the police car Thackeray went to meet the other couple.

Newsom greeted the policemen with a smile which was as close to tentative as he was every likely to achieve.

'This is Peter Macdonald from Mendelson, Green and Macdonald, solicitors,' he said, waving a hand airily at his companion. Thackeray nodded gravely.

'I'm pleased to meet you, Mr Macdonald,' he said. 'I've already had the pleasure of meeting your partner, Victor Mendelson. But quite honestly, I don't think your services will be needed here this afternoon. This is a very preliminary meeting we're having with Jason Carpenter. I don't think we've even brought the handcuffs with us, have we, Sergeant?' Mower shook his head, smiling dutifully at that, though he noticed that on this occasion there was no sign of amusement in Thackeray's eyes, which were like blue ice.

'The Globe felt that their interests would be best served if I were here, Chief Inspector,' Macdonald said.

Thackeray shrugged, turned on his heel and pushed through the heavy swing doors into the hotel lobby, followed by the three other men. The spacious hall was furnished like a comfortable lounge, with chintz-covered armchairs and settees arranged around a blazing log fire and the hotel's function confined to a discreet reception desk in dark wood in one corner. The lobby appeared deserted and Thackeray hesitated for a moment before his attention was caught by a lone figure sitting unobtrusively at a corner coffee table. As the draught from the door wafted across the room, almost imperceptibly disturbing the petals on the lavish flower arrangements and causing the fire to flicker more vigorously for a moment, the figure rose and turned towards them with what could only be described as a welcoming smile.

Jason Carpenter was a young man of astonishing good looks. Tall, slim, and expensively well-dressed in the sort of casual continental clothes Kevin Mower would almost have sold his soul for, he waited for the party of older men to approach him as if he were about to host a small and exclusive social occasion. He was broad-shouldered and slim hipped, and his face had something of the innocence of a Renaissance cherub – blue eyed, full cheeked and with golden hair falling softly across his forehead in a curiously old-fashioned style. He glanced at the four visitors in turn, nodding briefly to Vince Newsom and then fixing on Michael Thackeray a gaze of such open-faced charm that Mower found himself tempted to smile in response. Thackeray however remained unmoved.

'Is there somewhere private we can talk?' he asked Newsom coldly. The journalist nodded and gestured towards the door of a smaller sitting-room which stood ajar.

'They said we could use that room,' he said.

Carpenter led the way, and Thackeray noticed that he walked awkwardly, with a limp which swung him in a slight roll from side to side. The youth saw the chief inspector's curious glance and smiled crookedly as he held the door open for him with exaggerated politeness.

'Bent,' he said sardonically. 'From an early age.'

Thackeray allowed the other four to settle themselves in even more comfortable armchairs around a coffee table while he closed the door to the lobby firmly and stood for a moment watching them. Mower had dutifully taken out his notebook and positioned himself a little apart from the rest. Carpenter sat between Vince Newsom on the one hand, and the solicitor Macdonald on the other, leaning back comfortably in his chair, his legs elegantly crossed and his hands folded demurely in front of him. He was like some exotic young prince, a dauphin surrounded by his countiers and advisers, Thackeray thought, but a prince of darkness not of light in spite of his golden good looks. Carpenter made as if to speak but then, catching the full force of Thackeray's unfriendly gaze, apparently thought better of it and waited in silence for the chief inspector to begin.

Thackeray took his time, remaining on his feet and positioning himself, arms folded, against the wooden shutter to one side of the deep low window. His face was in shadow but the soft late afternoon light fell full on the group assembled around the fireplace, and full into the self-confident blue eyes of Jason Carpenter.

'Do you know why I wanted to talk to you today, Mr Carpenter?' Thackeray said at last.

The student looked uncertain for a moment and his eyes flickered between Vince Newsom and the lawyer before he answered.

'Not really,' he said at last. 'I don't believe I've done anything the police could be interested in.'

'Don't you?' Thackeray said drily. 'Well, I suppose this morning's revelations in the Globe are between you and your conscience. But I have good reason to think that there's a bit more going on than that, and some of it may very definitely be of interest to the police. So for a start, would you like to tell me who dreamed up the outing campaign that you and your friends have been involved in?'

'I did,' Carpenter said, unabashed. 'It's not illegal as far as I know. I spent some time in the States last year and it was all going on there at the time. They don't mess about over there, you know. They were sticking posters on walls

182

and lamp-posts – names, photographs, the lot – getting it all out into the open . . . Great! I thought it was time we did something similar here. Some of us are sick and tired of all these closet gays hiding behind the few of us with the guts to come out. They stay behind their nice comfortable barricades while those of us who are more honest get the shit kicked out of us in dark alleys, though of course that's one of the crimes you lot don't worry too much about, isn't it?'

Thackeray looked at the face of self-righteousness and was appalled, not for the first time, by the almost insouciant cruelty of the moral crusader.

'How did you draw up your list?' he asked, swallowing the anger which threatened to flow up uncontrollably from some deep well inside him which he normally kept tightly capped.

'Oh, some people, like Richard Thurston, we knew about anyway. From personal contact, you might say.' Carpenter grinned and even Vince Newsom looked slightly sickened. 'Others we found out about by asking around at the Blue Lagoon and places like that. It's not difficult if you're part of the gay community yourself. People trust you.' Carpenter seemed to see no incongruity in boasting about the trust he had evidently gained and betrayed so grossly.

'So people told you about the likes of Councillor Baxter?'

'Yes, him, and a few others. It wasn't very difficult, Inspector. It's a small world, you know? You may be able to keep it quiet from straights but it's almost impossible not to be known in the gay community itself. We just asked around.'

'And your list? How long was it in the end?' Thackeray asked.

'A nice round dozen,' Carpenter said lightly. 'A nice respectable dozen.'

'Which included Richard Thurston and Councillor Baxter?'

The boy shrugged. 'Yes, they were both on the list,' he said.

183

'But you knew about both those men's tastes quite a long time before that, didn't you?' Thackeray said, his voice hardening suddenly. Carpenter glanced at his two minders, the first faint flicker of worry in his eyes.

'I knew about Richard, obviously,' he said. 'I could hardly not, could I?' He laughed, with the first faint hint of nervousness at the way the interview was going.

'Did you know he was being blackmailed?' Thackeray asked.

Carpenter shook his head.

'Blackmailed?' he said. 'No, I knew nothing about that. Richard was always very cautious, very careful what he said. He was terrified his wife would find out about us.'

'Of course,' Thackeray said. 'But that didn't worry you when you decided to out these people, the fact that they all had careers or marriages or families which would be damaged by what you were proposing to do? In the case of Richard Thurston, it didn't worry you when you exposed him in the Globe this morning?'

'No, it didn't in the end. I think in the end getting these things out in the open is more important than protecting individuals from embarrassment.'

Thackeray's lips tightened and he turned away towards the window, gazing unseeingly for a moment at the hotel's well-manicured lawns. Embarrassment was not the way he would have described the damage this beautiful boy had inflicted on Thurston, he thought. He swallowed his own fierce emotion with difficulty, knowing that it came from a sympathy for Thurston that was both unprofessional and irrational, and turned back to the group round the table. Sergeant Mower, who had been quietly noting down everything that had been said so far, wondered if he was the only one of the group who caught the implacable dislike of Carpenter that he glimpsed in the chief inspector's eyes, a dislike out of proportion, he thought, to what was admittedly a messy and unpleasant case.

'Did you know Bill Baxter personally?' Thackeray asked.

Carpenter shook his head.

'He was just a name on the list,' he said dismissively.

'This list, where was it kept? Who had access to it?'

The boy shrugged and ran a hand through his fine gold hair, pushing it momentarily away from his brow.

'The executive of the Front,' he said. 'That's five of us altogether. I kept it most of the time, but if we had it in the student union we kept it locked in the office safe. We're not completely naive, you know.'

'I'd like a list of the people who have seen it,' Thackeray said. 'We'll need to talk to them all.' He looked at Carpenter again for a moment. 'Did it not strike you that the existence of your list laid those people open to blackmail?' he asked.

'That's the whole point about coming out,' Carpenter said angrily. 'If you're out you can't be blackmailed. There's nothing you can be blackmailed about.'

'Should we take it that your inquiries include the possibility of blackmail?' the solicitor, Macdonald, broke in suddenly. Vince Newsom's attention, which had been wandering, fastened on the detective again, his look eager, but Thackeray was dismissive.

'I am investigating more than one offence, Mr Macdonald, upon which Mr Carpenter's unpleasant little list may have some bearing,' he said with evident distaste. 'It certainly seems likely that the exposure of Dr Thurston may have been the culmination of blackmail demands he could no longer meet, which is something you may want to tell your editor, Mr Newsom, on the off-chance that he may not want to be associated any further with the results of criminal activity. But I can't confirm any of this yet. It's too early to know exactly what's been going on.' He stood up and glanced at Mower, who closed his notebook with a snap.

'There's just one last question, Mr Carpenter,' Thackeray said, apparently as an afterthought as he moved towards the door. 'Do you have access to a word processor?'

Jason Carpenter had risen to his feet and half-turned to face the two police officers, his eyes wide and unworried.

'Yes, of course,' he said. 'Who doesn't these days?'

FIFTEEN

THE WEATHER HAD TURNED COLD and windy and the red and gold posters urging the electors of the Heights to vote for Richard Thurston were beginning to flap disconsolately in every chilly gust. Laura knew that this was simply because they had now been attached to windows and doors and noticeboards for more than two weeks, but it still seemed symbolic of the shell-shocked state of Richard's campaign, blown almost to pieces by the Globe two days previously.

There had been no further revelations, rather to Laura's surprise, and certainly not for want of effort on the part of the dozens of London journalists who had saturated the constituency, to join the local reporters in prying into every cranny of Richard Thurston's life. But like everyone else who had been asking questions, Laura had discovered that Jake Taylor and Angela Thurston between them had effectively sealed Richard off from further intrusion. It was made very clear that Laura was to have a no more favoured status than anyone else, much to Ted Grant's irritation. The single interview was to be the end of it in Jake Taylor's book, and he was now very obviously calling all the shots with a air of grim determination.

If there was still a danger to his reputation from the reminiscences of other former boyfriends, as Richard had admitted there might be, then she assumed that Taylor had reached them first and somehow effectively ensured their silence, however far around the world they might have wandered. Without first-hand confirmation she knew that Vince Newsom, who talked freely in the pubs of further revelations to come, would be inhibited by the laws of libel. Jason Carpenter's word alone on what had gone on before he himself arrived at the university would not be good enough, as the Party's lawyers would no doubt have told the Globe by now.

Laura had spent the last two days burying her own grief for Rob Stevens and for Richard Thurston in a whirl of frantic activity. Her interview with Richard had made the front page and Ted Grant had been pleased enough with it to press her to greater efforts in covering the activities of the Thurston camp. Nothing came of it, but at least the relentless activity had enabled her to fall into bed each night after a session at the Lamb and Flag so exhausted by work and alcohol that sleep had overtaken her before remembrance could.

This morning her mission was to gauge the reaction to Thurston's exposure of his bedrock supporters on the Wuthering estate. For that exercise her grandmother's bungalow was the obvious place to start. She had not been to see Joyce since the day after the accident, unwilling to expose herself to either further sympathy or the sharp questioning which she knew she would be subjected to since the Globe's revelations. This morning, although she was deathly tired and fiercely hungover, she felt a sufficient distance had opened up from the moment she had been almost physically overwhelmed by Vince's betrayal for her to be able to stand back and talk calmly to Joyce about exactly what had happened.

She locked her car and pushed open the wooden wicket gate, held to its concrete post by a loop of thick wire, which separated her grandmother's narrow strip of garden from the littered pavement. There was no immediate reply to her knock but she could hear movement inside and she waited patiently, shivering slightly in the fresh wind from

188

the Pennines, her hair escaping from the clips with which she had carelessly fastened it up that morning and blowing in red-gold strands about her face. At last the door opened and Joyce beckoned her in, a smile of pure pleasure lighting up her creased features.

'I'm right glad to see you, lass,' the old woman said. 'Come on in and get warm. I've kept the heating on this morning it's so parky out.'

Joyce led the way slowly into the living room, still using her walking frame awkwardly and with resentment in every jerk of her body.

'Set you down,' Joyce said, waving to a chair, but Laura smiled faintly and shook her head.

'You sit down and I'll make the tea,' she said. For a moment the two women looked at each other searchingly. Her grandmother looked older this morning, Laura thought, older and more frail and disappointed. The smile with which she had been greeted had disappeared without trace. For her part Joyce could see the tiredness and strain in Laura's eyes, and the signs of tension around her mouth which she tried to hide with a gaiety that was sadly forced.

'How are you?' Joyce asked, 'You're sure it was just bruises, nothing worse?'

Laura nodded.

'I'm fine now, physically,' she said. 'Just a bit stiff. As for the rest . . .' She let her smile slip and shrugged dispiritedly. They both knew that there were hurts which took longer to mend. She had never been able to pretend with Joyce.

'It's all turning into a right mucky business, isn't it?' Joyce said, sinking into her favourite chair by the gas fire. She didn't need to explain which business she was talking about.

'Is he losing many votes up here?' Laura asked.

'Well, I don't think it fills folk with a lot of confidence,' Joyce said. 'There've been a few of the old stalwarts dropping out, people who've worked for the party for as

189

long as I can remember. They won't have it, you know. They won't say that's what's done it, won't talk about it, in fact. But the truth is they can't bring themselves to vote for him now. The youngsters aren't so bothered, those in the party, any road. They take it in their stride. They're all for gay rights and fashionable causes like that. They learn about these things in school nowadays, I'm told. But those who were brought up 'chapel' . . .' She shrugged and shook her head sadly.

Laura turned away to hide the pain in her own eyes. Bradfield had not had a Labour Member of Parliament now for fifteen years and she knew that her grandmother believed that this was the last election she would be able to fight and possibly the last she would see. For it to be lost in a mire of scandal and recrimination would break her heart, she thought. She made tea in the tiny kitchen and brought two mugs and a plate of biscuits back into the living room.

'You can't really tell what effect it will have,' she said, far more cheerfully than she felt. 'There hasn't been an opinion poll yet to show what it's done to people's voting intentions. After all he was six points ahead on the last one. That's a good solid lead. And the voters may be more forgiving than you think.'

'If he'd been having it away with his secretary then you might be right,' Joyce said grimly. 'But not with a lad. There's a lot of folk offended by that.'

Laura nodded, thinking how much more offended they would be if the knew it had been with three or even four lads.

'What if they knew he was being blackmailed?' she asked quietly.

Joyce sipped her tea and sighed heavily.

'I don't know, love, I really don't. In my day they fought elections about policies, not folk's private lives. They say Lloyd George was an old goat but that's not why my father helped chuck him out.'

*

Laura took her grandmother down to the local committee rooms where she introduced her to several of the other local campaigners who were, she discovered, equally gloomy about Richard Thurston's chances of taking the train to Westminster at the end of the week. The confidence which had characterised the first days of the campaign had been dissipated like the good weather and Laura drove slowly back into the centre of town through a dismal drizzle in the grip of a pessimism as deep as her grandmother's.

She wrote her feature quickly, knowing that Richard Thurston would hate its conclusions, and while she was waiting for Ted Grant's unpredictable reaction to what she had written, she rang Vicky Mendelson to check on her health.

'Blooming, of course,' her friend said dismissively. 'You may scorn motherhood as a career but I seem to have an exceptional talent for it. How are you, by the way? David said he'd heard you'd been in some sort of accident. I was worried.'

Laura gave her a sketchy outline of what had happened to Rob. She knew that Vicky's normal tendency to worry about all those close to her could become near neurotic during her pregnancies. As it was, she heard the sharp intake of breath at the other end of the phone and wished there was some way in which she could soften the word 'death', but none of the usual euphemisms bore any relationship to Rob's brutal passing.

'I'm all right,' Laura said. 'I promise. We'll have lunch as soon as this wretched by-election is over and I'm not so busy at work.'

'Did you see Michael Thackeray again?' Vicky asked. 'He was quite fanciable, I thought, in a dour Yorkshire way.' Vicky had come to Bradfield from the deepest Home Counties and to Laura's amusement had still not entirely

191

shed her preconceptions about the North in spite of having married into it. 'He followed you out of the house that night with a distinct gleam in his eye. David thought so too.'

'After Vince, I'm off men,' Laura said dismissively. 'All Michael Thackeray wanted out of me was the low-down on Harvey Lingard. Nothing more romantic than that.' She hoped she sounded convincing, not at all sure that she was convincing herself.

She noticed Ted Grant weaving his way through the desks towards her and ended the conversation quickly.

'Yep, that's fine,' he said, gesturing at the feature on her computer screen. 'Thurston's had it, I should say.' Laura nodded tiredly. The last thing she wanted was to get into a political discussion with Grant, but he was clearly not finished yet.

'Who did you have lunch with in the Lamb and Flat last Wednesday?' he asked aggressively. Laura had a distinct impression that he knew the answer to his question but would wait indefinitely for her response anyway.

'I don't remember,' she said, playing for time.

'Come off it, Laura,' Grant said angrily. 'Don't eff me about. You were seen. A little dark girl, punky hair, duffle jacket. It couldn't have been one of those dykes from the university, could it?'

'You told us to leave that story alone,' Laura reminded him.

'But not if she had the dirt on Richard Thurston! What I didn't want was a load of crap about outing and gay rights.'

'I told her the Gazette wasn't interested in gay stories,' Laura said flatly. 'I thought I was obeying your instructions.'

'Jesus Christ,' Grant said. 'If I find out we missed the Thurston story the day before Newsom got it, I'll swing for you, girl, I really will.' He spun on his heel and marched back to his office, fury in every jerky stride. Laura watched him go, aware of the eyes of colleagues turned curiously

192

her way. Her career, she thought, seemed now to be at the mercy of Dilly Jenkins and her friends and she doubted that the Front would be any kinder to her than they had been to Richard if exposure suited their book. She shrugged and wondered just how devastated she would feel if she were to be sacked. Not very, she suspected.

That evening she decided to give the Lamb and Flag, which she had for the last few evenings found a noisy and effective route to emotional oblivion, a miss. It was time, she thought, to sit and face what had happened and come to terms with it. She walked slowly through the thinning crowds in the town centre, doing some desultory shopping, before turning back towards the Gazette car park where she had left her car. As she approached the office again, keys in hand, a shadowy figure detached itself from the shadows on the darkest side of the building. With her heart thudding Laura moved quickly away from the car and back into the pool of light by the main entrance where she could see the comforting bulk of a security man behind the reception desk. The figure followed and as he too stepped into the light she took in the face and figure of a young man she vaguely recognised.

'I'm sorry if I frightened you. I'm not a mugger. You don't remember me, do you?'

The voice, like the figure, was youthful, but she could not immediately place it. The young man was conventionally dressed in an overcoat over a dark suit, a light blue shirt and sober tie. She looked harder at a thin face, clean-shaven, short-haired, with only the hint, in the dim light, of dark circles beneath the eyes to take away from the absolute normality of his appearance. It was that normality which threw her, but eventually she placed the voice.

'The accident,' she said, and he nodded.

'You look a bit different,' she said, recalling the black leather jacket and chains.

'I work in a bank,' he said. 'They're asking for witnesses

to come forward in your paper again tonight, but I can't. My boss would do his nut if he found out. They've no idea I spend my evenings in the Blue Lagoon.'

The excuses fell out in an embarrassed jumble and Laura was seized with a deep sense of depression.

'You too,' she said softly.

'Me too,' the young man said.

She drove him to a quiet surburban pub on the far side of the town where she guessed there would be no one who would recognise either of them. He insisted on buying her a drink and she took the opportunity to take a closer look at him than had been possible in the ill-lit car park or while she had been driving. He was, she thought, rather younger than she was herself, a little taller, slim, brown-haired and altogether unremarkable. If she had passed him in the street she would never have associated him, even face to face, with the white-faced, black-clad stranger in the dark alley who had held her in his arms above Rob's crumpled body and told her he was dead.

He brought her a vodka and tonic and a pint of lager for himself and sat down opposite her at a quiet corner table. His name was Steve, he said.

'I've been agonising ever since about coming to find you,' he said. 'The Gazette identified you both so I knew where to come.'

'You saw what happened?' she said. 'I never really knew what hit us. The car came from behind and it was all over so quickly.'

'I know. The car had been parked further up the street. I followed you both out of the bar, and as I came up the steps I saw the car start up behind you. It accelerated as you got to the narrow part of the street by the Copocabana.' He stopped, his face tense, his hands clasped nervously around his glass.

'I've thought about it and thought about it,' he said at last. 'And I've come to the same conclusion every time. I think the car was waiting for you. I think what I saw was a

194

deliberate attempt to kill you.'

Laura felt her heart lurch in fear just as it had done when he had approached her in the darkness outside the office.

'You can't be sure,' she said, wanting him to change his mind, hating what he was saying. He shook his head.

'If I really thought it was an accident, I wouldn't be here now. I'd have let it be. But I knew Rob. I'd seen him around. And it wasn't an accident. The car was there, its engine idling. What it did was bloody dangerous. It must have been going at about forty-five, fifty, by the time it hit you. It took nerve and determination to get through that narrow gap. It wasn't an accident. It couldn't have been. I'm absolutely positive.' He spoke jerkily, but with total conviction.

'Oh, God,' Laura said softly, a feeling of total desolation overwhelming her. She picked up her glass with a hand that shook and took a deep drink to steady herself.

'I'm sorry,' Steve said. He too looked distressed, as if putting what he had been thinking for days into words had given it a new and more horrific reality, a spectre made bloody flesh.

'You'll have to tell the police,' Laura said. The young man looked for a moment as though he might jump to his feet and take flight. He sat with his fingers tensed against the table top as if about to push himself into convulsive movement. Laura sat quietly, hardly daring to breathe, knowing that she could not hold him there against his will, until eventually he relaxed again and subsided slowly back into his seat, nodding dumbly.

'I thought you'd probably say that,' he said.

'Did you see what sort of car it was,' Laura asked, although she felt a deep unwillingness to hear the answer.

'Not clearly,' he said. 'Some big estate car. I couldn't see what colour, or the number plate. It was very dark at that end of the street and he didn't put his lights on. He was away before I'd really registered what had happened, it was so quick.'

'And you couldn't see who was driving?'

Steve shook his head glumly.

'Too dark,' he said.

They sat in silence and finished their drinks.

'I'll go now,' the young man said at last, pulling his coat back on and looking more determined. 'I will go to the police,' he promised. 'If I leave it any longer I'll start dithering again. Best to get it over with.'

Laura drove him back into town in an anxious silence and dropped him outside the central police station before driving slowly home. Her reactions seemed to have been slowed again by shock and alcohol. Too much alcohol again, she told herself guiltily. She parked the car clumsily on the drive in front of the house, going back twice to check that she had locked the doors and the boot. At the top of the two flights of stairs her flat felt cold and unwelcoming, and she went into every room closing the curtains and blinds against a darkness which suddenly seemed menacing.

Outside the wind moaned through the garden trees as if the world had been plunged back into the depths of winter, and an occasional flurry of rain against the window-panes rattled her nerves. For a long time she sat huddled in her coat by the unused fireplace in the living room, gazing unseeingly at the faded gold of an embroidered fire-screen she had found in a junk shop, and drinking vodka neat, because she could not find any tonic and did not even have the energy to retrieve ice from the freezer.

By now, she thought, Steve would have made his statement and added another vicious twist to the spiral of violence in which she and too many people she knew and liked had been caught up. Another flurry of sleet against the window made her jump. She stood up restlessly and checked for a second time that her front door was locked and bolted and that all the curtains were tightly closed.

Someone out there, she thought, horrified, had tried to kill her. Someone out there had actually killed Rob. She felt more afraid than she had ever felt in her life.

For more than an hour she sat turning the events of the last week over in her mind, losing count of the glasses of vodka she poured and drank. At last, tired and tense and not totally in control of her senses, she picked up the telephone and called the central police station. Chief Inspector Thackeray was not there, she was told, but they could pass on a message.

'Tell him,' she said wearily, her voice slurred, 'tell him that I'd like to see him urgently. Tell him that I think Rob Stevens was murdered.'

It was more than an hour before Michael Thackeray rang Laura Ackroyd's doorbell. He had eaten a solitary and stodgy meal in the Woolpack after leaving his office, and then gone reluctantly back to the flat which he could never bring himself to call home. It was, he conceded, comfortable enough in its spartan, purpose-built way, but many of his books still lay in boxes where the removal men had dropped them two months previously, and his furniture stood about the rooms with a curiously temporary air, dumped rather than arranged.

A television and stereo stood on a shelf-unit in one corner, with a jumble of tapes and discs below them, but there were none of the personal mementos or photographs which would have given the living room a feeling that it was anyone's permanent home.

Thackeray was hoping to spend the quiet fag-end of the day thinking, something he felt he had had too little time to do since Bill Baxter's suicide and Richard Thurston's confession that he too was being blackmailed. That had lent a new and unwelcome dimension to what had appeared to be a straightforward case of murder.

He was convinced in his own mind that the

angelic-looking Jason Carpenter had used the information he had gained about Bradfield's gay community to milk its most vulnerable members. That was an arrest he would enjoy, he thought grimly, his dislike of blackmail sharpening the urgency with which he always pursued his quarry whenever it lacked any vestige of compassion for its victims. It was a trait which worried him sometimes, fearing that it might one day distort the rationality with which he prided himself that he tackled his job.

It was no part of his role to act as avenging angel, he told himself sharply as he turned his mind from his instinctive dislike of Carpenter to Richard Thurston, the blackmailer's victim for whom he felt something very close to fellow-feeling, even though he was increasingly inclined to believe he might have murdered Harvey Lingard. His problem with that theory was that Thurston's alibi apparently stood up to all Sergeant Mower's urgent probings. Guilty or not, Thurston's position genuinely saddened him.

Still less did any urgency for justice on his part focus on Laura Ackroyd. He felt instead a deep reluctance to discover just what Laura had known, and how long she had known it, in spite of the accumulating evidence that she had not told him the whole truth the last time he had seen her, or even, he suspected, much of the truth at all.

Dissatisfied with the progress of the case, and his own uncertain reaction to it, he turned up the central heating, made himself a coffee and turned on the television for the nine o'clock news. It was then that the telephone rang and he was given Laura Ackroyd's message.

He sat for a moment gazing at the receiver after the duty sergeant had rung off. The buzz of excitement which he had felt when Harvey Lingard's body had been discovered, and which had since been overlaid by a deep distaste for the path this particular inquiry was taking, had unexpectedly and powerfully returned. But was it simply the thrill of the chase, he wondered, or did it have more to

198

do with the excuse the call gave him to see Laura again, something he had been putting off since his last interview with Richard Thurston because he distrusted his own motives. He knew that Laura must be asked to clarify some of the things she had already told him, but he had almost decided to ask Kevin Mower to see her in his place. At this time of night, and with a message as urgent as this one had sounded, that was no longer an option.

There was no entry-phone on the door of the converted Victorian house where Laura, according to the neat notices by the bank of four doorbells, lived on the top floor. Thackeray waited patiently for an answer, his coat collar turned up for protection against the sharp wind and the occasional squall of sleet. Eventually the hall light was switched on and the door opened a crack, secured by a chain. Laura herself peered through the gap and then closed the door briefly in order to unlock it.

'I'm sorry,' she said. 'I'm not in a mood to take any chances tonight.' Thackeray followed her into the dimly lit hallway and looked at her sharply. Her face seemed pale and pinched, her eyes sunk deep into their sockets, and she was huddled into an outdoor coat with the collar turned up as if the house had no heating. She waved him ahead of her up the stairs.

Once in the brightly lit living room he realised how ill she looked and could see that she was shivering. She appeared to try to say something, but then swayed towards him as if about to fall. He caught her by the arms and lowered her gently into a chair, where she sat with her head on her knees and her arms wrapped around herself, shivering convulsively. He put a tentative hand on her brow, which was cool and clammy. A bottle of vodka and a glass stood on the coffee table and he wondered how much she had drunk.

'Have you eaten anything tonight?' he asked. She shook her head, sick and miserable and hardly able to speak. He picked up the vodka bottle and went into the kitchen. He

199

stood for a moment by the sink looking at the almost empty bottle before pouring the dregs determinedly down the drain. His hand, he noticed, was not quite steady as he put the bottle in the rubbish bin.

He took a deep breath and looked around curiously. It was not a flat where expense or care had been spared and, unlike his own, it had a cheerful, lived-in look. He found bread in a crockery bin, butter and ham in the fridge, and made sandwiches and a couple of bright yellow mugs of instant coffee. As far as he could see, Laura had not moved by the time he carried a tray in and put it on the coffee table in front of her. He shifted her empty glass to one side and glanced at her quizzically.

'How many of those have you had?' he asked. She shook her head.

'I'm not sure,' she said. 'I lost count.' She took the coffee mug carefully and held it between her hands as if to warm herself, and gradually her shivering subsided. Slowly she sipped the scalding liquid and obediently ate a couple of sandwiches when he handed them to her. Gradually a little colour returned to her cheeks.

'I'm sorry,' she said at last, more normally. 'Getting drunk doesn't solve anything, does it?'

'I tried it on a grand scale once,' he said. 'It turned into a very dead end.' For a moment his face took on the look of a roughly carved sphinx, as though a shadow had passed across his soul, and he turned away from Laura as if to spare her his pain.

They sat in silence for a moment, each absorbed in their own thoughts, before Laura shook herself sharply, as if she had suddenly decided to move back into the land of the living. She stood up, attracting Thackeray's attention again, and took off her coat. Reaching behind her head with a gesture which made him acutely conscious of the curve of her breasts under her loose top, she unfastened the clips which were holding her hair back in an untidy coil and shook her curls free over her shoulders in a burnished cloud. She instantly looked years younger and slightly more relaxed and appeared quite unaware of the effect she was creating. She picked up another sandwich and bit into it hungrily.

'I haven't eaten properly for days,' she said. 'Not since the accident. Just snacks in the Lamb and Flag, dreadful gunk, and booze, lots of booze. Do you want a drink?' She looked round vaguely for the vodka bottle but he shook his head.

'I don't,' he said, his voice carefully neutral. 'Anyway there's none left. Are you here on your own now?'

She gave him an unexpected ghost of a grin, a faint flush of colour returning to her cheeks.

'I threw Vince out,' she said with some satisfaction. I bet you did, Thackeray thought, with a flicker of amusement. She's still drunk, he thought, drunk enough to have forgotten for the moment why she asked me here. She looked pale, vulnerable, very beautiful and infinitely desirable. He groaned inwardly and moved away to sit on the other side of the table.

'You rang the station,' he said quietly. 'You said you had something to tell me about Rob Stevens's death.'

The question dragged her back into the real world with sudden brutality and her face closed up again.

'I think he was murdered,' she said. 'And I think that whoever killed him wouldn't have much cared if I'd been killed too.' She said no more but the look in her eyes told him that she found the prospect both appalling and frightening.

'What makes you think that?' he asked, and she told him about her encounter with Steve and what he had told her he had seen as he came out of the Blue Lagoon that night. Thackeray listened impassively and when she had finished he crossed the room and picked up the telephone. It was clear to Laura that his sharp questions about a witness to the accident did not receive the answer he had hoped for, and in the end he put the receiver down forcefully.

'He never got as far as making that statement,' Thackeray said.

'He works in a bank. He won't be difficult to find again,' Laura said dully. 'Though he won't be pleased to see you. He's another gay who doesn't want to come out.'

Thackeray sat down again and looked at Laura thoughtfully. She seemed deeply depressed by the tale she had told him and he could sense the nervous tension in her again as she waited for him to make the next move.

'I think it's about time you started being a bit less economical with the truth,' he said.

'What do you mean?' she said but it was obviously only a token protest, made without conviction. 'I don't think I've told you any lies.'

'Perhaps only by omission,' he conceded. 'But you failed, for instance, to tell me that Richard Thurston had asked you to help him, that you knew he'd been Harvey Lingard's lover, that you'd been looking for Jason Carpenter. You even failed to tell me that Rob Stevens was gay, though it didn't take me long to work that out.'

'Hanging offences?' she asked, attempting lightness, but there was no answering amusement in Thackeray's eyes now, and eventually she looked away again.

'I would, I suppose, do anything for Richard,' she said, hearing in her words an echo of Angela Thurston's dogged expression of loyalty what seemed like a lifetime ago. 'Well, almost anything. I desperately wanted to help him out of this mess.'

'So tell me just what your efforts amounted to,' Thackeray demanded. 'Thurston told me some of it himself but I need to hear your version.'

She told him everything that had happened since Thurston had confessed to her that he was being black-mailed: the unexpected arrival of the student Dilly Jenkins at the Gazette offices, Rob Stevens's offer to come with her to the Blue Lagoon and its devastating consequences.

'You didn't report Dilly's visit to anyone at the Gazette?' Thurston asked curiously. Laura shook her head.

'You won't win any brownie points with your editor for that, will you?'

She shrugged.

'Vince says I'm in the wrong trade, too sentimental by half.' She made an attempt at a laugh but it was obvious that she was hurt by the accusation, however justified she felt it might be. 'I expect he's right,' she added.

'So you went looking for Jason Carpenter at the Blue Lagoon? You didn't go to meet him as you suggested originally?'

'No,' Laura said. 'Dilly promised to let me know where to contact him but when she failed to phone me back I panicked and decided to try to find him myself. Rob just volunteered to come for the ride. It was the worst offer he ever made. I expect he was too sentimental too.'

'Stick to the facts, Laura,' Thackeray said gently. 'Now think. Did anyone know where you were going and why? Did you or your colleague tell anyone, anyone at all?'

'I tried to contact Richard,' she said slowly. 'I left messages for him at his campaign office and with Angela.'

'Messages?' Thackeray persisted. 'What sort of messages? Can you remember exactly what you said?'

'I've been thinking about that all evening,' she said miserably. 'I was trying to be discreet. I said I was hoping to meet our mutual friend at a holiday bar.'

'The Blue Lagoon? Would he work that out?' Thackeray said sceptically.

'It's almost next door to the Copacabana,' she said. 'There's nowhere else it could be. Bradfield's not exactly littered with bars and nightclubs. He'd know of the Blue Lagoon's reputation. Most people do.'

'But he didn't turn up anyway?'

'No, I didn't really expect him to. The Blue Lagoon was the last place Richard would want to be seen during the campaign. I just wanted to keep him in touch, let him know I was doing something . . .'

'You still haven't met Jason have you?' Thackeray asked. 'Can you describe Rob for me? Height, what he was wearing that night, that sort of thing?'

She looked at him sharply and he knew that she had followed his own line of reasoning and intensely disliked where it was taking him.

'About five foot ten, I suppose,' she said, her voice shrinking to little more than a whisper. 'Brown hair, blondish really, and he had a dark jacket over his suit, a casual jacket . . . It was very dark.'

'Dark enough for one young man to look very much like another,' Thackeray said. 'The height's about right. And you had gone looking for Jason so it would be quite logical for anyone seeing you come out of the bar with a man to assume that it was him.'

'No,' Laura said, but they both knew that on this occasion no really did mean yes.

She slumped in her chair, twisting a strand of reddish-gold hair into a tight spiral. With her pale oval face and sweeping curls she should have looked like the Botticelli Venus, Thackeray thought, but her expression was one of unrelieved misery, her mind now clearly focused on the numbing climax to that night.

'You didn't see the car?' he asked at last, knowing that he had to see this interview through to the end however much it hurt Laura.

'No, it came from behind. I've told the police all this already.'

'I know. But now you're suggesting that what happened was not just a fatal accident. It might have been murder. Do you know anyone who drives a big heavy estate car?'

Laura looked at him with eyes full of tears.

'Richard does,' she said.

She sat for a moment staring at Thackeray intently.

'Don't you feel anything when what you do wrecks people's lives?' she asked eventually, her misery turning to

anger.

It was a question, Thackeray thought, which he could as easily return, but he refrained.

'In my experience the lives have been wrecked by the time we get there. We're just the boys with the sirens and the flashing blue lights who clear up the mess. And if you're asking whether it's painful sometimes, then yes, of course it is. You grow a thick skin, but sometimes it's not thick enough. Just like journalists, I imagine.'

'I'm sorry. It was a stupid question,' Laura said dully. 'You have to understand that Richard is special.'

'How special?' Thackeray asked quietly.

'I didn't go to bed with him, if that's what you're thinking,' she came back quickly, the flash of anger in her eyes again. 'Not that it's any of your business.'

Thackeray sighed. 'If you're right, and Rob Stevens was murdered, it will all be my business,' he said.

SIXTEEN

'WE DON'T MOVE UNTIL AFTER the votes are counted on Thursday night,' Superintendent Jack Longley said flatly. 'That's straight from the top, Mike. I went over every eventuality with them yesterday. Pursue the blackmail. Check out the witness to the car accident, if you're convinced it wasn't an accident. And check Thurston's alibi for the Lingard killing again. But as far as Thurston himself is concerned, you leave him strictly alone. You don't interview him, and you certainly don't arrest him. That clear?'

Thackeray nodded, unfazed by Longley's edict, but intrigued as to how far this pause in his investigation might be made to stretch. Electoral law, he knew, was arcane and little used, but fierce in its protection of candidates' and voters' rights. If the chief constable had decided not to throw a spanner into the now almost concluded electoral process this did not particularly surprise him.

'I'd not want to be flung into the Tower of London or whatever else they prescribe for interfering with a candidate. But what if he takes a shotgun to Carpenter, sir?' he asked mildly, proposing the most extreme eventuality he could conceive. Longley gave a snort of amusement.

'I can't see that,' he said. 'But you'd better keep an eye on Carpenter, though it goes against the grain to help the blasted Globe to keep a little toe-rag like that out of harm's

206

way. But do it all the same. Have you got any further on the blackmail?'

'Bill Baxter's son came up with the last letter – he found it hidden in his father's desk when he was going through his things. A demand for £25,000. There was no way Baxter could have got hold of that amount of money in cash in present circumstances, his son says. In other words, the business is on its uppers, so the suicide note he left at home wasn't that bizarre. Money was a problem, though Ian Baxter wasn't willing to admit that at first.'

Thackeray recalled with some satisfaction the admission he had eventually extracted from a squirming Baxter, who when it came to it had turned out to be much keener to conceal his company's financial difficulties than his father's sexual peccadillos in an interesting reversal of conventional morality.

'The note?' Langley asked. 'Handwritten, typed, cut out of newspaper headlines?'

'Word processed.'

'Bloody computers,' Longley grumbled. 'Can it be traced?'

'I doubt it,' Thackeray said. 'But it matches the letters Thurston gave us – same paper, same type-face, even the same phrasing, and of course the same sum of money – even more impossible for Thurston to lay hands on than Baxter, I'd guess. They've all gone to forensic anyway, to see what they make of them. With a bit of luck we'll get some prints at least. And I've sent Mower and a DC up to the university to have a look at the equipment the students use in the union and get some samples of paper and type. The trouble is, Mower tells me that even if the letters were run off on the printer there it doesn't prove much. Someone could have brought a floppy disk in from another machine and just fed it into the students' union printer. These machines aren't like typewriters with idiosyncracies in the key-faces or in the amount of pressure different people might put on the keys. That's all ironed out so you get a uniform product. Great for the criminals, a bloody nuisance for us.'

'I'm getting too old for this game,' Longley said heavily. 'I can't cope with all this electronic stuff. My five-year-old grandson's quicker than I am with the video recorder and all these remote control thingies they have about the place. It's time they put me out to grass with Harry Huddleston.'

'Cricket, isn't it, he goes in for? I can't see you tottering over to Headingley five or six days a week just yet,' Thackeray said dismissively, knowing full well that if Longley wanted to get to grips with electronics or anything else, the brain behind the amiable façade would find little difficulty in achieving mastery. It had not taken him long in Bradfield to learn that the avuncular manner the superintendent adopted could be cast off with uncanny suddenness to reveal the steel beneath.

'You're getting along with young Mower?' Longley asked.

Thackeray nodded non-committally.

'He's sharp,' he said. 'But I wouldn't bank on him not cutting himself.'

Longley nodded.

'Aye, that's about it,' he said. 'I told you how he blotted his copybook in the Met with some senior officer's wife? Daft begger. And then he rubbed the drug squad up the wrong way somehow last month. They wouldn't keep him when his attachment was up. He wants watching, that one, especially with women.'

Thackeray smiled wryly. If the cap fits, he thought, and wondered whether Mower's speculative tongue had incautiously betrayed to Longley what he reckoned was his own less than professional interest in Laura Ackroyd or whether the remark was sheer coincidence. If Mower gossips about me I'll make his life a misery, he thought vindictively.

Longley looked at Thackeray thoughtfully for a moment.

'I thought with your experience you might keep him on the straight and narrow,' he said. 'I reckon he's got potential. Folk can get over set-backs worse than he's had. You know that, better than most.'

Longley had never before mentioned the set-back which had nearly wrecked Thackeray's own career, although he knew that it would be spelt out on his record in all its shaming detail. It had evidently not deterred Longley from taking him on as Harry Huddleston's replacement, though he did not imagine it had not been discussed at length by the appointing board, nor would ever be forgiven or forgotten.

'Mower's far too calculating to get himself into that sort of mess,' Thackeray said equably enough, although his face had gone as still and cold as stone. Longley took the hint and did not pursue the subject.

'Right then, let's get our case in order and then see where we are by Thursday night,' he said. 'You'll need the chief's say-so, but if by that stage you still want to bring Thurston in, then we'll bring him in, whether he's our new MP or not.'

Sergeant Kevin Mower sat in his car looking thoughtful, with a young detective constable at his side. They were in the car park at the university, where Mower had just taken possession of a small box of floppy disks and some samples of printed material from the computer in the students' union office. Dilly Jenkins from the Gay and Lesbian Front had been in the office when Mower arrived and had fiercely disputed the police officers' right to inspect the computer.

'It's a witch-hunt,' she had hissed, to Mower's ill-concealed amusement. With her spikey black hair and ill-fitting dark clothes she was well qualified to be the object of just such a hunt, he thought unkindly. When confronted with a search warrant she had watched with simmering fury as Mower worked his way methodically through the contents of the machine's hard disk and rummaged through floppy disks left in a state of confusion in nearby drawers.

'You'll damage these disks, darling, if you don't look after them properly,' he had admonished Dilly cheerfully, choosing his words to provoke maximum indignation.

The box Mower had brought away with him was clearly marked with Jason Carpenter's name and contained just two three-and-a-half-inch disks which, when translated on to the screen, had offered little of interest, consisting mainly of correspondence between the Front and similar organisations in other parts of the country.

'That's about as useful as the files of the local rabbit fancier's circle,' Mower said in disgust. 'Come on Dilly, darling, where's this famous blacklist kept?'

Dilly shook her hedgehog head angrily, her ear-rings jangling.

'I don't know. I haven't got it. We're not stupid enough to leave it lying around on a computer disk for pigs like you to get access to, are we? And don't call me darling!'

Mower laughed. 'But you must have seen it,' he persisted. 'Can you make me a list of the names which were on it, or all those you can remember?'

Dilly's pale, pinched face took on an obstinate scowl.

'I can't remember the names,' she said. 'Apart from Dr Richard bloody Thurston, they didn't mean anything to me. They're not people I know. I've only been in Bradfield two terms.'

'So your mate Jason's got the list stashed away somewhere, has he?'

'I suppose so,' Dilly said. 'He didn't say.'

'And I don't suppose he said that he'd been running a nice little extortion racket with some of those names, did he?' Mower said contemptuously.

'He didn't! He wouldn't!' Dilly flashed back. 'The list was for outing people. It has to be the right thing to do.

We have to get away from all this hypocrisy. If people are out they can't be blackmailed, can they?'

'If you believe that, you'll believe anything,' Mower said. 'And believe me, someone's been taking some of these nice, respectable closet gays to the cleaners. You should ask your friend Jason how come he can afford his smart Chevignon jackets on his student grant if you think he's so pure.'

The crack hit home. Dilly's black leggings and droopy grey sweater with ragged holes at the elbow looked as though they had been picked up at a jumble sale, or worse.

'His parents aren't short,' she said sulkily.

'Nice for him,' Mower said. 'Tell him I'm borrowing his disks, if you see him, will you. Do you want a receipt?' The girl shook her head and watched in a hostile silence as Mower switched off the computer and printer and put his booty into an inside pocket of his jacket.

Back in the car, Mower came to a decision.

'Right then, Tony,' he said to the young constable at his side, who had simmered angrily but silently throughout his exchanges with the girl. 'I think while we're up this side of town we'll just see if Mrs Angela Thurston's at home. With her old man about to become an MP, we need a chat with her about security, don't we?'

'Come on, Kev. Isn't that crime prevention's job?' the constable said, not concealing his lack of enthusiasm for the chore.

'In this case, probably Special Branch's or even MI5's if the truth were known,' Mower said with an expansive shrug. 'But it doesn't stop us having a preliminary chat, does it?'

It took no more than five minutes to reach the Thurston house, and Mower pulled up outside, looking with interest at the small blue Renault parked on the drive.

'I'd like to get a look at their other car,' he said to his companion as they made their way to the front door. 'Just take your cue from me.'

211

There was no immediate reply to Mower's ring on the doorbell, although a dog could be heard barking somewhere at the back of the house. They both glanced around the immaculate front garden where rock plants tumbled and scrambled over small cliffs of soft sandstone in a profusion of purple, pink and gold.

'Someone likes their garden,' the constable said admiringly. Mower shrugged. Where he had been brought up gardens had tended to consist of a patch of oil-stained concrete, just big enough to accommodate a car at the front of the house, and an almost equally constricted area of football-scuffed turf and mud at the rear. His eye was caught by a movement at the tall window to their left and he turned to press the doorbell again more insistently. The door was opened quickly then.

'I'm sorry,' Angela Thurston said. 'I thought it might be the reporters again. We've been besieged for a week.' She had come to the door in her stockings, her feet looking incongruously small beneath a pair of baggy corduroy trousers and a heavy Aran sweater. She looked strained and tired, her hair wispy and in need of a wash, Mower thought uncharitably.

'I was in the garden,' she said vaguely, glancing at Mower's proferred warrant card and waving the two men into the house with hands which were mud-stained. They followed her into the kitchen where she went to the sink to wash. An amiable labrador met them, tail wagging enthusiastically. Mower avoided its welcoming pink tongue with distaste and the dog turned his attentions to the detective constable who patted its head abstractedly as his eyes roved around the room.

'What can I do for you?' Angela Thurston asked when she had dried her hands.

'Have you given any thought to the security of your house if your husband wins on Thursday?' Mower asked in return. He moved to the other side of the kitchen and gave what he hoped was a convincing inspection to the lock and bolts on the glass-paned back door. 'You're likely to be a target for all sorts of cranks, you know. Or worse. It always happens.'

Mrs Thurston hung the towel up on a rail with precision. She looked preoccupied, as well she might, Mower thought. She glanced at the kitchen window which gave onto the back garden, where a magnolia was dropping the last of its browning petals on to a lawn that was beginning to look unkempt.

'We keep on saying we'll get proper window locks and a burglar alarm,' she said. 'Richard keeps putting it off.' She patted the dog, which had taken up station at her feet. 'I always thought with the dog in the house I'd be reasonably secure if I was here by myself.'

'You'll be more vulnerable if your husband is elected,' Mower improvised energetically. 'Will you go to London with him?'

Angela Thurston shook her head emphatically.

'No, no,' she said. 'I'll stay here.'

'So you'll be here alone much more than previously,' Mower said, as if that justified his visit. 'You really do need advice on that.'

'Do you think he'll be elected?' Angela Thurston asked, turning anxious eyes on Mower as if seeing him for the first time. 'Can he be elected now?' There was desperation straining her voice, desperation which had already etched itself indelibly on what only a few days ago had been quite a soft and pretty face for a woman of her age, Mower thought, recalling the glimpses he had had of her on television with her husband during the early, less stressful days of the campaign before Vince Newsom threw his front-page hand-grenade into the proceedings.

'Can he be elected?' Angela repeated querulously.

'If I knew the answer to that, Mrs Thurston, I'd be down at Ladbrookes putting my shirt on the result,' Mower said lightly. 'Cheer up, it'll soon be all over. Look, I tell you what,' he went on in his most appealing manner, one hand resting lightly, for no more than a reassuring instant, on her arm. 'Let's pretend he's won, that it's all over, and you just show me the house and we'll work out what you might need to do in that situation, just to make yourself feel secure while Mr Thurston's away legislating for us all.'

'Doctor Thurston,' Angela corrected him automatically. 'He's a PhD.' She seemed almost persuaded, Mower thought, which was in itself a sign of how abnormal her situation was. If he had tried to patronise her ten days ago, he thought, those blue eyes would have seen straight through him and sent him packing. Now she seemed to be still in the state of shock which had been apparent when she had sat by her husband at his press conference and had read her prepared statement of support in the voice of an automaton.

She led him round the house with the dog bounding joyously at her heels, discoursing dully on the relative merits of window locks and grilles, infra-red alarms and sensor pads, while Mower distractedly attempted to point out the weak points of cloakroom windows and access from a flat garage roof while his sharp, dark eyes roamed restlessly around the comfortably shabby sitting-room and a study with two desks – one almost bare and the other cluttered.

'That one's mine,' Angela Thurston said apologetically, waving at the tidy desk, with its typewriter under a dust-cover and neat in- and out-trays. 'I do most of his administration, answer the letters, all that sort of thing.'

They went upstairs, with Mower pausing ostentatiously to examine the landing window as they went, and she showed him the bedrooms, two of which had obviously been abandoned by the Thurston's grown-up children as they were bare and tidy, the beds stripped down to a single cover over the mattresses. The largest room was clearly the marital bedroom, the big double bed still unmade. Next to that was another, smaller room, with a narrow single bed and a cluttered dressing table – her own, Angela Thurston acknowledged with a slightly embarrassed laugh.

'We decided to have separate rooms,' she said. 'He's keeping such erratic hours now, and I'm one of those people who needs their eight hours, and I get migraines . . .' She shrugged.

'So you don't always wait up for him?' Mower asked.

'No, I go to bed when I'm ready. It's the only way I can stay sane during all this . . .' Her voice trailed off again and she left the sentence unfinished, her face desolate.

'Oh, I'm sure you're going to remain perfectly sane, Mrs Thurston,' Mower said, laughing with what he hoped was encouragement. 'Now perhaps we'd better have a quick look outside – garage, outbuildings, that sort of thing.'

She led the way out of the back door of the house into the garden, from where Mower solemnly pointed out to the constable areas of weakness in the house's defences. The flat roof of the garage, a later addition to the stone Victorian house, aroused his particular interest.

'What cars do you drive, Mrs Thurston?' he asked with what he hoped was suitable casualness.

'I have a little Renault,' she said. 'Richard drives the big Volvo estate, though at the moment he's being driven everywhere by his campaign people. Candidates don't drive themselves, apparently.'

'So the Volvo's in the garage, is it?'

'No, it's not actually,' she said. 'It's out of action, being repaired. A headlight was smashed in the multi-storey car park the other day. Someone must have parked carelessly and hit it while I was shopping – I didn't notice the damage until I got home. They must have noticed when it happened but they didn't leave a note or anything. People don't care these days, do they.'

She laughed nervously.

'I'll be so glad when it's all over,' she said.

'You weren't out in the Volvo on Thursday evening, were you?'

She looked at him vaguely again.

215

'Thursday?' she said. 'That was the night the Globe story came out? No, no, that was Friday, wasn't it? Thursday I went to bed very early. I had a migraine. I didn't hear Richard come in. I did the same the next night, too, but then about eleven the phone started ringing and that woke me and he told me what had happened.'

'Did you really not know about his affair?' Mower asked, as if curiosity had finally got the better of his professional reticence. She looked at him with eyes that were unable to disguise an expression of deep hurt.

'Everyone must think I'm a fool,' she said. 'I had no idea. I hardly knew the boy.'

'You're pushing your luck, Sergeant,' Chief Inspector Thackeray said when Mower explained why he had come back into the office looking like a cat who had just lapped up a puddle of cream.

'Sir,' Mower said, deeply pained. 'The car's crunched. I saw it. According to Thackeray's driver he dropped him at home unusually early that night, well before ten, he thinks. He had plenty of time to pick up the Volvo and get down to the Blue Lagoon, no sweat. He set Laura Ackroyd up. Got her to do the legwork, find Carpenter for him and persuade him not to talk. But he'd already decided to ensure he kept quiet – permanently. He followed Laura with the intention of killing Carpenter – only he hit the wrong man. She didn't come out of the Blue Lagoon with Carpenter, as he expected. She came out with Stevens. But in the dark they're near enough in height and build for him to make the mistake. He had the motive and the opportunity.'

'It's a theory, Sergeant, but so far it's entirely circumstantial,' Thackeray said. 'And so far it's based on a conversation you've had with Angela Thurston which was unauthorised, deceitful and on which you've made no notes. So let's take it a step at a time shall we?'

'Sir,' Mower said with exaggerated respect and sat at his desk, his face a mask of indifference, his dark, eyes angry. 'How long is the inquiry on hold?' he asked.

'Until Thursday night, after the count,' Thackeray said calmly. 'We leave Thurston – and, by extension, Mrs Thurston – alone until then. In the meantime, let's apply a bit more science, and a bit less emotion to this inquiry, shall we? Get those disks of Jason Carpenter's to the computer people at county if you reckon they might be able to resurrect anything he thinks he's deleted. We'll be doing this town a favour if we can put that little shit away for the blackmail.'

'Right, guv,' Mower conceded reluctantly. 'And Thurston's car?'

'Ask the garage to delay work on that,' Thackeray said. 'We don't want the evidence, if it is evidence, resprayed and polished out of existence. Then we'll get forensic to have a look at it, and at Stevens's clothing. You'd better make sure the coroner knows what's going on, too. We're entirely within our rights to look at a suspect car after a hit and run without indulging in fantasies about murder. If that car hit Stevens hard enough to kill him and cause damage to the car then I'd expect the impact to have left traces on one or the other. If traffic have been doing their job properly on the hit-and-run inquiry they'll have asked for an examination of Stevens's clothing already, but check it out. Liaise, Sergeant, liaise. That's what police work is supposed to be all about these days.'

'Yeah, right, guv,' Mower said with all the enthusiasm of a Presbyterian instructed to discuss cooperation with the Pope. He picked up his phone and began to make the necessary arrangements. Across the room Thackeray turned back to the file in front of him which contained the statement he had persuaded a deeply embarrassed city-centre bank clerk to make that morning. As Laura Ackroyd had led him to expect, it accused the car driver who had hit her and Rob Stevens of premeditated murder.

Attempting to kill someone by running them down was an uncertain proposition, Thackeray thought. You could never be sure of success. But it was not beyond the bounds of possibility if the motive were strong enough, and in this case putting Jason Carpenter in hospital for a while might have served Richard Thurston's purpose just as well if he had been trying to protect his reputation until the election was safely over.

Thackeray sighed heavily. He had dealt with cases before where blackmail had backfired and had felt a sneaking sympathy for the worm that turned against a particularly cruel and vicious predator. He knew he would not enjoy arresting Richard Thurston, if that was what he eventually had to do. And he wondered bleakly what Laura Ackroyd would feel if her determination to find Rob Stevens's killer resulted in his charging Thurston with the offence. It would inevitably, he thought, cast a blight over a relationship he was increasingly tempted to pursue. And that, he thought, would be no bad thing.

SEVENTEEN

THE DAY OF THE BRADFIELD by-election dawned dark, gusty and wet, with a sharp north-westerly wind whipping low clouds over the Pennines and sending scudding rain almost horizontally across grey slate roofs and empty streets. Laura Ackroyd got up early although she was not due at work until much later in the day. The weather reflected her mood, she thought sombrely as she pulled back the curtains and grimaced at the bleak landscape outside where the cherry blossom lay in soggy brown heaps on the lawn.

Laura had been assigned a press pass to the town hall for the election count and a brief from Ted Grant to interview the wives of the winning and the losing candidates after the result had been declared at about one the next morning. That meant that most of the day was her own. Even so she was far too tense to lie in bed with so many of her hopes and fears in the balance. After tossing restlessly for an hour or more, she had showered, dressed, and eaten a spartan breakfast by eight o'clock, then left the flat carrying with her an impenetrable cloud of depression.

She drove only a short distance before pulling in to a parking space outside the local primary school, a solid, stone Victorian building diminished by the tatty accretions of the twentieth century which surrounded its arched central windows and church-like hall. This morning there were no children being hustled along the pavement and across the tarmac playground by anxious parents, concerned that they might be late. The school was closed and a trickle of adults, bundled up in macs and anoraks and looking far from cheerful, were making their way into the building to vote at the polling station in the echoing school hall.

Laura stood in the polling booth for a moment gazing unseeingly at the names on the ballot paper before putting her cross firmly beside Richard Thurston's name. It was hardly an act of faith, she thought, more of blind optimism, and one which she doubted would be copied by the grim-faced and sodden electors who waited to follow her into the booth.

She had slept badly. In fact she had slept badly for several nights now, ever since her last interview with Chief Inspector Michael Thackeray, an hour she looked back on with painfully mixed emotions. She was thoroughly embarrassed that he had found her drunk, and desperately afraid that what she had said that night, not all of which she could remember clearly, had put Richard Thurston at even greater personal risk than he already was politically.

She refused to take seriously the possibility that Richard had been involved in Rob Stevens's death, that he had mistaken Rob, as Michael Thackeray had implied, for Jason Carpenter. Even less could she contemplate that he might have been involved, by accident or with malice aforethought, in an attempt on her own life. The idea filled her with such deep revulsion that she pushed it into the furthest recesses of her mind. Only in the watches of the night did it come writhing out of the mists of sleep like some grinning Grendel from the bog, to be pushed away again with difficulty as she tossed and turned and tried to find again the dark comfort of oblivion.

She had been disturbed enough to telephone Richard the day after she had seen Thackeray and try, with unusual diffidance, to discover where he had been on the night of Rob Stevens's death. He had sounded strained and tired but not unduly worried by her questions. He had got her message that night at his campaign headquarters, he had told her, but had not felt that the message was intended to lead to any action on his part, which she had to admit was true enough. She had not expected him, by any stretch of the imagination, to come rushing to the Blue Lagoon that night.

After that, he had said easily, although she had wished she could see him face to face, he had gone home as weary as usual after a day's campaigning. Angela had already taken herself to bed with her migraine, as she had done most nights that week, and he had watched the late news and gone to bed himself soon afterwards.

And there her terrifying suspicions would have to lie, she thought, until after today. The police too, she suspected, would not be likely to pursue their inquiries with great vigour until after the election was over. The Gazette's crime reporter had told her the previous day that there had been no sign that Chief Inspector Thackeray had made any further progress in his investigations into Harvey Lingard's death and there was no hint of any further revelations in the near future. It was as if normal life had been temporarily suspended.

And there, she had decided, she would have to leave it. Not that she found waiting easy. Laura never found waiting easy. But neither personal interest nor professional curiosity would induce her to contact Michael Thackeray for information about the murder – or was it now murders? – or his view of Richard's part in them.

More than once she got to the point of picking up the telephone to contact the engimatic policeman and ask him directly what was going on, but every time she put it down again just as the line was connected to police HQ. It was not just her humiliation at the memory of their last meeting which prevented her from completing the call – though mentally she cringed at the idea of what

221

Thackeray must now think of her, and shied even further away from asking herself why she cared.

She was also, she reluctantly admitted to herself, too afraid of what he might know by now about Richard Thurston to venture into police territory again. So Laura remained in a sort of limbo, deeply suspicious that things were happening that were being kept from her, either deliberately or by chance.

Even the national newspapers seemed to have unaccountably backed away from the story Vince Newsom had so dramatically launched. The character assassination of Richard Thurston seemed to have petered out as polling day approached. Even in the Globe there had been nothing further from Jason Carpenter, although Newsom was still to be seen with the press pack looking unprecedentedly pleased with himself, clearly confident that his reputation was now established. Laura gained some slight satisfaction from ignoring him whenever their paths crossed.

Most of the newspapers had followed up the Globe story for a day or two: there had been portentous leading articles in the serious papers about the irrelevance of sexual orientation to the fitness of a candidate to become an MP, and a few no-holds-barred assaults on 'poofs' in general and Thurston in particular at the more outrageous end of the market. Yet even these had declined as polling day approached and the attention of the popular press had been distracted by the even spicier indiscretions of a soap opera star.

No one, not even Ted Grant and the Gazette, was much interested, it seemed, in the local campaign for Pink Power which the student gays had launched in Thurston's support, and Jason Carpenter himself was still noticeably absent from all his old haunts and quite unavailable for comment.

Her vote cast into the black ballot-box without a vestige of optimism, she drove slowly down into the town centre

222

and out the other side, past the town hall where the television outside broadcast vans were parked ready for the evening's events. If Richard lost the election, as Laura felt coldly sure now that he would, his humiliation would be broadcast across the nation in the early hours.

Laura would be there to see it in the flesh, a commitment she had to fulfil however reluctant she now felt about the assignment. If she could not face the town hall tonight, she thought, then she would have to admit to herself, and more crucially to Ted Grant, that Vince was right. She was too soft for the job. And once that was admitted then there would inevitably be no job.

She parked outside her grandmother's bungalow before nine o'clock without any very clear idea of how she had arrived at the Heights. Joyce Ackroyd was at the door almost before she had locked the car. This was not an area where you left a car unlocked for even a moment.

'Have you seen what those daft kids are doing now?' Joyce called, as she opened the gate. 'Have they got no sense? Can you not have a word with them? They'll finish his chances the way they're carrying on.'

'What's the matter, Nan?' Laura asked, aware that days of anxiety and lack of sleep were affecting her temper. 'Who's upsetting you now?'

Joyce Ackroyd peered angrily around the rainswept and apparently deserted estate and then pulled Laura through the front door into the narrow hallway. Laura had seldom seen her so angry. She was gripping her walking frame as if about to use it as an offensive weapon should an opponent be so ill-advised as to come within reach.

'The youngsters from the university,' she said. 'They've got a loud-speaker van and they're touring round making a right awful din asking folk to vote for their first gay MP. They're supposed to be intelligent, students, but they sometimes make you wonder. Pink Power! I've never heard owt so daft! And at eight o'clock in the morning, and all!'

'They must have moved on,' Laura said. 'I didn't see them as I drove up. But they'll be on the one o'clock news at this rate.'

'They've not got the sense they were born with,' Joyce said bitterly, wrapping a scarf round her neck with such vigour as to make the act look positively dangerous. 'They'll lose him the seat.' Joyce was dressed, Laura noticed with a smile, in the navy and white wool dress she reserved for funerals, weddings and parliamentary elections.

'If it's not lost already,' Laura said gloomily, helping her grandmother into her coat, which had a large red and gold rosette fixed to the lapel. Joyce had no truck with roses, she had said many a time. 'The last opinion poll wasn't very encouraging.'

She checked that her grandmother's back door was locked and then helped her into the car, securing the front door of the bungalow as carefully as she had the back. There were few people on the estate who had not been burgled or robbed, and age was no defence – more likely to be regarded as an incitement to crime.

She drove half a mile past the four looming blocks of the Heights proper and into an area of older council housing, uniform pebble-dashed semi-detached houses for the most part, some of them boarded up and most of them in a state of delapidation, interspersed with an occasional row of bleak little shops, some of these also closed down.

The estate eventually gave on to another main road leading steeply downhill towards the town centre, and Laura found a parking space between bus-stops and delivery vans close to the door of a building which had once been a chapel and now proclaimed itself the Longworth Road community hall. The windows and doors were plastered with Richard Thurston's campaign posters. Laura helped her grandmother out of the car and into the committee rooms for her ward, where she was greeted by a handful of party workers with warm enthusiasm.

'I thought you weren't going to meck it, Joyce,' said an elderly woman who was bent double over columns of names and addresses on a central table.

'I'd not miss a parliamentary, Dora,' Joyce Ackroyd said sharply. 'I said I'd be here, and here I am. My granddaughter brought me down.' She manoeuvred herself into position to take a seat behind the table and her glance softened as she looked at Laura, taking in the tension around her mouth and the dark circles under her eyes.

'Bear up, lass,' she said. 'Happen he'll make it yet.' She glanced sharply at the array of lists in front of her.

'Are they coming out?' she asked.

The woman completed ticking off a number of names on the lists before answering.

'Aye,' she said. 'But not as fast as they should. Fred's got t'figures from t'last general election and says we're down.'

'Fred's working, is he?' Joyce asked.

'Aye,' the woman said. 'Under protest, I think. And Stanley won't come out, he says. Of course, he's chapel. Very strict. The younger ones don't seem to think owt of it, though.' It was typical, Laura thought wryly, that the cause of the disaffection amongst some party members should be acknowledged but never spoken. As a generation, she thought, with a few exceptions like Joyce, they lacked the words.

'You can tell already how its going, can you?' she asked, interested in spite of the depression which threatened to overwhelm her. She had never spent an election day in a committee room but she knew vaguely that the parties used a system of checking off who had been to the polling station against their canvass returns, so that by the time the polls closed they had a good idea which of their supporters had taken the trouble to vote. Tardy people who had promised support were prone to be reminded of their obligation with some vigour as the day progressed.

'Come and check these off with me, love,' Joyce said,

225

picking up another sheaf of forms which had been brought in from the polling stations. 'You call the numbers and I'll cross them off.'

If it was intended as a form of therapy, it was kindly meant, Laura thought, and did as she was told. Very slowly the morning passed. At hourly intervals helpers appeared with more forms from the polling stations, which were carefully checked, and soon after a lunch of sandwiches and soft drinks, which Laura fetched from a neighbouring pub, troupes of helpers arrived eager to begin knocking on the doors of the uncomfortably large number of pledged voters who had not so far bothered to put their crosses on the ballot papers.

For much of the time Laura relapsed into an anxious reverie, her eyes fixed on the lists of crossed-off names. She was conscious of Joyce watching her anxiously but there was no opportunity to talk as the room filled up with helpers. It was obvious from the coming and going that the work was being done with dogged determination rather than buoyant enthusiasm. Very few of the party workers, Laura concluded, believed that Richard would win. They were going through the motions out of loyalty, no more. The list of promises fulfilled was growing too slowly and everyone knew it. No amount of anxious counting by Joyce could alter the fact.

'I've got to get out for a bit, Nan,' Laura said at last when the oppressive atmosphere got too much for her.

'You'll not wait to see the candidate, then?' Joyce said. 'He'll be round shortly.' Laura shook her head. She did not think that she wanted to face Richard Thurston at all today. Her sense of guilt at having let him down was compounded by the nagging fear that there was worse to come — far worse, in fact, than the loss of the election, which now looked inevitable. She did not want him to read that in her eyes, and doubted that she could hide it if she met him face to face.

'I'll get some fresh air and make sure your place is all

right,' she said. It was a lame excuse and she knew that Joyce could see through it but the older woman simply nodded, confining her anxiety to a troubled look which compounded Laura's guilt.

'Drop back in later, then.' It was half question, half plea, and Laura agreed quickly. There had been a time when she would have shared her worries with Joyce, but the distance between them was growing too great for that now. Laura was not sure whether Joyce was withdrawing from her. Perhaps that was what old people did in the end, to make the inevitable parting more bearable, she thought. More likely her own emotions had become too complex now to share, her morality too different.

Casual, had been the word Joyce had used tartly when Vince had dominated Laura's life with such all-consuming vitality that visits to the Heights had become too infrequent for comfort on either side. Good riddance, Joyce had said with satisfaction, when Vince had eventually departed and Laura had tentatively tried to take up with her grandmother where she had left off. The distance between them had remained unbridged, the estrangement unmentioned and unforgiven on both sides.

Laura drove back up the hill towards the flats and parked outside her grandmother's house again. All was peaceful down the row of old people's homes – net curtains neatly arranged to keep out prying eyes, doors and windows tightly closed against the drizzling rain and the ever-present possibility of intruders.

But as she sat for a moment in the car with the window open and gazed across at the bleak expanse of muddy grass and littered concrete which separated the four massive blocks of flats, her attention was caught by the sounds of a loudspeaker and confused shouts from the far side of the estate. She could not define later what convinced her that something was badly wrong. It was, she supposed, only the hint of a scream amongst the confusion of sound, but it was enough to make her swing the car in a vicious U-turn and acclerate to the far side of the estate with a sense of sharp alarm.

Passing between two of the blocks and into the main road which passed close under the north side of the flats she had to brake sharply to avoid a group of youths running wildly towards her. The solid phalanx split up as she approached, and passed her on either side without slowing their frantic run, one or two of them banging threateningly on the roof of the Beetle as they swung around it. Taking the corner more slowly she pulled in to the side of the road and gazed in horror at the scene ahead.

A loud-speaker van plastered with red and yellow party posters interspersed with the shocking pink of the Pink Power campaign was drawn up at the kerb. In front of it, right at the foot of the flats where walkways overhung the road on every alternate level, a group of young people were gathered around someone lying on the ground. Laura got out of her car feeling faintly sick and elbowed her way to the front of the crowd. To her slight relief the body crumpled half on and half off the pavement among the sodden litter did not appear to be anyone she knew. But that sense of lessened anxiety was short-lived. The girl who lay there with her short blond hair and once white T-shirt soaked in blood, her head cradled in Dilly Jenkins's arms, showed no sign of life.

For a moment Laura felt herself pitched back to the night of Rob Steven's death, and terrified revulsion threatened to overwhelm her. She ran her hands frantically through her damp hair as she struggled to hold down the panic which urged her to turn and run. The moment passed and she grabbed the arm of one of the students, who seemed stunned into an immobility even more shocking than her own. She shook the boy angrily.

'Have you sent for an ambulance?' she asked. The youth turned towards her, his eyes filled with horror, and nodded.

228

'Someone's gone to phone,' he whispered from lips which looked blue against the ashen pallor.

'What happened?' Laura asked. The student looked at her, the first tears beginning to run down his face, unable to reply. At length he took a deep, shuddering breath, and forced the words out between gritted teeth.

'The yobs began name-calling and throwing stones,' he said, his face crumpling now with unashamed grief. He glanced up at the peeling façade of the flats, where not a face was visible at a window or balcony, and then at the pavement and road, which were littered with stones and other rubbish – some recognisably part of a television set, smashed and shattered into jagged shards of plastic and glass.

'There was a lot of shouting and screaming,' the boy went on. 'Then someone threw something from up there.'

Laura too glanced up at the grim façade above. It was not unusual, she knew, for rubbish, worn-out electrical appliances and even occasionally a child to hurtle down that cliff face, usually by accident but occasionally by design.

'And that hit her?' The boy nodded dumbly, too overcome to speak.

'Dear God, you should have had more sense than to come up here,' she said, horrified by the naivety of the students. 'Queer-bashing is a spectator sport round this part of town.'

The ambulance and police came quickly, sirens blaring, and the unconscious girl – not dead apparently but not, Laura guessed, far off – was stretchered away. In the huddle of distraught students who were left behind to talk to the uniformed police who now swarmed around the estate, Laura caught Dilly Jenkins's eye.

'Tell me about it,' she said. 'I'll have to write something.'

'Don't you get sick of battening on other people's misery?' the girl said waspishly, clutching her duffel jacket around herself in a vain attempt to calm her convulsive shivering, her face, chalk white, her lower lip trembling.

'Oh, shut up, Dilly,' Laura snapped. 'At least I don't go

round stirring up trouble like you and your friend Jason. And this.' She waved an exasperated hand at the spilt blood which lay smeared across the road and mingled with the rain to run in a pinkish-grey trickle into the rubbish-choked gutter. 'This was just bloody stupid.'

She would have gone on, venting all her own pent-up emotion on the girl, but she reined in her outrage as she took in Dilly's pale face, ugly with misery, and her hands still smeared with her friend's blood. Impulsively she put an arm around the girl's shoulder and pulled her close.

'Do you want to go to the hospital?' she asked. Dilly shook her head.

'Her partner's gone with her.'

'Then let me take you home,' Laura said with a sigh.

Bradfield town hall was noisy, packed and overheated in the glare of the television lights. In the well of the hall, tables were set out in rows and at every table the skilled fingers of off-duty bank clerks earning pin money flickered through the bundles of votes and piled them neatly in stacks of hundreds ready for the returning officers to check and place in the final piles on separate tables at the end of the room.

The platform had a festive appearance, with the dais – where the microphones stood ready for the election result to be declared – surrounded by banks of flowers already looking less than fresh in the torrid atmosphere. Beneath the platform the candidates and their wives stood anxiously with their agents and a few of their supporters who acted as scrutineers at the count.

Laura Ackroyd was watching the proceedings from the balcony, which was packed with a motley collection of reporters, television crew and party workers who had not been lucky enough to gain access to the body of the hall. She could see some of her colleagues below. Ted Grant and the political reporter Fred Jones were ingratiating

themselves with the group around Tim Lennox, the Tory candidate, and in the throng Laura spotted the bulky figure of Councillor Stan Treadwell looking even more self-satisfied than when she had met him at Vicky Mendelson's dinner party. His doubts about his party's candidate seemed not surprisingly to have evaporated during the unforeseeably vicious campaign of the last few weeks.

Richard Thurston's supporters were on the whole younger – many of them, she guessed, probably his students. His minder, the MP for the neighbouring constituency of Eckersley, Jake Taylor, was not in evidence and Laura wondered if that was a case of a rat abandoning a sinking ship. Richard, as far as she could see from her vantage point, looked haggard and tense, and his wife, in the Paisley wool dress that Laura recognised from her interview with her what now seemed a life-time ago, was twisting the strap of her shoulder-bag nervously between her fingers as the count continued. She had apparently made no particular effort to look smart, Laura thought, for her dress was teamed with flat brown shoes and a purple scarf which hung forlornly around her shoulders. Her face was impassive, her emotions almost but not quite under control, but she still looked irredeemably and deliberately dowdy beside Antonia Lennox, a tall slim young woman in a fashionable black and white suit and blue rosette, who stood chatting to her husband's supporters as if she were enjoying a day at the races.

Just after one o'clock there was a flurry of activity below. The piles of votes were now all gathered in and the returning officer, looking slightly anxious, consulted with both the candidates and their agents. On the balcony the TV crews finalised their preparations for broadcasting the announcement of the result, but within minutes the tension had subsided again as the news that there was to be a re-count was relayed round the packed hall, giving rise to a deep growl of frustration from the waiting crowds and

231

audible curses from the press. Laura caught Vince Newsom's eye in the crowd below and deliberately turned away from his flashing smile and cheery wave. She was pleased to realise that at least the sight of him left her totally unmoved.

They're almost all here, gathered together in one place, she thought, the victims, the predators and the jackals alike screwed up in nervous anticipation of the kill. But the longest shadows were cast by those who were not there. For Laura the ghosts of Harvey Lingard and Rob Stevens were very real tonight.

She sighed and moved away from her vantage point at the edge of the balcony. She needed some air and pushed her way through the crowds and down the stairs into the lobby. It was a cool and airy space, rising the full majestic height of the building in a series of tall gothic arches over the main stone staircase. The hallway was floored in deep blue and white Victorian tiles and she stood still there for a moment to allow the cooler air to take the flush from her cheeks. A couple of security men in their municipal navy blue stood guard at the mahogany swing doors which led out into the town hall square, while two uniformed policemen barred the entrance to the main hall and the continuing count.

Laura desperately wanted to escape. If she could have found any excuse not to take her official place in the hall and watch the imminent conclusion of the electoral drama she would have done so. She stood gazing at a sepia representation of Bradfield's town council in 1897, a solemn collection of mutton-chopped, waistcoated and watch-chained worthies who gazed complacently out of posterity. What she would give, she thought, for that sort of certainty and self-confidence, the virtues which had built this monument to municipal self-aggrandisement in which events were unfolding. It was not, she thought, a suitable place for the sort of self-doubt which currently tormented her.

The sound of the main doors swinging open and the draught of cold air they caused made her turn and to her surprise she found herself face-to-face with Chief Inspector Michael Thackeray, closely followed by Sergeant Mower. Thackeray's face was glacial and when he did not speak Laura wondered if she had imagined the flicker of compassion in his eyes as he met her look of undisguised dismay.

'Is the count over?' Mower asked, giving her what she had come to recognise as the inevitable glance of appraisal he offered to anyone of the opposite sex. She could see from the approval in his eyes that her short brown skirt and cream shirt under a darker jacket passed muster although to her they felt hot and sticky at the end of a long day. She shook her head, partly in response to his question and partly in irritation at his presumption.

'There's a re-count,' she said sharply. 'It'll be another half hour at least.' The two men looked at each other.

'We'll wait in the car,' Thackeray said shortly and turned back towards the main doors.

'Please,' Laura said, her voice sounding thin and child-like in the vast empty space of the hallway.

'Please,' she said again more quietly as the two men hesitated and turned back towards her. 'What happened to the girl who was hurt up at the Heights? The gay student? Is she all right?' Mower glanced at the chief inspector again. Thackeray had gone into one of the withdrawn moods with which Mower was becoming familiar but he still needed at least the nod of consent which the chief inspector gave him before speaking.

'She's out of danger,' he said. 'And we've got the yobbo who chucked the tv set over the edge. A lad by the name of Regan we've had our eye on for a while. Lives on one of those walkways. We're arresting Jason Carpenter tomorrow, too, for the blackmail offences. He wasn't quite as thorough in wiping his computer disks as he thought he'd been. Our forensic people have retrieved some very

233

interesting correspondence he'd been engaged in.'

'And Richard Thurston,' she said, forcing the name out in a near whisper. 'Are you here to arrest Richard?' She addressed her question directly to Thackeray and she did not mistake the look in his eyes as this time he spoke for himself, although apparently with reluctance.

'I'm sorry,' he said. 'There'll be a press statement later. That's all I can say now.' He turned away abruptly and pushed his way out of the double doors, letting in a flurry of rain. Mower gave an almost imperceptible shrug and followed him out, leaving Laura standing in the middle of the hallway, which suddenly felt as cold and desolate as the tomb.

Very slowly she walked up the shallow stone steps, showed her pass to the policemen on the door and entered the main body of the hall, where expectancy now seemed to have reached fever pitch. She pushed her way through the crowds of over-excited party workers and tellers towards the front. She knew who it was who put an over-familiar arm around her waist before she heard Vince Newsom's voice in her ear.

'It looks as if we've done it, doll,' he said.

'Done what?' she asked, extricating herself irritably from his embrace.

'Done Richard Thurston to a turn,' Vince said cheerfully.

'Is that what it's all about?'

'It's what the Globe's all about, my sweet,' he said, unabashed. 'And don't you forget it.'

'Ah, there you are,' Ted Grant said, seizing her arm as she turned away from Newsom and made to pass him blindly. 'Right, they're ready to declare. It looks as though Lennox has won so grab the fair Antonia first. You can catch up with Angela Thurston later. We'll not be wanting to waste much space on her now.'

With the movements of an automaton Laura pulled her tape-recorder out of her bag, and watched as the

candidates and their wives assembled on the dais and the returning officer took centre stage to an expectant silence. It did not take much percipience to see that Ted Grant's estimate was right. Richard Thurston took a position a little behind his rival, his face grey and gaunt. Angela held his arm comfortingly, but she too looked distraught and on the verge of tears. For his part, Tim Lennox stood close to the returning officer, smiling broadly at his supporters below, one of whom tossed a bouquet of blue and white flowers to his wife, who caught it expertly and made a little mock curtsey in return.

Laura hardly took in the final figures, which gave Lennox a three-figure majority in place of the lead of thousands which Richard Thurston had confidently expected when his campaign began. When the cheering had ended, she pushed her way through the exultant crowds of Lennox supporters and conducted the brief interview with Mrs Lennox to which she was committed.

That done, she turned away to catch a glimpse of the Thurstons moving dispiritedly towatds the doors of the hall, a disconsolate crew of supporters in their wake. She hurried after them and was in time to see Chief Inspector Thackeray and Sergeant Mower move in to speak quietly to Thurston in the doorway. Frantically she pushed her way through the crush and, as a stunned silence fell amongst the Thurston supporters, she heard Thackeray's clear voice pronounce the familiar words of the caution.

'I understand,' Thurston said. He glanced at his wife and then around the tightly packed group in the doorway behind him, finally catching Laura's eye with evident relief.

'Look after Angela,' he said, before turning abruptly on his heel and leaving the hall with the two police officers.

EIGHTEEN

IT WAS THREE IN THE morning before Laura was able to leave the Gazette office and drive wearily out of town, past the silent university buildings and into the quiet avenue where the Thurston house stood in unremarkable darkness amongst its neighbours. She had not been able to approach Angela Thurston in the uproar which had followed her husband's arrest before Ted Grant had seized her arm and demanded to know what was going on.

His look of horror when she told him was a purely human response and surprised her, but it was swiftly erased by the professional excitement she expected. By now they were surrounded by the rest of the press pack jostling for position.

'But what have they arrested him for?' Ted had demanded.

'In connection with the death of Robert Stevens,' came a voice from the crowd, confirming what Laura desperately feared but had not herself heard Thackeray say. 'But who the hell is Robert Stevens?'

'Christ!' Grant had muttered, his sharp blue eyes fastening on Laura's pale face for a moment before assessing the expectant mob which surrounded them both.

'Back to the office,' he said sharply. 'Come on, lass, move! This one's ours, if ever a story was. It's too late for these buggers from the nationals to get anything much in the last edition so it's all ours. Just keep your fingers crossed he's not charged before we can do it justice.' With a feeling of utter despair, Laura had followed him.

Under the harsh lights of the interview room at the central police station, Michael Thackeray found it hard to pin down the reason for his dissatisfaction. Richard Thurston sat across the table from him in his shirt sleeves, his long thin hands spread palm down on the table in front of him and a look of resignation on his face. He had said nothing at all on the brief journey across the town hall square to the police station, nor while he was going through the humiliating rituals of arrest in front of the custody officer.

He had emptied his pockets of keys, loose change and handkerchiefs, read his rights silently, refused the services of a solicitor and even voluntarily unfastened the forlorn red rose from his lapel and handed it over with its pin and a faintly ironic smile.

And now he was quietly, if wearily, answering Thackeray's questions with no attempt at prevarication or bluster, and little apparent surprise at the situation in which he found himself. He had, he said, as he had told the chief inspector before, returned home earlier than usual on the night of Rob Stevens's death. He had not gone out again. His wife had not seen him come in, he repeated. She had been asleep in bed. And no, if he had chosen to go out again in his own car, the Volvo which was normally kept in the garage, she would not have seen him go or return.

'Did you go out again, Mr Thurston?' Thackeray asked. Mower, who was standing near the door, rubbed his sweating palms on the inside of his trouser pockers with distaste. The small room with its tape-recorder and bright lights was hot and every one in it was obviously exhausted. Thurston, he thought, looked on the point of collapse and Thackeray as grim and tense as he had ever seen him, did not look in much better shape.

'No, Chief Inspector, I didn't,' Thurston said. 'I went to bed.'

'Though you knew that Laura Ackroyd was hoping to see Jason Carpenter that night at the Blue Lagoon on your behalf?'

'Yes, I knew that. I got her slightly cryptic message and worked that out.' Thurston gave the ghost of a smile, apparently at the thought of Laura, but it quickly turned to a look of sadness.

'You can't seriously think that I would hurt Laura,' he said tentatively and then, catching Thackeray's implacable gaze, gave a shrug of resignation. 'You do think that,' he said.

'Shouldn't we call it attempted murder?' Mower said harshly from the back of the room, seizing his chance. 'That's what I'd call it. Your friend Laura Ackroyd was lucky not to be killed.' Thurston switched his gaze to Mower and both officers thought for a moment that the detective sergeant had shaken the interviewee out of his apparently calm resignation, but although there was a momentary flicker of anger in Thurston's eyes he said nothing.

'We're wasting time, Dr Thurston,' Thackeray said. 'Your car, the Volvo, was damaged in a collision.'

Thurston nodded.

'My wife was using it,' he said. 'It was hit in the multi-storey car park, she said. She didn't notice till she got home.'

'That day?'

'The collision was that day, yes, or was it the day before? We've seen so little of each other the last couple of weeks it gets difficult to remember what happened when. She told me about it the next morning over breakfast. She'd already booked it into the garage to have it fixed, she said.'

'A collision in the car park. That's what she told you, is it?' Thackeray came back, sceptically. 'Could she have taken the Volvo out that night without your knowing? About ten o'clock?'

Thurston shook his head emphatically this time.

238

'Of course not,' he said. 'I was there. I'd have heard her. I told you, she was asleep when I got in.'

'You saw her asleep?'

'I looked in on her before I went to bed, yes.' Thurston said emphatically. 'She takes pills for her migraine. She didn't wake.'

'So it would come as a complete surprise you to learn that our forensic people tell us that fibres found adhering to the damaged light and bumper match fibres taken from the clothes Rob Stevens was wearing that night?'

Thurston did not answer immediately. He sat silently looking down at the table for a long time, his head bowed. Press him, press him now, Mower thought impatiently, but Thackeray was as impassive as Thurston and said no more. The silence lengthened until suddenly Thurston shrugged and turned his hands up in a gesture of surrender.

'I thought it was Jason, of course, in the dark,' he said. 'I expect you've worked that out. I didn't intend to kill him. I just thought I could put him out of action until the election was over. I never meant to hurt Laura at all. I didn't even realise I'd hit her until the next day. It was a mad, bad thing to do and it went terribly wrong. I'm more sorry than I can tell you.'

Thackeray pushed his chair away from the table abruptly. He turned to Mower.

'Take his statement and charge him with the murder and attempted murder,' he said, surprising the sergeant with the anger in his voice. 'Tomorrow, Dr Thurston, after you've appeared in court, I shall want to talk to you again about Harvey Lingard.'

Thurston watched the chief inspector go with a look of stunned acceptance.

Thackeray went upstairs to his own office and sat for a moment trying to control his emotions. Then he rang Superintendent Longley, who had left instructions that he was to be told the outcome of Thurston's interview no matter what the time.

'He's admitted the Stevens thing,' Thackeray said curtly when a tetchy sounding Longley answered his call. 'Though we may have difficulty making a murder charge stick. He could get away with manslaughter.'

'Leave that to the CPS and the courts,' Longley said cheerfully. 'It's a good result, Mike. Congratulations. And Harvey Lingard?'

'Tomorrow,' Thackeray said. 'Thurston can't take any more tonight.' And nor can I, he thought.

Laura was surprised to find the door to the Thurston house ajar when she arrived. Even so she rang the doorbell, unwilling to enter uninvited, and waited for several minutes before eventually pushing the door open and stepping into the hall. The house was completely silent and the only light visible was a thin thread of yellow from beneath what she recalled was the kitchen door.

Tentatively she called Angela, but got no response and was seized with the certainly that there was something dreadfully wrong. Relying on the dim light which filtered through the hall window she knocked on the kitchen door itself. Again there was no reply, and becoming more and more afraid of what the silence would reveal she turned the knob and opened the door.

The kitchen was in disarray, but empty. Cupboards and drawers stood open, their contents revealed but not greatly disturbed. It was as if someone had been looking for something which they had not found.

A faint sound made her jump and set her heart thudding wildly. It seemed to come from the far side of the room, and when she moved around the large central table she realised that Angela's dog was lying in its basket, apparently oblivious to her presence. Puzzled she crossed the room and put a hand on the animals's head. The dog gave another great shuddering sigh, the noise which had startled her, and then lay still again. Very gently Laura ran her hand over the animal's neck and back but there was no further movement, no sign of a breath, and she realised that the dog was now dead.

She was overcome with real fear then. Urgently she ran back into the hall, turning on lights where she could find the switches and opening the doors to every room. She could find no one, nor anything untoward on the ground floor nor, when she ran upstairs, in any of the bedrooms or bathrooms.

Uncertainly she stood in the middle of the Thurstons' bedroom, where the double bed was unmade and Richard's discarded clothing lay untidily on the floor – abandoned no doubt as he had hurriedly dressed for what should have been a day of electoral triumph. There was, as far as she could tell, no one in the house. Angela, if she had been here and was responsible for the death of her beloved labrador, had gone. She turned out the bedroom light and as she did so happened to glance out of the window into the garden behind the house. There, as the light was extinguished, she caught a glimpse of a faint orange glow. Cautiously she approached the window and looked out. She had not been mistaken. There was a faint light coming from the shed at the bottom of the garden.

She ran downstairs, through the kitchen and outside into the cool night air. She had no sense of danger now, only a frantic impulse to prevent Angela from doing whatever it was she planned to do in the obscurity of her garden. Running half blind through shrubs and plants, which whipped across her face as she passed, she stumbled towards the glow of light at the shed window, making no attempt to disguise her approach. The door was not locked and she flung it open and stepped inside totally unprepared for the ferocious blow which took her legs away from her and flung her in a heap against the shed wall opposite the door, stunned and breathless.

Behind her she heard the shed door bang shut and a key turn in the lock.

241

'I might have guessed it would be you,' Angela Thurston said furiously as Laura struggle into a sitting position against a pile of compost bags and tried to collect her scattered wits. Feeling sick with shock she focused her eyes with difficulty on her attacker, who stood with her back to the door holding a heavy spade in her hands. Incredulously it came to Laura that Angela had hit her very hard with the flat of the spade as she had come through the door into the shed, catching her heavily behind the legs and pitching her across the narrow space to catch her head a glancing blow against a metal shelf.

'For God's sake, Angela,' Laura said desperately, aware of a sticky trickle of blood on her temple and of the numbness in her legs giving way to a fierce pain above her left ankle. Gently she tried to flex her foot and gasped, wishing immediately that she had not bothered, as another wave of nausea overcame her. The light in the shed was dim, coming as it did from a bare, low-watt bulb in the ceiling, but it was bright enough for her to see that her left shoe and stocking were soaked in blood, and she guessed that the spade had probably cracked a bone.

'Don't move,' Angela said, matter-of-factly. 'If you do I'll have to hit you again.'

'I don't think I can move,' Laura said faintly, aware that she was beginning to shake with shock and that Angela, for all she was twenty years or more older, was a strong woman quite capable in her present mood of using the spade to deadly effect.

'Good,' Angela said. Her voice was harsh and Laura could see that her eyes were very bright in a pale, gaunt face. She seemed to be gripped with a remote passion which left no room for any other emotion. Not mad but dangerous, Laura thought, and distinctly beyond the reach of reason.

'Why?' Laura asked, more faintly. Angela seemed to consider the question seriously for a moment but she did not reply. She put the spade down, evidently content that

Laura was immobilised for the time being, and turned to a pile of papers tucked between empty plant pots and seed packets on the mud-stained work-bench which ran down one side of the shed.

'In some ways it's quite a good thing that you're here,' she said, in a voice of apparent normality. 'You can tell me if you think I've left anything out.' She spoke almost as if they were discussing some administrative problem of mutual concern.

Laura tried to edge herself into a more comfortable position in the corner into which she had fallen but the slightest movement of her leg sent a searing pain from ankle to thigh which made her draw breath sharply.

'What do you mean?' she asked as soon as she could speak again.

Angela assembled her papers into a pedantically neat pile, as if undertaking some routine administrative chore, and turned her burning eyes to meet Laura's with a look of fierce pity. 'You didn't really understand, did you, that day you came to interview me for the Gazette? I told you then that I would do anything for Richard. You didn't understand how far I'd gone already. It's odd that it should be you, Laura, because you were here at the beginning. I suppose it makes sense if it comes full circle and you're here at the end as well.'

'The beginning?' Laura said.

'With that evil genius Harvey Lingard,' Angela said. 'How I hated that young man. I'll never forget you two coming to the house for the first time, you know. You made such a stunning pair, the red hair and the blond, both beautiful. It even crossed my mind that of all the attractive students Richard had had, you might be the one he fell for. I'd always expected him to fall for someone in the end. All that temptation, year after year. It wasn't much of a surprise when it finally happened. If only it had been you, all this need never have happened. He could probably have got away with it if the affairs had been with

243

women. The real shock was to discover that it was Harvey he was sleeping with. That I didn't expect. I thought I knew him so well, but he surprised me there.'

'You knew about Harvey?' Laura whispered.

'Of course I knew. I've known about all of them. Richard is so innocent, really. He thinks I can't tell when he's in love. Thinks I couldn't tell when things began to go wrong and he was rigid with worry over the blackmail. Thinks it's all passed me by, all ten years of it. It took me about half an hour to discover where he had hidden the blackmail notes. Men are so stupid. And the stupidest thing they do is to imagine that their wives are stupid as well.' She ended on a note of bitter contempt.

'You killed Harvey?' Laura asked. Angela nodded.

'I saw him that day in Market Street, quite by chance. I hardly recognised him at first, he'd lost so much weight, but then he looked straight at me across the street and I was sure. I'd have known those eyes anywhere. He didn't recognise me, of course. One middle-aged woman looks much like another to the young.'

'But why?' Laura said desperately. 'It was all over years ago. Why did you kill him? He was dying of AIDS anyway.'

The image of Harvey as she had known him, full of energy and life and laughter, the image which had haunted her ever since she had learned of his death, was more vivid tonight than it had ever been. 'We all loved Harvey,' she whispered, tears in her eyes.

'I thought he was the blackmailer, of course.' Angela said, as if to an uncomprehending child. 'It seemed obvious that that was why he was in Bradfield. I followed him on the spur of the moment. I sat behind him on the bus to Heyburn, and got off after him and a couple of women from the village. He made it easy, you see, going up that lonely path on his own and just sitting there, looking at the view, as if he hadn't a care in the world. It was as if he was waiting for me.' She stopped as if reliving that moment, a distant look in her eyes. Then her gaze flickered back to Laura.

'It was very quick,' she said, reading the horror in Laura's face. 'He never knew a thing about it. I rolled his body down towards the stream where it would be difficult to see, and then I kept walking across the moor to Haworth. It's a beautiful walk. Then I got the bus home from there. It was all so easy, I never thought anyone would ever find out . . . And they wouldn't have done, but then when another blackmail letter came and Richard was almost beside himself with worry I knew I must have killed the wrong person.'

She stopped, her face becoming remote again as the full import of what she had said struck her, words making a new and horrific reality of something which had never before been expressed.

'I realised then that it must have been Jason all the time,' she said, so quietly that Laura had to strain to hear her. 'But I didn't even get that right. When you left that message here for Richard it wasn't difficult to work out what it meant and I drove down to the Blue Lagoon and there you were, waiting outside. I watched you go in and when you came out, I thought the young man with you must be Jason. It was dark and I've only met him once . . .' She turned away from Laura and bent her head over the papers on the worktop, her face wracked with fierce emotion. She had been carried along for years, Laura thought, by this enormously warped loyalty – like some sort of engine thrust into overdrive by Richard's reckless disregard for his own safety and liable now to destroy them both.

'I got it all wrong,' Angela went on. 'I do get it wrong with people, you know. Plants and dogs are much easier. But you have to understand why. It was all for Richard, you see? You have to understand that. Tell him that.'

'But the police think Richard . . .'

'I know!' Angela's voice rose almost to a scream. 'Do you think I don't know, you stupid girl. Don't you see? That's what this is all about, because they think that Richard is to blame and he's probably fool enough to admit it, to protect me. I've got to tell them now what really happened. I've written it all down, and Harvey's wallet and credit cards are here, too, I took them out of his pocket after I . . . after he was dead. I thought it might delay things, they might not identify him. It was all on the spur of the moment. You will tell them, won't you?'

Angela broke off abruptly and ran her hands through her dishevelled hair.

'I don't understand,' Laura said faintly, although she had a horrible feeling that she did. The pain in her leg was getting worse and Angela seemed to be becoming more remote from her, receding in the dim light, the browns and reds and golds of the familiar Paisley dress fading into the dun brown background of the shed, the distraught face becoming a blur. 'You can't let them think Richard was driving the car that night . . .'

'No of course not. I've told you. It's all here. All the details. It's perfectly clear.' She sounded quite business-like again for a moment and put the documents neatly at the end of the work-bench close to the door. Then she picked up a green bottle which had been obscured from Laura's view and unscrewed the top.

'I thought this was in the kitchen,' she said almost inconsequentially. 'I tend not to leave the most dangerous stuff out here in case children get in and fiddle about with things. But it was here all the time. It's the best thing I can find. The most effective anyway. I looked it up. It's just as well I never went organic. I did think about it.' She laughed without mirth.

'Everything by the book,' she said. 'There's a handbook for it all, isn't there? Kitzinger for childbirth, Dr Spock for the babies, the Consumers' Association for buying a house, getting a divorce, finding the right poison . . . you name it.'

'No,' Laura said desperately, trying to push herself upright but forced back by the fierceness of the pain which

246

ran like fire up her leg again. 'Don't Angela, please don't,' she pleaded desperately, but Angela only looked at her with an expression of puzzlement in her tired blue eyes.

'There's nothing else to do,' she said. 'There's no other way. Can you see me in Holloway? That would be much worse.' She made to take a draught from the bottle but seemed suddenly to change her mind. Her look softened for a moment, her face seeming to take on some of its fading prettiness again as she gave Laura a glimmer of a smile and unlocked the shed door.

'Not here, though,' she said. 'There's no need for you to watch.' She went out of the door, closing and locking it behind her. Laura groaned in frustration and strained her ears for any further indication of whether Angela had done what she intended, but all she could hear was the soft sigh of the wind and the occasional rustle and squeak of night creatures in the garden beyond.

'Oh God,' Laura said faintly. 'Please help me, someone.'

She never knew quite how long she lay in the shed, drifting in and out of consciousness as the pain in her leg grew worse and threatened to overwhelm her, but eventually she was aware of the door opening and a voice she knew exclaiming in horror.

'How did you know I was here?' she asked faintly as Michael Thackeray examined her injured leg with competent hands and then half-carried her out of the shed, shielding her from the sight of the rigid body which lay sprawled face down on the grass in the dim starlight quite close to the shed door. She let herself relax against the solidity of his body and as they moved into the light from the house their eyes met, and there was unashamed relief in both faces.

'I couldn't sleep,' he said. 'There was something not right about Richard Thurston's confession. I'm sorry. I got it quite wrong. Thurston had concealed so much that it seemed obvious that he must have been concealing his part in the deaths as well. If I hadn't been so bloody tired I'd have worked out sooner that he was lying again, and why, but it came to me in the end. You don't know Jason Carpenter, do you?'

He sat her gently in a chair in the Thurstons' kitchen. She looked up at him and shook her head.

'I never found him,' she said.

'Richard Thurston couldn't have mistaken Rob Stevens for Jason. You might have done, in that dark alleyway, and Angela might have done, but not Richard. Jason walks with quite a pronounced limp.'

'She's written you a confession. It's in the shed,' Laura said. 'She killed Harvey as well.'

'Yes, I know. I saw what she'd left there, but I can't move it until the scene of crime team has had a look round.'

'Is she dead?' Laura asked.

'Oh, yes. There was nothing I could do for her. I almost fell over her body in the dark.'

'I couldn't stop her,' Laura said with a shudder. 'I couldn't get near her.'

'You mustn't blame yourself,' Thackeray said. He picked up the phone extension by the kitchen door, although he felt a deep reluctance to make the call which would bring the whole weight of the forces of law and order trampling in on them. 'I was far too slow making the connection with Angela, though Thurston himself virtually told me she could have been driving the car. He must have worked it out as soon as he realised we were interested in the Volvo.'

'She told me weeks ago she would do anything for Richard,' Laura said. 'But it's the sort of thing people say without really meaning it. I didn't take it seriously. I never imagined for a moment that she would go this far. What sort of love is it that can kill to protect a reputation?'

'It was not all one way. He was willing to carry the can for her for the hit-and-run death,' Thackeray said. 'And I was almost fool enough to believe him.'

'I'm sorry,' Laura said, as she began to cry, the tension

and shock finally overwhelming her. 'They were my friends,' she said through her tears as Thackeray tried awkwardly to comfort her.

'The pain will get better,' he said. 'It's difficult to believe now, but it does pass in the end.'

'I suppose so,' she said dully, aware that he was trying to convince himself as well as her of something he only half believed. Abruptly he pulled away and made the call to police headquarters.

They waited in silence. As her tears dried and the worst of the shock wore off, and they caught the first faint echo of an approaching siren, Laura glanced impatiently at her ankle, making sure that Thackeray did not catch the glimmer of excitement in her eyes which she could not quite suppress. I need to get that foot strapped up quickly, she thought. I've got a cracker of a story to write.